PRAISE FOR MYST

MW00846842

Distinctive characters and fun anecdotes about beer and brewing help make this a winner. Readers will want to keep coming back for more.

— *PUBLISHERS WEEKLY* ON *BEYOND A REASONABLE STOUT*

Exciting and irresistible...this absorbing mystery will not let you leave it unfinished. Ellie Alexander is a formidable mystery novel writer.

— *WASHINGTON BOOK REVIEW* ON *DEATH ON TAP*

With its beautifully described small-town setting and seamlessly intertwined details about brewing beer, this cozy will appeal to beer lovers everywhere as well as readers who enjoy mysteries highlighting family relationships and independent female main characters.

— BOOKLIST

Likable characters, an atmospheric small-town setting, and a quirky adversary for the amateur sleuth. The engaging premise and pairings of beer and food should appeal to fans of Avery Ames's 'Cheese Shop' titles.

— LIBRARY JOURNAL

A delight for foodies, craft beer fans, and lovers of twisty mysteries with a touch of humor.

— *KIRKUS REVIEWS* ON *WITHOUT A BREW*

Charming...featuring a clever protagonist and talented brewer whose knowledge of the science and art of brewing beer is both fascinating and fun. The cozy village and the quirky characters who inhabit it are a delight, and the intriguing mystery will keep readers enthralled to the very end.

— KATE CARLISLE, *NEW YORK TIMES*
BESTSELLING AUTHOR OF THE BIBLIOPHILE
MYSTERIES AND THE FIXER UPPER MYSTERIES

Ellie Alexander's prose bubbles like the craft beers her protagonist Sloan Krause brews—a sparkling start to a new series.

— SHEILA CONNOLLY, *NEW YORK TIMES*
BESTSELLING AUTHOR OF THE ORCHARD
MYSTERIES AND THE CORK COUNTY
MYSTERIES

A concoction containing a charming setting, sympathetic characters, and a compelling heroine that kept me turning pages way past my bedtime.

— BARBARA ROSS, AUTHOR OF THE MAINE
CLAMBAKE MYSTERIES

Death on Tap is an entertaining sip of the world of brewpubs and tourist towns. Sloan, a foster child turned chef, brewer, and mother, is an intriguing protagonist. Pour me another!

— LESLIE BUDEWITZ, TWO-TIME AGATHA AWARD WINNING AUTHOR OF THE FOOD LOVERS' VILLAGE MYSTERIES

A 'hopping' good cozy mystery...Readers will enjoy listening to local gossip and tracking a killer along with her in the charming German-style 'Beervaria' setting of Leavenworth, Washington.

— MEG MACY, AUTHOR OF *BEARLY DEPARTED*

ALSO BY ELLIE ALEXANDER

THE SLOAN KRAUSE MYSTERIES

Trouble is Brewing

Death On Tap

The Pint of No Return

Beyond a Reasonable Stout

Without a Brew

The Cure for What Ales You

Hold on for Beer Life – Mystery Short

Beer and Loathing

A Brew to a Kill – Mystery Short

Ale I Want for Christmas is a Clue – Mystery Short

STANDALONE NOVELS

Lost Coast Literary

THE BAKESHOP MYSTERIES

Meet Your Baker

A Batter of Life and Death

On Thin Icing

Caught Bread Handed

Fudge and Jury

A Crime of Passion Fruit

Another One Bites the Crust

Till Death Do Us Tart

Live and Let Pie

A Cup of Holiday Fear

Nothing Bundt Trouble

Chilled to the Cone

Mocha, She Wrote

Bake, Borrow, and Steal

Donut Disturb

Muffin But the Truth

Catch Me If You Candy

A Smoking Bun – Coming Feb 2024

Books 19, 20, and 21 coming in 2024/2025!

THE SLOAN KRAUSE MYSTERY SHORTS

THE FIRST POUR

ELLIE ALEXANDER

Published by
Sweet Lemon Press LLC

Cover design by Gordy Seeley

This is a beerish, bookish love letter to you. I know you've been wanting a print version of the Sloan Krause Mystery Shorts, and I'm so thrilled to be able to share this with you. Thank you for coming along on Sloan's journey. I hope you enjoy these shorts, and stay tuned because there's more brewing in Leavenworth.

HOLD ON FOR BEER LIFE

A SLOAN KRAUSE MYSTERY SHORT

ELLIE ALEXANDER

AUTHOR OF THE CURE FOR WHAT ALES YOU

FOREWORD

This book is dedicated to you. I can't thank you enough for the outpouring of love and support for Sloan, Garrett, the Krause family, and yes, even April Ablin. Never in my career have I received so many emails, private messages, and handwritten notes asking me to please consider reviving the series after it was canceled.

Full disclosure, I was shocked when the series wasn't renewed. I had just finished writing *The Cure for What Ales You* and was starting to think about what was next for Sloan when my agent called with the news. Instead of sketching out book six, I suddenly found myself having to re-write book five to try and wrap up as much of Sloan's backstory as I could. The worst part was that Sloan had really begun to find her readership. Building a series takes time. I know that from writing my long-running Bakeshop Mystery Series, and just as Sloan was connecting with readers like you, my publisher pulled the plug.

I had thought that was the end of Sloan's story, but then I heard from you. Again, and again, and again. And that reignited my fire and passion for this series. There's so much more I want to tell. There's more beer to be brewed, more delicious Bavarian food to be consumed, more charming village festivals to celebrate, and more growth for Sloan as she finally begins to tear down the walls that she's built around herself and step into the new life she's cultivated in Leavenworth.

This brings me to you. If it weren't for your excitement and unwavering insistence that Sloan's story should continue, I might have let the series die a slow painful death. But here we are.

Think of *Hold on for Beer Life* as a little taste of what's to come. I hope this novella brings you a beerish escape as we pick up where things left off with Sloan and Garrett. There are bonus recipes included if you want to create your own delectable farm-style feast!

I'm working on book six which will be a full-length mystery. In the meantime, I'm sending you huge gratitude for coming along on this series journey with me.

Prost!
Ellie

CHAPTER
ONE

MY HAIR FLEW in the lofty, warm breeze as the car sped along the winding highway. I couldn't believe I was doing something so spontaneous and something just for me. It had been years since I had a getaway like this. Long before my marriage had disintegrated and before everything I thought I had known about my past had come into question.

The weekend trip had been my brewing partner Garrett Strong's idea, after a harrowing experience during Maifest when my teenage son Alex had been taken and a manhunt involving our entire village of Leavenworth, Washington had ensued. Fortunately, Alex had been found unharmed. Unfortunately, I wasn't sure I could say the same for myself. Physically speaking, I was fine, but emotionally not so much.

I had finally learned some answers about my past from my aunt Marianne. She had arrived in Leavenworth to warn me, but then had become entangled in the strange turn of events and had disappeared again before I had a chance to dive deeper.

Maybe I wasn't meant to fully understand my own origin story. Maybe it was time to let the past go for good.

This weekend was a fresh start. Garrett and I had been invited to the soft launch of Confluence Brewing's immersive beer retreat. The itinerary included a beer-inspired farm dinner, lodgings in the brewery's converted farmhouse, a beerish brunch, a hop field tour, and a bonfire. Not only was it going to be a much-needed break, but it was also going to give us a chance to spend time together outside of work. I was hesitant to call the weekend an official date, since we planned to use the opportunity to get a sense of whether we might incorporate some of what Confluence was offering at Nitro as we continued to look to innovate and expand on the booming market of beer tourism. However, spending an entire weekend in the dreamy orchard setting with Garrett had left me feeling jittery with anticipation for the last few days. I had packed and re-packed my suitcase three times, trying to decide what to bring and what to wear to dinner tonight.

I glanced out the window as we passed the turnoff to Peshastin Pinnacles State Park. The sandstone pinnacles were a favorite spot for rock climbers this time of the year. Scrambling up the slabs came with quite the reward—the view from the top of the hillside offered climbers a sweeping view of the Wenatchee valley orchards.

"Have you climbed the Pinnacles?" Garrett asked, keeping his attention on the road.

Sunlight flooded through the trees on either side of the two-lane highway as if shining a spotlight on our route. The first days of summer were upon us. Patches of purple lupine and yellow balsamroot mixed in with varying shades of green as we cut through the alpine forest.

"A long time ago." I chuckled at the memory. "It wasn't pretty. Somehow Mac convinced me to give it a try when Alex was just a toddler. I basically clawed my way to the top and was paralyzed at the summit. I didn't even really get to appreciate the view because all I could think about was that I had to rappel back down. It wasn't my bravest moment. Let's just say I might have freaked out before I worked up the courage to launch myself off the top of the craggy peak." My eyes drifted to the prominent rockface as visions resurfaced of clenching my eyes shut and clutching the belay ropes with a death grip.

Garrett let out a half-laugh like he thought I was exaggerating. "Sloan Krause freaking out. Now that I would like to see."

I shot him what I hoped was a playful look. "Don't mess with me, Strong. If you're not careful, I might freak out at Confluence tonight. There's no rock climbing involved with this retreat, is there?"

"No. I promise. The only adventure this weekend involves is putting your hoppy palate to the test, but seriously, you should freak out. I'd like to see it." Garrett egged me on. "You've held so much in while holding our entire town together these past few years. If anyone deserves a freak-out, it's you." His tone had shifted.

I could hear the emotion in his voice. I didn't want to run from it. That was the pattern of my past, a protection strategy I had implemented from a young age. But I also wasn't ready to bring down the mood of our first official date. If it was a date.

"Thanks," I replied with sincerity. "Really, I mean it, but let's talk about lighter things. It's so beautiful, and I'm excited about this weekend. Tell me everything. I want the beer and food details."

For the briefest moment, Garrett looked like he wanted to say more, but instead, he steered around a sharp turn and brushed a strand of wavy hair from his eye. "As you know, Confluence Brewing is fairly new to the scene. They started out

7

like us—nano, small batches, brewing in the old barn on the property for over six years. From what I heard, they did pop-up events at the orchard that sublets them barn space for their brewing equipment, and they gained a cult following. They did a huge renovation and are officially opening a tasting room, lodgings, and doing weekend beer getaways. It sounds like they're gearing up. They've been gaining notoriety and had that write-up in Brew Magazine. I'm excited to check them out. When Ben, their head brewer, reached out, he sounded like he might want to talk about some potential partnerships, which could be cool, assuming that their beer is good, of course."

The craft beer community was relatively small. I had heard of Confluence but had yet to visit our colleagues to the east. Wenatchee was about a thirty-minute drive from Leavenworth. It was bigger than our Bavarian village and known for its apple orchards, artisan market, breweries, wineries, and historic downtown.

"Dinner is in the orchard, right?" I asked Garrett.

"Yep. Five courses under the stars. Each course has a beer pairing, which will put your 'nose' to the test."

I laughed. Otto Krause, my father-in-law, well, technically soon to be ex-father-in-law but forever family, had declared that I had the "nose" for hops many years ago. He had helped me cultivate my tasting palate and mentored me on every aspect of the brewing process. Without his guidance and expertise, I would probably still be working odd jobs, waiting tables, and managing booths at the farmers market. Although my relationship with Mac had ultimately failed, I was indebted to the Krauses. They had welcomed me into their family and to Leavenworth. We had been through so much together that I knew without a shred of doubt that we would stay connected even once my divorce with Mac was finalized.

"It's so much pressure." I touched the tip of my nose. "I hope my senses bring their A-game tonight."

"Hey, your palate on its worst night is better than mine," Garrett teased.

Our conversation drifted to summer plans and brainstorming new beers for Nitro, the nanobrewery that we ran together. For the next couple of months, we would see a reprieve from the huge festivals like Maifest and Oktoberfest that brought thousands of visitors to our mountainous retreat every weekend. Instead, summer would bring steady crowds of adventurers. Leavenworth was the perfect basecamp for hiking, climbing, and rafting. It should be good for business, and it was always fun to serve frothy pints and pub snacks to beer lovers after they had spent a long day out in nature.

I loved the intimate feel of Nitro. It was a place where our regular customers were like family and where tourists were greeted and welcomed like old friends. We had been housing guests in four converted suites above the brewery that were themed after the four key ingredients in beer—water, hops, grain, and yeast. As part of any stay, we gave our overnight guests a free pint, special tastings, tours of the brewery, and a beer-infused breakfast. The idea of potentially partnering with Confluence on excursions to hop farms or collaborating on a new brew was exciting.

The drive to Wenatchee didn't take long. The Columbia River cut through the center of the vibrant town with views of the surrounding Cascade Mountains to the east. Wenatchee had become a hub for foodies and growers of all sorts. Its downtown public market was a community gathering spot where visitors could find fresh fruits and vegetables grown in the region as well as artisan crafts and gifts.

We soon found ourselves on the outskirts of town, where suburbs transformed into orchards and vineyards. A small sign

9

to our left pointed to Confluence Brewing. Garrett turned off the highway and followed a gravel drive through the orchard. McIntosh, Gala, and Honeycrisp apple trees stretched on either side of the path as far as I could see. In the distance there was a classic red barn, a farmhouse, and numerous outbuildings.

The orchard was clearly still operating because heavy equipment like tractors and machinery, along with stacks and stacks of crates for apple picking, lined the left side of the gravel drive.

An intentionally weathered sign reading CONFLUENCE BREWING hung from the barn as we pulled into a gravel parking lot in front of it. The farmhouse was a few hundred feet away, nestled in apple trees in every direction.

"I guess we're this way." Garrett steered into a parking space. Before we got out, he reached for my arm. I felt a surge of energy rush up my spine as his eyes met mine. "I'm happy we're here together, Sloan. I've been looking forward to this weekend for a while." His voice deepened.

My heart pulsed fast. I'm not prone to blushing. My olive skin and gift (or curse) of concealing my emotions tended to make me appear aloof, even when my internal feelings threatened to pull me under. In this moment with Garrett's wide eyes locked on mine, maintaining strong eye contact and studying my face with a look of such tenderness, my heart pounded against my chest. The faint hint of hops on his skin and the warmth of the car made heat rise in my cheeks.

"I'm glad we're here, too," I said softly.

For a second, I thought he was going to lean in and kiss me, but instead, he squeezed my arm and released me. "Let's go get hoppy."

"Oh, no, not beer puns." I reached for my wrap. June evenings tended to cool down with the setting sun. I had opted for a red wrap dress with a floral print and a pair of strappy sandals. Garrett, who usually hung out in shorts and beer T-shirts, had dressed for the occasion, too, in a pair of khakis and a sky-blue button-down shirt. I had to admit that my heart had skipped a beat when he had shown up in the outfit holding a bouquet of wildflowers.

I pushed the thought aside as I got out of the car. The air smelled sweet, like apple blossoms. The barn was stained a rustic burnt shade of red with bright white trim and a sloped roof. Its doors were propped open to reveal a gorgeous tasting room and bar inside.

We were greeted immediately by a young woman in her early to mid-twenties. She balanced a tray of beers in one hand and a stack of nametags in the other. "Welcome to Confluence. Are you joining us for the brewer's dinner and the weekend retreat?"

"We are," Garrett replied with a smile.

"Okay, great." She held out the stack of nametags and set the tray of beers on a folding table that had been set up in front of the barn. There were welcome packets and itineraries stacked on the table. "Could you do me a favor and find your names? I was supposed to have help here at the greeting table tonight, but Josh is missing like always, and I'm on my own."

"No problem." Garrett flipped through the nametags.

"Can I get you started with our welcome beer?" the woman asked me, pointing to the tray of golden ales. "This is our summer pilsner. It's going to be really soft with a nice mouth-feel. We used hops from Central Washington, which are going to give it that nice aroma and then a crisp finish."

Someone had trained her well in craft beer speak. "Sounds lovely." I took a glass of straw-colored beer from her. "Have you worked at Confluence long?"

She shook her head. "No. This is my first summer. I just

graduated from the CWU brewing program. Josh did, too. We're both interning with Ben."

"That's fantastic," I replied, taking a sip of the beer. The program she was referring to was Central Washington University's school of brewing science. It was one of the first of its kind, offering students an accredited Bachelor of Science in Craft Beer. Students who graduated from the program went on to do a variety of jobs in the field, from laboratory research to positions as head brewers.

Garrett found our nametags. "Is Ben around?"

She took the remaining nametags from him and positioned the tray so he could take a pint. "Yep, he's around somewhere. Although you should call him Big Ben, that's his nickname. I'm Miri, by the way. Sorry, I should have introduced myself. But, like I said, Josh is supposed to be here, so I'm trying to do like a thousand things."

"Can we help?" I asked without even thinking. "We're brewers, too. We're from Nitro in Leavenworth."

"Oh, my God." She clasped her hand over her mouth. "Nitro? You guys are the best. I did a term paper on nanobreweries in the state, and you were one of my case studies. Ben loves you guys, too. He talks about Nitro all the time. He's super excited that you're here this weekend." Her freckled cheeks flamed with color. "Now I'm really embarrassed. You two are VIPS tonight. There's no way I can let you help."

"It's fine." I looked to Garrett to make sure he agreed.

He gave Miri a decisive nod. "Absolutely. Put us to work. What do you need?"

Miri chewed on her bottom lip. "Well, if it isn't too much trouble, would you mind taking the menus to the table with you? They are right inside the barn—in the tasting room. I was supposed to go set them out at the table, but Josh bailed on me, and guests started arriving."

"No problem." Garrett was already moving toward the rustic barn doors. "Let us know if you need anything else. Sloan and I have firsthand experience with what it's like to wear a lot of hats when you run a small brewery."

"Thanks." Miri smiled with relief as another car pulled up.

Garrett and I headed inside the barn. I was expecting the interior to match the vintage exterior, but to my surprise, the space had been completely modernized. Refurbished hardwood floors gleamed under strings of white and gold twinkle lights that swept in arcs across the ceiling, giving the appearance of sparkling waves of dazzling stars. Keg barrels and bar stools were spaced throughout the open room. Greenery in the form of potted ferns and cuttings of apple blossoms brought a touch of nature inside. A long bar with dozens of taps took over the far end of the barn.

I was about to comment on how cool the space was, but the sound of voices stopped me.

A man wearing knee-high rubber boots stood with his back to us. He was tall, at well over six feet, and built like a Sasquatch.

He shouted at another man who wore a Confluence T-shirt and cowered next to him. "I don't care if you've looked everywhere. Go look again. Find him and bring him to me, or you're both done."

The other man nodded frantically and hurried out the back door.

Given the boots (a must for any craft brewer) and the fact that the man could have passed as a giant, I had to guess this must be Big Ben.

He muttered something under his breath and then turned around. The sight of Garrett and me made him take a step backward. "Oh, hey. Oh, sorry, I, uh, didn't know there was anyone in here. The tasting room is closed for a private event tonight."

"We're here for the dinner," Garrett replied, pointing to his nametag.

"Gotcha. Great, great. Welcome." The man cleared his throat and moved closer to us. He had scruffy hair and matching facial scruff like he hadn't shaved for a couple of days. "Uh, the dinner is outside, though."

"We came to pick up the menus," I interjected. "Miri was shorthanded outside, and Garrett and I are brewers, so we figured the least we could do is help a fellow brewmaster out."

"Oh, crap, you're Garrett Strong and Sloan Krause?" Realization dawned on him. He extended his hand and gave Garrett a hearty shake. "I'm Ben. It's awesome to have you guys here, but man, I told my team to treat you like VIPS, not put you to work."

I didn't want Miri to get in trouble. "Not at all. We volunteered."

Garrett lifted his beer glass. "Plus, we have your pilsner to start us off, so it's all good."

Ben forced a smile. "I appreciate it." He let out a long sigh. "Staffing issues. I guess that's what I get for hiring recent college grads. I'm ready to kill them. I swear, whatever happened to work ethic?"

I didn't want to get into it with Ben, but we had had the opposite experience with our staff at Nitro. Maybe we had lucked out with Kat and the twins.

"Are these the menus?" Garrett motioned to a stack of creamy cardstock paper with silver and gold lettering sitting on a nearby keg barrel.

"Yeah, but I can find someone else to get them down to the field." Ben waved him off with a meaty paw. Neither Garrett nor I were small, but Ben towered over both of us.

"No, don't sweat it." Garrett picked up the stack. "Sloan and I are heading that way. You take care of your staff and get ready for the dinner. We'll bring these menus with us."

"Thanks. It's good to have beer celebrities here. I hope you enjoy tonight's tasting. As long as I can round up my team, we should have a good spread for you. It's kind of busy now, but I'd love to chat with you about what you're doing at Nitro when we have some time this weekend. I've got some ideas for a collab, and my business partner and I are getting ready to launch a second space in Seattle, so I'd be totally open to doing some marketing with you on that since you guys get so much traffic from the area."

"Sounds great," Garrett replied. "We're looking forward to the weekend and always game to talk shop."

"Awesome." Ben pointed to his left. "Just follow the tractor path through the orchard, and eventually, you'll come to a fork. Stay to the right. The lower orchard is to the left, and we've got that area closed off due to some problems with wildlife—nothing to worry about. Just stay to the right, and you'll get to a clearing. You can't miss it. The tables are already set up, and feel free to grab another pint. We'll keep the beer flowing tonight."

We left Ben and followed the path on the other side of the barn. The smell of apple blossoms and fresh-cut grass was even stronger as we navigated the dirt road. I also caught a hint of something strong, which I guessed to be hemp. Hemp and pot fields had become abundant in the valley. The distinct smell was overpowering, but fortunately, the aroma dissipated when we came to the fork in the road. That was a con of having the "nose." I could pick up scents like a bloodhound for better or worse.

Everything was a wash of variegated shades of green from the grass to the trees as we continued on.

"This is the quintessential farm experience, isn't it?" Garrett said, motioning to a small field adjacent to the orchard where peonies, bellflowers, and salvia bloomed. There were u-pick flower signs and a stand with shears and galvanized tin buckets.

"It's so gorgeous," I agreed.

We came to the clearing where two long tables had been set up in front of rows of late-blooming Pink Lady apples.

"This must be it." Garrett came to a stop in front of the tables.

Any romantic inklings I had felt were heightened by the sight of the spot where we would be dining. Both tables had been draped with sheer white tablecloths. There were place settings with each of our names, vases of wildflowers, and dozens of candles waiting to be lit. Additionally, the trees had been strung with lights and paper lanterns. It was like a scene from a fairy tale.

"Looks like we're the first ones here." Garrett set the menus on the edge of the table. "Should we toast to something?"

I had taken small sips of my beer on the walk down so as not to spill it all over my dress. My glass was still nearly full. "Sure. What should we toast to?" I blinked rapidly as Garrett moved closer to me. The jittery feeling returned.

He touched his glass to mine. His eyes were locked on me. They had a glowing quality to them, like the lights wrapped around the trees. "To new adventures."

My throat tightened. I could feel my body pulling toward his.

At that moment, a scream cut through the orchard, breaking the spell and causing both of us to jump.

"Someone help! I need help. Help me, please!"

TWO

WE BOTH SET our beers on the table. Garrett sprinted toward the apple trees. I followed behind as fast as I could. The screams sounded close.

"Help! Someone help!"

We followed the sound of a woman's high-pitched voice through the tidy rows of organic apple trees. The ground was uneven with rocks and holes. Leaves crunched under my feet as I sprinted to keep up with Garrett. I'm naturally tall, but Garrett was even taller, and he was obviously on a mission to help. The scent of fresh-cut grass mixed with hemp lingered in the air as I sucked in deep breaths and forced my legs to move faster.

The screams continued as we raced through endless stretches of trees until we finally made it to the source of the frantic screams—another clearing that must have been in the lower orchard. A rusty tractor, farm pallets, rickety scaffolding, and ladders were clumped together in an open section of dirt surrounded by another field of apple trees. In the distance, I could see several outbuildings and a large fence. I wondered if we were near the edge of Confluence's acreage.

Miri, the college grad who had greeted us upon our arrival, was kneeling down next to a young guy who appeared to be passed out.

I froze and clutched my stomach.

Oh, no.

He was lying face up a good ten or twelve feet away from the farming gear, and he wasn't moving.

Was he dead?

Miri glanced up at us with wild eyes. "It's Josh. I just found him like this." She looked from the ground to a ladder propped next to a tree at the edge of the orchard. "I think he must have fallen, but he's not responding."

I moved closer as Garrett reached into his pocket for his phone.

Part of my training at the brewery involved being certified in first aid and CPR. "He might have a concussion," I said to Miri.

"Should I call EMS?" Garrett asked, his phone in hand.

"Let me assess him first." I bent down next to Miri. Josh was flat on his back. His eyes were closed, but his breathing and pulse were steady. There were no obvious signs of injury. He wasn't bleeding or bruised. "When did you find him?" I asked Miri.

Miri's voice cracked as she spoke. She rocked back and forth on her knees. "Uh, I don't know. A couple of minutes, maybe. It all happened so fast. I was supposed to be greeting the guests, but Ben came out of the barn not long after I met you. He was furious about Josh disappearing and told me to go look for him." Her body quivered like she was cold. Only it was warm in the orchard. I hoped that she wasn't about to go into shock. "Do you think he's going to be okay?"

I gently nudged his shoulder. "Josh, Josh, can you hear us?"

He let out a low moan.

That was a good sign.

Miri gasped. "Was that him?"

I nudged him again, careful not to move his head. If he had fallen, he could have sustained a neck or head injury.

His eyes fluttered open. He blinked rapidly. "Where am I?"

"You're on the ground in the orchard," I replied. "We think you might have fallen."

"No, I didn't fall." His voice sounded groggy, like he had just woken up from a nap.

I watched as he attempted to sit up. "Take it easy," I cautioned him. "You may have hit your head."

Josh swayed from side to side after getting himself semi-upright.

Garrett caught my eye. "Should I call for help?"

"Let's give it a minute." I turned to Josh. "I'm Sloan. I'm trained in first aid and CPR. Can I take a look at your eyes?"

Josh squinted. "Yeah."

I checked his pupils and ran him through a concussion protocol. His eyes were reactive. Another good sign. "Do you remember what happened?"

He ran his fingers through his shaggy dark hair. Like Miri, he was young, not that much older than Alex. His face still had a boyish quality.

"You fell," Miri interjected. "You fell off the ladder."

"No. No, I didn't fall," Josh insisted. His eyes were glassy, but his speech was clear.

"You did. I found you here—passed out on the ground." Miri thrust her finger toward the ladder. "You fell off the ladder."

"Miri, what's your deal? I didn't fall. Okay?" Josh glared at her.

"How did you end up on the ground, then? And where have you been? Ben's pissed," Miri countered. Her body had stopped shaking, but her eyes darted from the ladder to Josh and back again.

Why was she so convinced that Josh had fallen? I wasn't sure her theory was correct. The trees were at least twelve feet away, and the ladder was still propped upright against one of them. It didn't seem possible that Josh could have fallen off the ladder and ended up on the ground next to the tractor and pallets. Not unless he had launched himself from the ladder, and why would he do that?

"I was doing my job. You know that. I told you I was coming out here." His teeth clenched as he spoke with forced restraint.

Miri flinched. She shook her head. "No, you just disappeared."

Josh sat all the way up. Color had returned to his cheeks. His eyes looked brighter. "Are you the one who has a concussion? We had a conversation in the barn, remember? Saachi told me she wanted apple branches on the tables. I told you I was coming out here to clip some before the guests arrived. You were getting everything ready. Maybe you didn't hear me, but I swear I saw you nod."

Miri folded her arms across her chest. "I definitely did *not* hear you say that."

"Who is Saachi?" I asked.

"Our boss," Miri responded, not taking her eyes off of Josh.

"Well, I did. Like I said, I came out to the orchard to clip some branches for decoration, and then the next thing I knew, someone smacked me on the back of my head, and I woke up on the ground."

"Why would anyone smack you on the head, Josh?" Miri's tone had shifted from concern to irritation.

"You tell me." He shrugged and started to push to his feet.

I stopped him. "We should make sure you don't have a gash on the back of your head."

"I'm fine." He stood up. "I have to get to work."

"If you were knocked unconscious, it's probably a good idea to go to the hospital and make sure everything's okay. Are you feeling dizzy? Nauseous? Do you have a headache?" I stopped him from moving too quickly by holding onto his arm. "Can I take a look at the back of your head? I want to make sure you're not bleeding."

"Go ahead."

I checked for any sign of bleeding or cuts. The skin didn't appear to be broken, but I did feel a lump on the back of his head. "Do you feel this?" I moved his hand to the spot and watched his eyes narrow as he touched the contusion. "Does it hurt?"

"Nah, it's not too bad." He brushed dirt from his jeans and Confluence Brewing T-shirt. "I'm fine."

Garrett seconded my concerns. "Are you sure? I can call for help. You don't want to mess around with a concussion."

Josh was already moving toward the barn. "It's fine. I'm fine. I need to go check in with Ben before he freaks out. Thanks for helping me."

He raced off with Miri on his heels.

"That was weird," I said to Garrett, watching the young brewery interns arguing as they followed the path through the trees back toward the barn. "He thinks someone hit him?"

"Really weird." Garrett nodded in agreement. His eyes landed on the ladder. "His story checks out, though. How would he have fallen off the ladder and ended up here?" He pointed to the ground and then to the patch of trees. "He was flat on his back. It doesn't make sense."

"Yeah, that's exactly what I was thinking." Getting hit

made more sense physically speaking, but why would someone try to hit the aspiring brewer?

"I feel like we should do something else, but what?" I brushed my hands together and smoothed down the front of my dress.

Garrett shrugged. "I don't know. If the kid is refusing medical help, I'm not sure there's much else we can do."

"I'll mention it to Ben, and if Josh is helping out at dinner, we should keep an eye on him. The fact that he has a goose egg is actually a good sign. You really worry with a head injury if the swelling is internal, but still, if he were to start slurring his words, have blurry vision, or feeling nauseous, we need to call for help right away."

"Yeah, got it." Garrett returned his phone to his pocket.

I took a minute to study the area. My intuition told me something else was going on. How had Miri gotten down to the lower orchard so fast? What had Josh been doing here? Ben and Miri had both made it sound like everyone was helping with check-in and dinner prep. Something didn't add up.

Garrett held out his arm. "So, should we head back for dinner? It's not quite the romantic start I imagined, but hopefully, this night will turn around once the beer really starts flowing."

I took his arm and sighed. "I have a weird feeling about this, but you're right. I'm not sure there's much more we can do."

We returned to the tables in the upper orchard. Other guests had arrived in the interim. No one was aware of what had just happened, and I decided it was best to keep it that way.

Introductions were made, and the first course was passed around. As Garrett had hoped, the evening took a turn for the better as we munched on a trio of bruschetta. There was an apple chutney on sourdough with tart raisins, walnut pesto and goat cheese, and traditional tomato and basil with a drizzle of balsamic vinegar. Ben came out with a tray of hoppy spring honey pale ales to pair with our starters. The ale was light and delicate, with a lovely touch of sweetness from the honey. He stood at the head of the table and held up one of the pint glasses for everyone to see.

"Everything you'll be sampling tonight comes from this farm and orchard or from our neighbors," Ben explained. "You can say hi to the goats who produced the milk used in this cheese on your way to your rooms tonight. The apples in the chutney are from last year's harvest, and the heirloom tomatoes and basil were hand-picked from the garden next door. At Confluence, we want you to taste the region in which we live and work in every bite and every sip. You've probably heard the adage, 'What grows together, goes together.' That's our philosophy here. Every ingredient you taste in our beer is grown in this valley. The honey in our pale is from those beehives you see in the distance." Ben pointed to the far side of the orchard, where numerous beehives dotted the grounds. He was clearly passionate about the local growing region, which is something I appreciated about the community in Leavenworth and Wenatchee.

The hyper-local focus came through in the food and the beer. Each bite was truly a delight.

"This is seriously good," I said to Garrett, taking a long, slow sip of my beer. It was the color of straw and sparkling clear without a speck of trub floating in it. Trub is the sediment that collects at the bottom of the tank during the brewing process, and something no one wanted to get a mouthful of while drinking a pint. Ben obviously took great care when it came to the brewing process, too. Unfiltered beers had been trending lately, but both Garrett and I were purists when it came to filtering. I wanted to drink a clean pint and leave the trub for the bottom of the barrel.

"Yeah, the honey notes really hit you at the finish," Garrett said.

I took another taste. "I feel like there's something familiar about this."

"Familiar?" Garrett tried his beer again, too.

"Could it be the hops? I know I'm getting Simcoe." I held my nose to the rim of the glass to get a better smell. "Maybe it's the honey?"

"You're right." Garrett swished a sip of beer around in his mouth. "My nose isn't on par with yours, but there is something almost familiar about it."

Ben wandered over to us. "How are you liking the honey pale?"

"It's great," I answered honestly. "It's reminding us of something, but neither of us can put a finger on what. Maybe it's close to a batch of honey that we brewed this spring."

"All the honey in the region tastes the same." Ben raised his eyebrows and gave me a dismissive nod. "You can't make anything original in the valley anymore. Those days are over. That's what I've been telling my interns."

I wasn't sure I agreed with his perspective, but I took the opportunity to bring up Josh. "Hey, did you know that Josh took a fall earlier?"

Ben took a step back from the table. "What?"

We proceeded to tell him about Josh's injury.

"Thanks. I'll take it from here."

I almost got the impression he was upset that we had brought it up as he moved on to talk to another group.

We enjoyed the tasting bites with our beer and the warmth of the sun. A band had been hired to serenade us. I listened to their sultry sounds and watched butterflies and hummingbirds dart between the trees. A feeling of contentment came over me. I was here in the middle of a blooming orchard on a warm June evening with a man whom I had grown close to and developed a solid friendship with over the past couple of years. If someone had told me on the fateful day I had caught Mac with the beer wench that I might find happiness like this, I probably wouldn't have believed them.

I'd been through so much. The breakup with Mac. Starting a new chapter at Nitro. Learning that Otto and Ursula had been less than honest about their past and their reasons for settling in Leavenworth. Navigating new relationships with the entire Krause family and finally understanding my roots. After being abandoned and growing up without anyone to lean on, I almost couldn't believe that I had such a strong connection with Garrett and a network of friends and family in Leavenworth who would support me through anything.

It was good timing, too. Alex would be leaving for college soon. I was going to be on my own again, but this time it felt different. I might be living alone in my sweet little Bavarian cottage in the center of town, but I wasn't alone. That was a distinction that I was inordinately grateful for.

CHAPTER
THREE

OUR APPETIZER course was followed by a summer salad made with greens grown on the farm, candied pecans, grilled beets, goat cheese, and fresh herbs. It was accompanied by a rosehip pale ale. My thoughts ventured away from finding Josh knocked out amongst the apple trees and to the food in front of us.

A woman joined Ben. She had long dark hair that she wore in two braids and a severe smile. I wasn't a great judge of age, but I guessed her to be closer to thirty.

She held baskets of baked bread and a tray of clarified butter while Ben told everyone about the next beer.

"Everyone, let me introduce you to Saachi. She manages operations here at Confluence and keeps us all in line, isn't that right, Saachi?"

Saachi forced a smile and set the baskets in the center of the table. "This is spent grain bread accompanied by a variety of butter. A spicy chipotle, rosemary, cranberry orange, and a garlic and sea salt."

Ben kept his eyes on her as he spoke. "Saachi is also our

resident bread queen. She bakes our bread using the spent grains from the brew cycle. Please, help yourselves. Don't be shy. We think you'll agree that bread made from the by-products of brewing enhances the tasting experience."

He paused to pour the next round—a classic hoppy Northwest IPA.

I was familiar with using spent grains. Baking with beer and beer by-products was common in Germany. Otto and Ursula had introduced me to the techniques many years ago. They didn't let anything at Der Keller go to waste. One of the most popular kinds of bread served at the restaurant was called biertreberbrot, a traditional German bread made by adding spent grains to the dough and incorporating nuts and raisins. The result was a delicious nutty loaf chock-full of extra protein and fiber.

Garrett and I had played around with different recipes for using Nitro's spent grains. From a timing perspective, we had landed on using our brewery by-products to make dog biscuits instead of bread. On special occasions, I would bake a couple of loaves of biertreberbrot, but otherwise, because we were such a small and nimble operation, making batches of dog treats from our spent grain was the least time-consuming. We kept the special bone-shaped snacks at the bar and outside for any four-legged friends who happened to stop in with their owners. The dog treats had become so popular that we had a rotation of "regular" pups who trotted in for their daily fix.

"Ready for round two?" Ben interrupted my thoughts and offered me a pint of Confluence's IPA as he explained to the table that the beer was brewed with Yakima Valley hops and white peaches. The combination of the fruity, hop-forward beer and rustic bread slathered with cranberry-orange butter had my tastebuds singing.

"This is even better than I expected," I said to Garrett,

keeping my voice low. "But again, there's something oddly recognizable about this beer, too."

He savored a mouthful and nodded. "Yeah, it's kind of blowing me away, which is saying a lot. It's not as if we aren't surrounded by world-class restaurants in Leavenworth, but it definitely is bringing up a beer memory for me. Do you think it's just the hops? Maybe it's because we use Citra and Mosaic, and so does Der Keller. Maybe it's a regional thing?"

"Could be," I agreed.

He was right about Leavenworth in terms of the food and beer scene. Even though our Bavarian village boasted a population of just over two thousand permanent residents, Leavenworth's food scene rivaled that of any big city because we were a tourist destination. Sure, delectable German fare was easy to find, but world cuisine was also on the menu, as were locally sourced farm-to-table provisions. I loved living in a small community that was so connected to food.

Ben and Saachi shared a brief exchange as he handed out another round of pints to the table. I tried not to eavesdrop, but from how her brows furrowed and how she yanked her arm away from him, I got the sense that things weren't exactly going smoothly between them.

"Saachi, would you like to tell everyone what's next up after they finish their bread?" Ben's tone was light and jovial when he finished passing out drinks. Too jovial.

She inhaled deeply and tucked an empty tray beneath one arm. "Sure, Ben. I'd love to." Her sarcastic tone said otherwise.

Garrett kicked me gently and leaned closer to whisper, "Are you getting a vibe that things are tense between those two, or is it just me?"

"Yeah, it's like they're trying to hold it together."

Saachi flipped a braid over one shoulder. "The next course

is a creamy yellow squash soup made with root vegetables from a farm a few miles from here. It has a touch of our North-west red ale that you'll be sampling with it. We used fresh garden thyme, organic garlic, onions, and a healthy amount of cream as the base, along with our handmade chicken stock."

"Sounds delish," one of our tablemates commented.

"It is." Saachi didn't even attempt to be humble about her cooking. Instead, she glared at Ben. "Is that good? I need to get back to the kitchen."

Ben's smile grew wider, but his eyes betrayed him. They were filled with rage. "Yes, yes. A quick round of applause for our chef."

Everyone clapped half-heartedly. Surely Garrett and I weren't alone in picking up on the tension between them. The food, beer, and setting were amazing, but Confluence clearly had some serious staffing issues to work out.

Saachi stomped away.

Ben circled the table with a growler, topping off drinks.

Josh and Miri showed up shortly, both carrying trays of the yellow squash soup. Maybe it was my upbringing, but I couldn't shake the feeling that something was wrong between them as well. Spending years hopping from foster care home to foster care home had taught me to be a careful observer. Their rigid body language and the way Miri continually stole glances at Ben had me on edge. What was going on with the Conflu-ence crew?

"How's the head?" I asked Josh when he delivered my soup. I studied his face for any sign of a concussion.

His hand instinctively rubbed the base of his skull. "Fine. I'm good." He sounded like he didn't want to talk about it.

Miri gave me a pleading look, shook her head, and nodded toward Ben. "Can we not talk about it right now?"

"I just asked how he was doing."

Ben came our way. "Is something wrong?" He looked at my soup.

"Nope. Everything is amazing," I replied truthfully.

"Are these two bothering you?" He gave Miri and Josh a warning look. "I know they're both super fans of Nitro, but I believe we made it clear at the team meeting that Sloan and Garrett are here as dinner guests tonight, right?"

Miri gulped and nodded.

Josh started to say something, but she elbowed him in the stomach, and he shut up.

"We're happy to chat about anything," Garrett said, kicking me under the table.

Ben's tone shifted. "Not on my watch. You're paying guests, and I've made it abundantly clear to my interns that they are to serve you and walk away. Right, guys?"

Miri's face flamed with color. Josh hung his head.

I had to say something. "Ben, I appreciate that, but really, I was the one who was checking in. Josh took a fall, and I wanted to make sure he's feeling okay."

"Yeah, why didn't you come to me?" Ben's eyes bulged. "I can't believe I had to hear about this from a guest—a VIP guest."

The rest of the table had fallen silent as Ben's voice grew louder and more forceful. An awkward silence washed over the orchard as all eyes turned toward us.

"It's not a big deal," Josh said. He hunched his shoulders and stared at his feet. "I fell off a ladder when I was clipping branches for the table. They found me and made sure I was okay."

Why had his story changed? An hour ago, he had insisted that he hadn't fallen off the ladder.

Miri's head bobbed in agreement. "Yeah, we would have

told you, but it was a whirlwind. Everyone showed up at once, and we needed to get beers and direct people out here to the orchard."

Ben scowled. "Did you let Saachi know? And how far did you fall?"

"It wasn't that bad." Josh's hand went to the base of his skull again.

I wondered if he was aware that he was touching the spot where he'd been hit.

"This needs to be reported and documented. We've been over this. Any incident or injury must be reported to management. Understood?"

Josh kept his chin down. "Yes."

"What's that?" Ben wiggled his ear. "I don't think I heard you."

"Yes, understood." Josh spoke louder but didn't meet Ben's steely gaze.

"Good." Ben's fake smile returned to his face. "Go find Saachi and fill out an incident report."

"But what about the next course?" Miri asked.

"I'll come help." Ben motioned toward the barn. "Incident report—now."

Garrett took a bite of soup. Silence hung thick in the air like the puffy white clouds on the horizon.

Ben brushed his hands together and made his smile tighter. So tight it made my cheeks hurt. "Sorry about that, everyone. The joys of running a nanobrewery and having young interns, are you with me?"

A few people chuckled uncomfortably.

"Let's get into this beer," Ben continued, seemingly oblivious to the awkwardness. "You can't live in the Pacific Northwest and not love a hoppy red."

I listened to his description of hops and his step-by-step

brewing process as I ate my soup, which was on par with the rest of the courses. However, I couldn't shake the feeling that there was more brewing at Confluence. Who had hit Josh hard enough to knock him out? And why had his story changed?

The sun had begun to sink behind the apple trees. Music continued to waft through the air, and conversations returned to the table. I tried to stay in the moment. This was my first official date with Garrett, after all, but I couldn't stop the litany of questions running through my brain. Was Confluence simply having growing pains? Maybe they had bitten off more than they could chew tonight. A five-course dinner with beer pairings was no small undertaking. Perhaps the tension I was picking up on was that. But it felt like more. The friction between Ben and Saachi had been palpable, and unless Josh had been lying, his head injury was no accident.

I sighed.

"Everything okay?" Garrett asked.

"Sorry, I didn't realize that I'd sighed so loudly." I dipped my spoon in the creamy soup. "I don't know. It's weird. I can't stop feeling like something else is going on."

"Same." Garrett stirred his soup. "I have to say I'm starting to wonder about Ben."

"Me too. I'm getting that gross feeling in my stomach, and it's not from the food."

"What should we do?"

I shrugged. "What can we do?"

Garrett rested his spoon in his bowl. "I heard Ben telling one of the other guests that there is going to be a brewery tour after the main course. A stretch break before dessert. I vote that we both keep our eyes open on the tour. I don't want to think the worst, but do you think there's a chance that these interns and other staff members are being exploited, or..." He trailed off.

I had a feeling I knew what he was going to say. Or worse. Could Josh and Miri be in danger?

CHAPTER
FOUR

As MUCH AS I tried to relax and enjoy the main course, I could feel my spine stiffen and my jaw tighten every time Ben passed by us to check on how we were liking dinner. I had no complaints about the meal. The main course was grilled chicken marinated in a citrus IPA, fingerling roasted potatoes, corn on the cob, and blackened Brussels sprouts. The hearty feast paired wonderfully with the bright, fresh citrus notes of the IPA. It was hard not to fall in love with the food. And, if it weren't for the chaos and animosity amongst the staff, I would gladly have wanted to partner with Confluence on a joint beer.

One of the best parts of the craft beer community was collaborating. When I gave brewery tours at Nitro, a recurring question was always about how we dealt with our beer competition. The truth was that there was little competition between craft brewers. If anything, most of us went out of our way to promote each other. Marketing the craft was more important —it helped all of us. Plus, as brewers, we understood and appreciated the work that went into each individual pint. You would never hear Garrett, me, or any of our staff throwing shade at another craft brewery.

Der Keller had set that tone when they first opened their doors nearly thirty years ago, mentoring new brewers and collaborating whenever the chance arose. That was the kind of community I wanted to be a part of, but there was no chance we were going to spend more time with the dysfunctional team at Confluence. Brewing was meant to be fun and creative not that it wasn't work, too, but I couldn't imagine what brewing with Ben would be like, and I didn't want to spend another minute imagining it.

As promised, Ben encouraged us to take a break to stretch our legs after dinner.

"We're going to give you the full access tour to the brewery," he said, holding up an empty pint glass. "Bring your glasses with you, and you can fill up on any tap you like. While we check out the equipment firsthand, our team will clean up and prepare the incredible final dessert course that we have planned for you. How does that sound?"

Everyone nodded.

His style was odd. On the one hand, he was over the top with schmooze, and on the other, he seemed slightly irritated that we were taking him away from the brewing process.

I couldn't get a good read on him.

"You ready for this, Sloan?" Garrett asked as we followed the group toward the barn. "Let's see if we can get to the bottom of the barrel and figure out what's really up with Confluence."

"I'm on it." Although I wasn't sure how we were going to get to the bottom of anything without talking to Miri, Josh, and Saachi. Hopefully, an opportunity would arise on the tour.

Regardless, I was glad for a chance to move. The food and

beer had been world-class thus far, but if I had stayed at the table much longer, I might have nodded off.

Garrett reached for my hand on our short walk to the barn. A pulse of electricity surged through me. I hadn't felt like this for a long time, and I'd forgotten about the rush that came with attraction. But with Garrett, it was different. When Mac and I had gotten together, I was barely an adult myself. Now I was a fully grown woman ready to explore a new relationship.

My thoughts drifted to Alex. I wondered what he would think if Garrett and I became a couple. I knew he wanted me to be happy, but I also knew that there would probably always be a part of him that wanted Mac and me together. How couldn't he? It was normal for kids to want their family system to stay intact. That had always been my dream. I couldn't even begin to count the number of times I had created elaborate fantasies about my birth parents coming to rescue me from whatever temporary foster home I'd been in at that time. Even long after I realized that was never happening, I spent an inordinate amount of time imagining all the reasons they hadn't come for me. Of course, none of the stories I'd told myself ended up being true.

I guess the good thing with timing was that Alex was preparing to venture out on his own. If Garrett and I had connected a few years ago, it might not have worked. But I didn't have that excuse now.

That's what it is, Sloan—an excuse.

My inner voice was right. I had mastered the ability to deflect. To deflect emotions. To put my needs and desires last. And quite honestly, to sabotage my own happiness sometimes. I understood why. The coping strategies I had adopted at a young age had served me well during a time when I had needed to guard my heart. But I didn't need them anymore. It was okay to release them and let go.

Stay present, Sloan, I told myself as I looped my fingers through Garrett's. His touch was soft and tender, which made my stomach flop.

Inside the barn, Ben continued his speech about the brewing process, giving us a close-up look at the brite tanks and kegging equipment. He reminded me more of a performer than a brewer as he talked through each step of the brew. There was something almost salesy about his approach. But then again, everyone in attendance seemed captivated by his style.

"He's making brewing sound so sexy," Garrett whispered.

I laughed. "I know. What about all the grunt work and cleaning?"

"Not sexy." Garrett winked.

Ben gave a half bow when he finished walking everyone through a brew day at Confluence. "As I said, don't be shy. Pour yourself a pint. The taps are open. Go get your drink on before we head down to the field for dessert." He motioned to the rustic bar. It had been crafted from old barn doors. The tap handles were made from recycled wood with chalkboard paint. Mason jars converted into lights hung overhead.

"You want a refresher?" Garrett asked.

"No, I'm good for the moment."

"Same." His gaze landed on the couple who had been seated next to us at dinner. They were filling their pint glasses to the brim.

I had to resist showing them the proper way to pour a pint. It's an art form. But from the way they had been downing drinks at dinner, I got the sense they were more interested in quantity over quality. Earlier, I had overheard them talking about being sure to "get their money's worth."

For most of my colleagues in the craft brewing industry and me, beer was about the experience. There were so many factors that went into creating each style of brew, from the time we steeped the grains to when and how many hops were added. I appreciated pulling out each nuanced flavor when I was sampling a pint. Craft beer was meant to be sipped slowly. Not guzzled.

Our tablemates clearly didn't care about that. They had already finished off their foamy pints and were pouring another round.

I surveyed the rest of the barn. Guests had drifted off to individual tables. A handful of people stuck by Ben, asking him more questions about the process. Josh and Miri were nowhere to be seen, but Saachi and the man I'd seen Ben talking to earlier came in through the back door.

The man left Saachi at the bar and headed straight for Ben. He was on some kind of mission. Saachi busied herself wiping down tap handles and stacking used pint glasses in the large farm sink behind the bar.

"Maybe I could use a refresher after all," I nodded in her direction.

Garrett caught on immediately. "Yeah, right, me too. I'm suddenly parched." He puckered his lips.

We made our way to the bar. Saachi tossed a dish towel over one shoulder.

"Did you want a refill?" Saachi sounded annoyed, like we were bothering her, but she plastered on a fake smile.

"I'll try your saison." Garrett offered her his glass.

She shook her head in disgust. "I'm not going to serve you a farmhouse style in that after you've already had another style of beer." She took his glass and promptly put it in the sink. "If anyone here except for me would do their job, you would have had fresh glasses."

I didn't disagree with her. Beer tasting flights mimicked wine tasting and were meant to be sampled in a particular order. At Nitro and Der Keller, we always started with our lightest beers first, working our way up to ESBs and stouts.

"Are you short-staffed?" I asked, hoping that she might open up if we could connect about running a small operation. "We know that pain all too well, don't we, Garrett? There are so many pros of owning a nanobrewery, like flexibility and being involved in every aspect of the business, but staffing is such a challenge."

Garrett agreed. "Yeah, without Sloan here, I don't know how I would have gotten through the first year."

Saachi handed him his beer and looked at me. "What do you want?" She must have realized how short she sounded because she smacked the side of her head. "Sorry about that. That sounded rude, didn't it? I'm almost at my breaking point, and I'm barely holding it together tonight."

"Is there anything we can do to help?"

"Can you murder a couple of flaky interns?" She laughed. But after discovering Josh unconscious on the ground earlier, I didn't find it funny.

"You mean Josh and Miri?" I asked.

"They think they own this place just because they have fancy college degrees. A piece of paper does not amount to being able to run a brewery, but try telling them that. This generation has no work ethic. They want everything to be handed to them on a silver platter. They want to make six figures right out of school and not have to put in any effort. I'm so over it."

Her statement surprised me, in part because she couldn't be that much older than Miri or Josh. I would put her in her early thirties at most. Not to mention that we'd had the opposite experience with our staff. They were young, but they were eager to work. I had never found Kat or the twins unwilling to do any task we put before them. And there was also the issue that college tuition had skyrocketed in the last decade. There could be truth to Miri and Josh wanting high-paying salaries, but that could be because they were drowning in student debt.

"How long have you worked at Confluence?" I asked.

She rinsed my glass. "Six years. You know what I've done in those six years?"

I wasn't sure if she was waiting for us to respond. Apparently she wasn't, because she scrubbed the pint glasses with such force I thought they might break in half. "Everything, that's what I've done. Everything. Do I get any credit for being the one who has scrubbed every brite tank? Who has literally shoveled manure out of this barn? No. I get nothing. Absolutely nothing."

"Aren't you the manager?" Garrett took the tiniest step backward as he asked the question as if he was worried that she would swat him with the dishtowel that she had twisted into a tight rope.

Saachi's jaw clenched like it had been locked shut. Her hands flew as she responded, the dishtowel waving like a flag. "That's only a title. Do you know what I learned today? He's paying those damn kids more than he's paying me."

"I thought they were interns." Garrett voiced what I was thinking.

"Paid interns. *Paid.*" Saachi's hand slipped. She knocked over a stack of glasses in the porcelain sink, shattering one of them. "Great. Ben's probably going to dock my paycheck for that, too."

"Why would he do that? He seemed so effusive at dinner about how integral you are to Confluence's success," I said, walking around the bar to help her pick up the glasses.

"I've got this." She held up her hand to stop me and tossed the dishtowel on the counter. "That's what Ben does. He's all for show. It's his Big Ben persona that he likes to put on in front of guests. He has such an ego. He has to be loved and adored by everyone he meets, but it's all fake. He should have been an actor. The guy can't brew."

"Can't brew." Garrett pointed to his beer. "This is one of the better saisons that I've had in recent memory."

"Ha, I bet it is." Her voice was laced with anger.

Garrett looked at me in confusion. I shrugged.

"That would be thanks to me." Saachi pressed a shard of glass between her thumb and index finger. "Who do you think brews?"

"You?" I couldn't hide my surprise, and I wanted to grab the piece of glass from her hand. Was she intentionally trying to cut herself?

She reached beneath the sink and dropped the glass into a garbage can. "Yep. I'm not even exaggerating. Ben likes to talk a big game, but the guy doesn't know the difference between a mash tun and a fermenter. He takes credit for my work. Pays me nothing, and then when anyone shows up around here, he pretends like he's the best boss on the planet."

"I'm confused, though." I handed her the towel she'd been using earlier. "Miri and Josh told us they were unpaid interns."

"I bet they did. That's part of Ben's façade, too. He hires young, bright-eyed brewers and calls them his interns. They're tasked with coming up with new recipes, testing small batches, that kind of thing. Which he takes credit for, but no, he pays them. He pays them to keep quiet and let him stay in the spotlight. None of that is new. This is the third round of 'interns' we've had since I started. What I didn't know until this afternoon is that Ben has been paying them nearly double my salary."

Could that account for why Josh had been knocked out? Was Saachi upset that he was making more than she was and, in a fit of anger, had hit him? Maybe it was a spur-of-the-moment decision. Or maybe she was plotting something worse. Could Miri be in danger, too?

She restacked the pint glasses that she had knocked over. "I'm keeping it together for the moment—barely. But let me assure you that the minute the last guest is gone on Sunday, Ben and I are going to have it out. I'm done being his lackey. I could get a job at any brewery around here. He knows it. He's terrified, and he should be. This ends tonight." Saachi whipped the towel over her shoulder. "I've got to go track down those slackers. Help yourself to another pint. Tell everyone to drink it all. I don't care."

She left without another word.

I stared after her. Saachi's rant had been illuminating. Is that why Ben had plastered on a fake smile through dinner? Did he know that Saachi had learned his secret? Was it true that he really couldn't brew? And why would he pay Miri and Josh more than Saachi if Saachi was doing the bulk of the work? That was asking for trouble. It didn't make sense.

"Well, that was more than I had bargained for." The stunned look on Garrett's face matched how I felt inside. "I guess we got our wish. We definitely learned something from that exchange."

I gave him a silent nod in agreement. However, I couldn't shake the feeling that Saachi was a woman out for blood. I could only hope that she didn't decide to literally spill anyone's in an attempt to resolve her situation.

CHAPTER
FIVE

GARRETT and I moved away from the bar. He got drawn into a conversation with a couple visiting from the East Coast about the difference between New England and West Coast-style IPAs. I took the opportunity to see if I could find Miri or Josh. As fate would have it, I spotted them outside the massive front barn doors. They were balancing a large tray of desserts and heading toward the orchard.

"Be back in a second," I said to Garrett and hurried to catch up with them. "Do you need a hand?"

Josh gingerly turned his head. A flash of pain crossed his face. He gripped the tray so hard that his fingertips went white. "I think we got it."

Miri held her side tighter as they navigated the unstable dirt path that led to the dinner tables.

"How's your head, Josh?" I felt silly not helping, but wasn't going to pass up a chance to see if I could learn more about their situation as interns at the brewery and figure out if there was any truth to what Saachi had told us.

"Uh, fine, I guess. I'm kind of fuzzy."

That wasn't a good sign.

"Are you sure you don't want to get it checked out? If nothing else, you should really fill out an incident report," I suggested. "Since it was a fall at the workplace, it's important to have it documented."

This time he didn't correct me about having a "fall." "Nah, it was my bad. I should have been more careful on the ladder." He was about to say something more, but Miri cut him off.

"Have you seen this dessert?" She thrust the tray in front of my face. "Isn't it gorgeous? Vanilla custard with orchard apple butter and shortbread with crystallized honey. You're going to lose your mind over this."

The desserts did indeed look elegant and simple at the same time. That was my favorite kind of food—beautifully prepared but without a lot of extras. Simplicity was under-rated, in my opinion. I much preferred food and beer that kept its focus on ingredients.

"I can't wait." I could tell that they were both going to stay tight-lipped, so I decided to try a different approach. "Listen, can I offer you some 'mom' advice?"

Miri wrinkled her forehead. "I guess."

"I have a son who's not that much younger than either of you. He's heading off to college soon, and I've been trying to impart as much wisdom as I can before he's out on his own in the world. I don't know what is happening behind the scenes here at Confluence, but as a mom and business owner, I want you to know that if you're in a position that feels uncomfortable, it's important to speak up. Not only for your own health and well-being but also because if you're being mistreated as staff, the odds are good that other people are, too."

Josh looked to Miri, who rolled her shoulders in a half shrug.

The first stars appeared overhead as we navigated the path down through the trees. Lanterns with glowing candles illuminated our way. We arrived at the tables before the rest of the group. They set the tray of desserts in the center of the first table and began placing them at each seat.

"Would it help if you talked to me? I'm in this industry and can advocate for you if necessary." I took my seat. A mild chill had fallen over the orchard as the sun made its descent for the night. I was glad to have brought along a wrap, which I tied around my shoulders.

Again, Josh waited to see how Miri would respond. He busied himself rearranging flower vases while Miri finished putting out the desserts.

When she was done, she reached for a stack of fresh napkins and folded one in a perfect rectangle. "It's complicated."

"I have time." I motioned toward the barn and tasting room. "I have a feeling that the beer is going to be flowing up there for a while."

Miri ran her teeth along her bottom lip. "I don't want to get anyone in trouble."

I kept my face passive, glad for my ability to keep my emotions at bay. "Who would be in trouble?"

She swallowed and gnawed on her lip. "It's sort of awkward."

"You look like you want to talk about it," I said in my best "mom" voice. It was true. I had learned to read body language over the years with Alex, and Miri was clearly conflicted. "I won't pressure you, but I'm here to lend a listening ear and any advice I can from my years in craft brewing."

"I know. You're like my idol. I have so many framed articles of you with the Pink Boots Society. You paved the way for women. You're my hero, and now you want to help us. It feels

45

so surreal." She shook her head like she didn't believe her own words.

"Trust me, I'm not a hero, but I am grateful to have had other women support and mentor me, and I want to do the same for you." Everything I was saying to her was the truth. Women had long been underrepresented in the world of craft beer, and I was extremely fortunate to have mentors like Ursula and my colleagues at the Pink Boots Society, who had not only been steadfast supporters of my work but who were committed to raising up women in every aspect of the craft.

She stacked more napkins on the table before letting out a long sigh. "Okay, I guess it's probably fine to talk to you. What do you think, Josh?"

Josh pointed to the base of his skull. "I have a goose egg that says yeah."

Was he admitting that he had been attacked?

"Fold these." Miri handed him half of the napkins. Then she turned to me. "I'm not sure where to start, so I'll give you the long story."

I nodded.

"Josh and I met Ben in college. He came to speak to our class and talked about the internship program at Confluence. It sounded great. You probably know as well as anyone how hard it is to get a job as a brewer right out of the gate. Josh and I both understood that we would have to put in some blood, sweat, and tears. You know, do the grunt work and work our way up to brewing jobs. Our professors made that clear in school. The odds of getting a job even as an assistant brewer right after graduation were slim. They encouraged us to take any jobs in the industry that we could. They talked about the importance of learning every aspect of the trade and how that would serve us well long-term, even if beertending or cleaning the tanks weren't the most glamorous work."

Everything she was saying matched my perspective. Craft brewing had gained major traction in the last decade. Breweries of all shapes and sizes had launched from coast to coast. The industry was booming; however, head brewing jobs were harder to come by. Unless Miri or Josh had enough cash to start their own venture right out of college, working their way up the chain was the most practical approach.

Miri had stopped folding the napkins and proceeded to pace around the table as she spoke. "Ben is a good salesperson. Big Ben can be pretty persuasive. He got us both so excited about working here. He promised that the pay wouldn't be great, but we would actually have a hand in the brewing process and do the bulk of the manual labor. He said it would be a great résumé builder and that after our first year, we would both be considered for more permanent positions if we wanted to stay on."

"That sounds standard for the industry," I offered. "And you're being paid? I was under the impression from what you said earlier that your internships were unpaid."

Miri caught Josh's eye. He was now folding the napkins with extreme focus as if they were ticking time bombs. "This is where it gets weird." She continued to pace. "We were told that we wouldn't get paid or that we'd get some tip money and free beer and food while on shift. Plus, we get free housing for the summer. Not a bad gig. We were cool with that, right, Josh?"

Josh's eyes didn't stray from the stack of napkins. "Yeah."

"I was able to defer my student loan payments for a year, so I figured this was the ideal setup. I would intern for a year. Learn the ropes. Get some practical experience and hopefully an awesome recommendation, and then look for a real job. But on our first day, Ben pulled us aside and said he had a special proposition for us."

Now we were getting somewhere.

"What kind of proposition?" I didn't like the sound of that.

"He told us that his business partner had come into some cash and that they were going to be busy building out a second pub in Seattle, so that if Josh and I took on the brewing on our own, they would pay us."

"Okay." I was confused.

Miri must have sensed my hesitation. "It sounds good, right? But there were strings attached."

"Like what?" I took a sip of my water and waited for her to say more.

"First, Ben made us swear that we would not tell anyone that we were getting paid." She tapped her fingertips to her forehead. "Especially Saachi. Anyone. He wanted us to complain and make a big deal of not getting paid. He didn't want anyone to suspect that we were anything other than starving interns. Second, they were only going to pay us in cash under the table. And third, he was going to take all the credit for brewing. We had to brew at off-hours when no one else was around or pretend like we were cleaning the brewing equipment."

She was right. This was an extremely odd setup.

"I take it you agreed?"

"I mean, yeah, why not? We're getting cash under the table. My student loans are already deferred. I didn't care about taking the credit for brewing. Ben promised that he would write us letters of rec that would land us jobs anywhere we wanted to work, so what was there to lose? It was like a dream."

"Except that it turned into a nightmare," Josh interjected.

"How so?"

Miri cleared her throat and answered for him. "Saachi caught on pretty quick that something was up. She's been here

48

the longest, and she does everything around the brewery. It didn't take a genius to figure out that every time she came in when we were brewing, and we would scurry to grab a bucket of cleaning solution, maybe we were up to something. She started following us around. She kept trying to get us alone. She'd ask us straight up if we were brewing for Ben, but we both lied. I think she thought if she could get us away from each other, that one of us would confess."

"And did you?"

"I didn't." Miri's tone was laced with anger.

Josh let out a long, slow breath. "I didn't mean to. She wouldn't stop bugging me. Plus, she was the one who told me that she knew that Ben couldn't brew, so I figured she already knew. I mean, come on, she's not stupid. She had to know that what we've been dabbling with on that rundown equipment isn't enough to sustain the brewery. We're basically glorified homebrewers, and Saachi knows it. She does the books. She has to know what's up." He gingerly touched his head. "That woman creeps me out. She's always lurking, or worse..." he trailed off.

"Yeah, well, as you can see, we didn't exactly keep our end of the bargain," Miri muttered. "That's why we're both kind of freaked out right now."

"Because you think that Saachi is going to tell Ben that she knows about your arrangement?" I pulled my wrap tighter around my shoulders. I wasn't sure if it was from the cool breeze blowing through the orchard or from our conversation. I had a bad feeling that Josh and Miri were in way over their heads. It made me think about Alex. I would hate for him to be in a position like this shortly after graduating from college.

"Saachi already told him." Miri sounded sure of herself. "She came after me when Josh couldn't keep his mouth shut."

"Came after you?" I repeated.

"She confronted me last night. I was here working late to prep for the dinner, and we were the only two people left. I thought she was going to hurt me, to tell you the truth. She was furious. She demanded to know what Ben was paying us, and she wanted every single detail about what Josh and I had agreed to."

"Did you tell her?"

"I didn't exactly have a choice. She wasn't going to let me leave without telling her."

"Do you think Saachi's the one who hit you on the head earlier?" I asked Josh.

He mumbled something I couldn't make out.

"Speak up, Josh," Miri commanded.

I wondered about their relationship. Were they colleagues? Friends? Something more? It was evident that Miri was in charge.

"I said, I don't know. Maybe." He kept eyeing the barn like he was trying to plot out an exit strategy.

"Saachi could have knocked him out. But it also could have been Chase."

"Chase? Who's Chase?" The more I learned from these two, the more questions I had about Confluence's legitimacy.

"He's Ben's business partner." Miri sounded put out that I didn't recognize the name.

"Is he here tonight?" I wondered if that's who I had seen Ben talking to earlier.

"He's always here." Miri rolled her eyes.

"Why would Chase have hit Josh?"

"Because he's the enforcer," Miri responded. "We broke our promise to Ben. That was our fatal mistake. Saachi told Ben. And I'm sure Ben told Chase. Now Chase is after us. If we're not careful tonight, I'm scared that one of us is going to end up with more than a bump on the head."

I stared at Miri. That was quite an accusation. I wasn't sure why Ben had opted for so much secrecy or whether Saachi was upset enough to harm either of the young brewers physically. But, I knew without a doubt that Garrett and I weren't leaving until we got to the bottom of this.

CHAPTER
SIX

I DIDN'T HAVE much time to ponder the situation because the sound of voices brought a halt to our conversation. Ben and Saachi were leading everyone toward us. The boisterous sounds of laughter and the sight of rosy cheeks were proof that the beer had most definitely been flowing while I was getting the lowdown on Confluence from Josh and Miri.

Garrett tore himself away from the couple who had been bombarding him with brewing questions. "So, any news?" His head tilted toward Josh and Miri.

Ben was busy handing out the last round of drinks. Saachi had made her way over to the interns and was waving her index finger in their faces.

"You won't even believe it." I shot a quick glance to make sure no one was listening.

"Try me." Garrett leaned closer.

I kept my voice low, not that it mattered. The rest of our dinner companions were happily oblivious to any tension brewing. "It sounds like Confluence is a disaster." I gave Garrett a brief recap of what Miri and Josh had told me.

"Chase. The name sounds vaguely familiar to me. I'm trying to remember why." Garrett tapped his temple as if hoping to trigger the memory.

"He could be in the brewing world. They said he's Ben's business partner but didn't mention anything about him brewing either. I don't get it. Why would Ben and Chase open a brewery and be in the middle of opening a second location in Seattle when neither of them brews—assuming that's true? And how are they keeping so many beers on tap?"

"Good questions. And why keep brewing a secret?" Garrett added. "Hire a good head brewer. Tons of breweries use that model. Most business owners, especially in the food and beverage world, aren't chefs or brewers themselves, so it's not like by hiring a head brewer, they would lose customers or even be judged. I don't get it."

"Neither do I." I shook my head. "I don't get the impression that Miri and Josh are being dramatic, either. They seem genuinely scared. We saw Josh knocked out. He was so insistent that he hadn't fallen off the ladder, and then suddenly, his story changed. That sounds like the behavior of someone who feels threatened."

"Everyone, please take your seats," Saachi said, dinging her pint glass with the tip of a spoon. "Dessert is served."

"I hope she's not intending to serve her just desserts." Garrett winked at his own joke.

I rolled my eyes. "You and your puns."

"They're so bad, they're good, yeah?" His eyes twinkled under the starlight.

I made a goofy face, glad for a moment of reprieve from worrying about Miri and Josh. Ben gave us the rundown on our final beer of the evening—a chocolate raspberry stout with notes of toasted coconut and pecans. The beer was thick and the color of molasses. Fortunately, they were serving the stout in small snifters, just enough to accompany dessert. A heavy beer like this was meant to be enjoyed in smaller portions.

"We have a lovely light custard to go with your dessert stouts," Saachi explained. She had sent Miri and Josh off again. "The musicians will be back for one last set. We've lit the candles, and the string lights will be coming on soon once the sun has finally set. Enjoy. Linger. Your rooms are ready, but if you decide you need a nightcap before you turn in, we'll keep the tasting room open until our staff has finished cleaning up."

I had to give her credit for her ability to switch into professional mode. Whatever was happening between her and Ben and the rest of the staff had been momentarily put aside while she was "on" in front of the guests.

The creamy vanilla custard balanced beautifully with the hearty, fruit-forward stout. It was like a marriage of chocolate and vanilla swirl ice cream—my childhood favorite. I was glad that Saachi had opted for a light offering to let the stout shine. She certainly knew beer and food. Which made my thoughts return to Ben—did he have anything to do with the brewery other than being the outward face of the pub?

There was one way to find out. Garrett and I needed to get him alone, too. We both had enough industry experience to be able to tell if someone was faking their way through. Ben might be able to talk a good game to the craft beer novices around the table, but it wouldn't take much for us to suss out if he were lying. A few targeted brewing questions should do the trick.

Saachi didn't stick around for the dessert course. She excused herself and made sure everyone had her cell number in case we needed anything overnight. "Your bags have been delivered to your rooms. Breakfast will be served in the farm-house starting at nine, and then the charter bus for our hop field tour will pick us up at ten, so I'll see you all bright and early."

"We could easily incorporate some of this for our B & B guests," I said to Garrett as we ate spoonfuls of the creamy dessert. "I hadn't thought of a charter. Yakima is only an hour and a half drive from Leavenworth. Actually, getting beer lovers out into the hop fields would be a once-in-a-lifetime experience."

"I'm right there with you, Sloan. Maybe it's a package we offer for the harvest season. It's good timing because that coincides with the fall leaf festival. It would be a beautiful drive at that time of year. We could make it a day trip and partner with a few Yakima Valley breweries. Do the hop field tour and tastings, and then have guests return on the bus. We wouldn't even need to be involved. We could organize it as an add-on and send them on their merry way."

"That's exactly what I was thinking. It would be too much time away from the brewery for us, but since we're a beer destination, I love the idea of finding ways to enhance that experience and send some love to fellow brewers in the region."

We brainstormed other possibilities as the evening wound down. A slight chill came over me as more stars appeared overhead. The orchard was aglow with candlelight and shimmering flickers from the strings of twinkle lights hanging between the apple trees. If it weren't for the chaos amongst the Confluence team, this night would be nothing short of perfection. I let my body sink into Garrett's as music lulled me into an almost dreamlike state. Despite the internal chaos amongst the Confluence staff, they had certainly outdone themselves with the food, beer, and lush setting. Everything felt like a fuzzy dream—the flashes of starlight, the glow of the moon filtering through the apple trees, the scent of melting wax from the candles, and the lofty sounds of violins. If it weren't for Josh's accident and not being able to shake the feeling that something here at Confluence was very wrong, this might have been the most romantic night ever.

Garrett's arm was solid around my shoulder. He smelled like the forest, with a hint of hops.

When the band finished their last piece, he squeezed my shoulder. "Are you ready to head to our rooms, or should we take Saachi up on her offer to top off our pint glasses in the barn?"

"Top off." I held up my empty glass. I didn't want another drink, but I knew I wasn't going to be able to sleep until I was sure that Josh and Miri weren't in any danger.

We said goodnight to everyone and strolled to the barn. It was impossible not to feel light on my feet or ignore the hum of energy between us as we meandered under the canopy of stars with the aromas of late spring lingering in the night air.

"What's our plan?" Garrett asked once we were out of earshot.

"If we can pepper Ben with some technical brewing questions, we should be able to get a good sense of how much he actually knows about the process."

"Good thinking."

"I don't know if he'll be around tonight. If he's not in the barn, we can try in the morning. I'd also love to find Chase. He's been a bit of a ghost this evening."

"Are you feeling okay about staying here?" Garrett studied my face with a concerned look in his eyes. "We could go find a hotel?"

"Me?" I wrinkled my nose. "I'm good. I'm not worried about my personal safety, but I want to make sure that the staff is safe before heading home to Leavenworth. I don't know if it's the mom in me or my personal background, but I can't leave, knowing that we might have been able to do something."

"That's why everyone loves you, Sloan Krause." Garrett's voice was thick with emotion.

Was he including himself in everyone?

I wasn't sure I was ready for love yet, but I was definitely ready to take the next step. I hoped that would be enough for him, but the truth was, if it wasn't, then we weren't meant to be. I knew what I needed now. I had learned that much from my breakup with Mac, and that was to take things slow and see how they progressed. Garrett and I had already built a strong friendship which felt like the perfect foundation for potentially building something more.

Something crashed in the barn. We picked up our pace.

"Not again."

I held my breath, anticipating seeing Josh or Miri on the ground again. Or worse.

Instead, when we got inside, we were greeted by the sight of three of the keg tables turned on their sides. The rustic oak barrels were heavy. They had to weigh close to a hundred pounds empty. Half of the chairs had been knocked over, too. Someone had ransacked the tasting room. Why?

"Hello?" I called.

A face popped up from behind the bar. It was Chase. He was holding a long aluminum brewing paddle like a baseball bat. "Get out of here! What are you doing? Did you do this?" he demanded with wild eyes, pointing the brewing paddle at the knocked-over tables.

"What?" I looked to Garett, whose face appeared as dumbfounded as mine.

"We were told that we could get a nightcap," Garrett responded, holding up his hands in surrender.

"Someone did this. Someone tried to trash this place." Chase repositioned his hands on the paddle.

"Are you okay?" I asked, taking a step closer.

Chase clutched the paddle tighter. "Stay back. Stay where you are."

"What's going on? Are you hurt?" Garrett pointed to the wooden barrels and tipped chairs. "Do you need help?"

"You shouldn't be in here." Chase didn't let go of his grip on the paddle. "Did you see anything? Did you see who did this?"

"No, like we said, we just came up from the orchard," Garrett said, taking a small step forward. "The other dinner guests will be here soon. Why are the tables and chairs on the ground? You think someone did this intentionally?"

"Yeah, obviously someone is out to get us—to ruin our grand opening." Chase stared from us to the bar, his eyes twitching as they scanned the room. "Someone trashed the place."

"Why are you hiding behind the bar?" Garrett asked. He had rolled his shoulders back and stood taller in a protective move.

Chase held the paddle higher. "I was looking for a weapon. I had to be ready to defend myself."

From what? I thought to myself.

"We've been having some... uh, some problems at the brewery, but from the looks of this place, it's escalated quickly." Chase's speech was stilted like he was having trouble finding the right words.

His frantic demeanor didn't match Miri and Josh's description of him. He didn't strike me as an enforcer. If anything, I got the impression that he would run away and hide if given the opportunity.

"Do you have any idea who could have done this?" Garrett was calm as he walked over to pick up a barstool.

"I don't know if you should touch those," Chase cautioned.

"Why?" Garrett reached down to pick up another.

"What if the police need to dust them for prints or something?" Chase had finally loosened his grasp on the brewing paddle and rested it on the bar. "I should probably call them." He seemed to be processing his thoughts as they came. He nodded in agreement with himself. "Yeah, yeah, I should probably head over to the main house and call the police."

"Really?" Garrett set the barstool upright. "I don't know if they would respond to a few knocked-over chairs and tables. Unless you know something else? Is there cash missing? Is anyone hurt or in danger?"

Chase ran his hands through his hair. "No. No. I mean, I don't think so, but isn't this destruction of property? You don't think the police will come if I call?"

"We can certainly call the authorities, but I don't think picking up a chair or two is going to hurt." Garrett started to lift the edge of one of the barrels. I went over to give him a hand. "It doesn't look like anything has been destroyed. I'm going to guess that the police would assume one of your dinner guests had too much to drink and decided to go table tipping."

"Do you think that's what happened?" Chase sighed with relief. "I uh, I might have panicked when I saw the tasting room like this. Things have been out of control around here, so I probably went to the worst-case scenario. Sorry about that."

"No need to apologize," I said, lifting with my legs. The barrels were indeed heavy. "We haven't been introduced, I'm Sloan Krause, and this is my brewing partner Garrett Strong. We're from Nitro in Leavenworth. Let us know if there's anything we can do to help."

Chase's mouth hung open. "Crap. You're Nitro."

That wasn't exactly the reaction I had expected.

"No, sorry. Sorry. I didn't mean it like that. I know Nitro. Ben made a big deal about how you guys are VIPs and should be treated like beer royalty."

Garrett winced. "Nah, we're not royalty. Are we, Sloan?"

I put my hand to my head. "Last time I checked, I wasn't wearing my beer crown."

Chase laughed uncomfortably.

The sound of voices nearby made him startle.

"Look, I gotta split. Thanks for putting the tables back." Without another word, he took off through the back door.

Garrett held his arms out in disbelief. "What is going on at Confluence? I feel like we're in some sort of an alternate reality."

"And not a good one," I added.

CHAPTER
SEVEN

A HANDFUL of tipsy dinner guests stumbled into the barn in search of late-night refreshers as Chase vanished out the back.

"What do you think, Sloan? Are you ready to call it a night?"

"Is it that obvious?" I rubbed my eye. Garrett and I tended to have opposite brewing hours. I was an early riser. I loved to tinker in the brewery and Nitro's commercial kitchen with a coffee and hot apple strudel in the mornings. Garrett, on the other hand, was a master of midnight brew sessions. Since he'd gotten his start homebrewing while working for a tech company in Seattle, he had trained himself to stay up after hours and brew through the night. It worked well at Nitro. I opened the pub, cooked breakfast for our B & B guests, and departed in time to have dinner with Alex, while Garrett kept the beer flowing until the last call.

"You've been fighting to keep your eyes open for a while." He patted my shoulder. "You're a trooper, but why don't you head to bed? I'll hang around for another half hour or so and see if I can learn anything more."

I felt bad leaving him, but I knew I wouldn't be functional tomorrow if I didn't get some sleep. "As long as you're sure," I hesitated, not able to hold in a yawn.

"Absolutely." He leaned in and kissed my cheek. His lips were warm on my skin. "Thanks for a great night, Sloan."

A jolt of electricity pulsed through my body. "Thank you," I replied, hearing the throaty quality of my voice and not wanting the moment to end. "I'll see you at breakfast." I sucked in a breath and headed for my room before I changed my mind about taking things slow.

Guest accommodations were located in the original farmhouse on the property, just a short walk from the barn. Like what we'd done at Nitro, Ben and Chase, or whoever was actually running the show, had renovated the house built in the early 1900s, dividing the space into separate guest rooms, some with private baths and some with shared bathrooms. Additionally, the kitchen, dining room, and living rooms were all communal spaces. It was a very similar setup and on trend with brewery tourism.

I was eager to see what sort of fare would be served at breakfast and whether Confluence used our model of infusing our food with touches of our beer.

I thought I might have trouble falling asleep, but I was out after I shot off a goodnight text to Alex and placed my head on the pillow.

I woke to the sound of birds chattering in the orchard the next morning.

Not surprisingly, it was early, before seven, which meant that I was probably one of the first, if not the first, people up. Given how much some of our dinner companions had had to drink last night, I had a feeling it might be a slow start.

I took a long hot shower and pulled on a pair of capris, a T-shirt, a sweatshirt, and a pair of lightweight tennis shoes.

Since we would be walking through hop fields later, I wanted to be dressed appropriately. My cheeks, which were naturally olive-toned, had even more color from spending time in the sun. It was interesting to watch my appearance slowly change. Some of my friends, who were also in their forties, complained about wrinkles and bags under their eyes. For me, I felt younger than I had in years. Maybe it was releasing my past, or maybe it was coming to terms with my divorce, but I felt like I was fully embodying who I was meant to be for the first time. It was empowering. I liked the reflection I saw in the mirror. This woman was strong. She was standing in her power. She had learned to nurture herself. The effect felt like a facelift. My skin glowed, and my eyes were bright. I don't even think I had realized the weight I'd been carrying internally and how putting walls around my heart had dimmed my internal light.

With that thought in mind, I headed down to the dining room in search of coffee. Breakfast wouldn't be served for a couple of hours, but a hot cup of coffee and a morning stroll sounded like the antidote I needed to face the day. I was eager to hear whether Garrett had learned anything else last night and hopeful for an opportunity to talk to Ben and Saachi.

The dining room had a variety of two- and four-person vintage farmhouse tables and chairs. Sunlight spilled in through large bay windows. Each table had a red and white gingham tablecloth and a small vase with wildflowers. There was a buffet table on the back wall with tea, coffee, hot chocolate, and apple cider. Black and white photographs of the farm and orchard over the years hung on the walls.

I breathed in the scent of the coffee and helped myself to a mug. Purple packets of hot chocolate caught my eye.

Huckleberry hot chocolate.

A note tied to the packets explained that the hot chocolate

mix was made by a local chocolatier and made a great addition to any morning coffee.

Why not?

I stirred the mix into my coffee and added a splash of cream. The result was delicious. The creamy hot chocolate elevated my basic cup of Joe, and the sweet, tangy notes of huckleberries finished it off beautifully.

I savored my drink creation for a moment, and then I poked my head into the kitchen. Someone on staff must be awake if there was already coffee. Plus, I could smell the baking bread.

"Good morning," I called into the doorway.

Sure enough, Saachi was at the stove. She had a floral apron tied around her waist and was stirring a sauce. "Oh, you scared me." She clutched the wooden spoon in her hand.

"Sorry. I wanted to thank you for the coffee and for the recommendation to add huckleberry hot chocolate. It's next level, as my son would say."

She returned to stirring. "That's a guest favorite. There's a fudge company that we get that and all of our chocolate from. I can't remember who decided to add it to coffee one morning, probably Miri, but now it's our signature breakfast drink."

"For good reason." I took another sip. "You're up early."

"Not by choice. Breakfast doesn't cook itself." She didn't bother to disguise the bitterness in her tone.

"What's on the menu?"

She lifted the wooden spoon from the pot. A caramel liquid dripped down like splatters of golden raindrops. "Caramel sticky beer buns."

"I wondered if you incorporated beer into the menu. We do the same thing at Nitro."

"Beer tourism is so popular. We can't keep up with the demand. Guests want beer in everything—breakfast, lunch, dinner. The classic beer flights and tastings are fine, but we're looking to stay in front of trends. Have you followed that spa in Germany that's offering beer massages and beer baths?"

"Yeah." I nodded and drank more of my coffee. "It's pretty incredible to see how trendy craft beer has become." The spa she was referring to offered beer lovers a chance to soak in a hot tub of beer. Believe it or not, the tradition of bathing in beer was longstanding, and the benefits of beer spas included softer skin and hair and the calming aroma of hops. Similar beer-inspired spas had popped up all over the place as of late. I had yet to try the experience, but April Ablin, Leavenworth's self-appointed ambassador, had been bugging Garrett and me to install a beer hot tub at Nitro. Not only did we not have the space, but we also didn't have the capacity to brew extra batches of our small craft for bathing purposes.

"How was the rest of the night?" I asked, changing the subject.

"Terrible." Saachi stirred her caramel sauce with such force that her long braids swung back and forth in rhythm. "Ben and Chase got into a huge fight. I'm surprised you didn't hear it. Didn't they wake you up?"

"No. When was this?" I glanced out the kitchen window in the direction of the barn. It wasn't that far away. If there had been a big argument, I was surprised that I hadn't heard it.

"Maybe around one or so. I'm not sure." She turned the burner to low. "I was so tired. The last guest had finally left the barn. All I wanted to do was close up, but then those two got into it."

"What were they fighting about?" I nursed my coffee.

"The usual—everything. I didn't stick around to listen. I've heard it all before. I tossed the keys to Ben and told him he could lock up. Then I came inside, put my earplugs in to drown out their voices, and went to sleep."

"Do you sleep here?"

"Not usually. Only on event nights. It doesn't make sense to drive to my apartment only to turn around and be back for breakfast prep a few hours later." She motioned to a door next to the fridge. "There are a couple of small rooms for staff on this side of the house. It's like Downton Abbey."

"Where does Ben live?"

"In town." She turned the heat off and removed the pot from the stove. "Chase is the only one who lives on the property. It's his family's land, you know?"

"No." I shook my head. "I didn't know that."

"Yep, they have big money. They own half the farmland in the valley. Some of it they've sold off to other farmers. Some has been transformed into hop fields and vineyards. The new subdivisions you passed, driving in—those used to be part of his family's property. They gave Chase this as a passion project. He lives in the new house at the south end, but the rest of us commute unless there's an event."

"What about Miri and Josh?" I finished my coffee. "I got the impression they were living here."

"Technically, yeah. They have RVs. Chase has a few RVs on the other side of the orchard. The plan has been to use them for farm staff, and then the interns have the other two."

It's like summer camp, I thought to myself. Not a bad gig for someone fresh out of college, but sleeping in an RV for months on end didn't sound appealing. I appreciated my memory foam mattress and espresso maker.

"Did anything else go down with them?" I took my empty cup to the sink.

"They ditched clean-up duties. That's nothing new. I swear this generation reeks of entitlement."

I wasn't going to get into a repeat conversation with her on the subject. "Where are they now? Do they help with breakfast?"

"Good question. They were supposed to be here forty-five minutes ago. Neither of them has shown their face yet. Classic."

"Is that typical? Are they normally late for their shifts?" Worry began to build. Saachi might be able to write them off as flaky, but after the threats and physical violence last night, I couldn't shake the feeling that there might be another reason they hadn't shown up yet.

"This is our first overnight event of the season. We're doing one of these a week for the next eight weeks, so let's just say they're not off to a great start."

"But do you think something could be wrong?"

She poured the thick caramel sauce into a Mason jar. "Why?"

"Well, after last night." I didn't feel like I needed to expand.

"No. I'm sure they're just sleeping in like slackers."

"Maybe." I wasn't convinced. "I think I'll take a walk before breakfast."

Saachi glanced at her watch. "You've got time. This won't be ready for a while."

I went out the front door. The air was crisp but already slightly warm. Everything smelled like fresh-cut grass and honeysuckle. I paused to drink in the view of the morning light hitting the tops of the apple trees and listen to the sounds of birds and frogs greeting the day.

A path started at the barn and led down toward the opposite side of the orchard from where we'd had dinner last night. That must be the direction of the RVs. I decided to follow it. Saachi could be right about Miri and Josh, but I didn't want to risk it.

Walking through nature was the best way to start the day. That was one of the things I appreciated most about moving into the village. My mornings always began with a short walk through town to Nitro, which was really much the same as this. Our village of Leavenworth boasted two thousand residents, so unless it was a busy festival weekend, my daily walks were filled with birdsong, mountain views, and cool breezes blowing up from the river.

In the pinkish light, it was easy to get a better sense of how vast Confluence's acreage was. I passed more tractors and farming equipment along with outbuildings and greenhouses before the RVs were within sight. In the distance, the massive fence that I had seen last night was visible. It was at least ten feet high and stretched for hundreds of feet. I couldn't tell if the fence belonged to Confluence's neighbors or if it was part of the property. The fence looked foreboding, like someone obviously didn't want to let anyone in. It didn't match with the rest of the grounds.

The RVs were grouped together in a small clearing. Each of them had awnings and outdoor seating with two camp chairs and firepits. It looked like a cozy space for summer camping. I wasn't sure if they were all occupied, and I didn't want to wake any unsuspecting workers, so I paused to think about my next move.

I didn't have to think long because a moment later, Josh was running toward me with Miri right on his heels.

CHAPTER
EIGHT

JOSH BARRELED toward me at a full sprint.

"Josh, stop! Please!" Miri chased after him.

He ignored her pleas and dashed by me like he was being chased by a pack of wild wolves.

Miri gave up when she got to me. She bent over, clutching her stomach in an attempt to calm her breathing. Her face was bright red from exertion.

"What's going on?" I asked.

She held up a finger as she sucked in air. "Cramp." She massaged her left rib. "He used to run in college. I don't know why I thought I could keep up with him."

"Why were you trying?"

"He's going to get himself killed." She stood upright and blew out a long breath. "I warned him, but he won't listen."

"Slow down." I tried to model easy and calm breathing. "Can you give me more specifics?"

She gasped for breath. Her cheeks were as red as the apples would soon be on the trees. "He's going to confront Saachi."

Saachi?

Now I was really confused.

"Why?"

Miri reached up and yanked a leaf from an apple tree, still breathing heavily. "He overheard Ben and Chase arguing last night, and now he's convinced that Saachi is the one who tried to kill him in the orchard before dinner last night."

Kill him? We had gone from Miri originally dismissing Josh's injury as a fall to it now being attempted murder. That seemed like quite a leap.

As if reading my mind, she continued. "I thought he was making it up yesterday. I figured that he had tried to get out of work again. That's his MO. He likes the brewing, but he hates the grunt work we have to do, so he's always sneaking off to the orchard and disappearing for hours. When I found him on the ground, I thought he'd been messing around and fell, but he kept insisting that someone hit him."

"I know, but then his story changed at dinner."

She brushed a fruit fly from her face. "We talked about it and decided it was better to pretend like it was an accident. That way, it wouldn't raise any suspicion with the person who hit him."

"And you think that's Saachi? What does Saachi have to do with Chase and Ben fighting?"

She balled up the leaf in her fist. "We were bringing in the last of the tables and chairs to the barn. Chase and Ben didn't realize we were there. We came in through the back door. They were arguing about Saachi. Chase told Ben that Saachi had gone psycho in the tasting room. He said that he found all of the tables and chairs knocked over, broken pint glasses and that the cash box was missing."

That lined up with what I'd witnessed when Garrett and I bumped into Chase after dinner. However, he hadn't mentioned anything about missing cash.

"We weren't trying to eavesdrop. We were doing our jobs, but Ben and Chase weren't exactly being quiet, either." Miri sounded apologetic. "Chase told Ben that he had to fire Saachi. He threatened to end their partnership if Ben didn't."

How had so much gone on in one lovely evening under the stars? I kicked myself for not staying awake longer.

"Ben refused. Flat out. Said it was non-negotiable and that Saachi was staying."

"Okay, but again, what's the connection with Josh? Why is he confronting Saachi? Wouldn't it make more sense for him to speak with Ben and Chase?"

"No, he's going straight to Saachi because he found proof that she's the one who knocked him out."

"What kind of proof?"

"I don't know. He wouldn't tell me. That's why I tried to stop him. I don't know what's going down between the three of them—Chase, Ben, and Saachi, but I think we should stay out of it. And if Saachi is really the one who hit him, it's stupid to confront her. What's going to stop her from doing it again?"

She had a valid point, but I could tell from the way her breathing remained shallow and her cheeks flushed that she was also in high-stress mode, which could mean that she wasn't thinking rationally. "First of all, it's broad daylight. I saw Saachi cooking a while ago, and she seemed fine. I can't imagine her hurting Josh."

"You don't know her. She's desperate to keep her job, and she'll do anything, even if it means resorting to violence."

"I didn't get that impression from her." I tried to offer an alternative narrative and a voice of reason. "Wasn't Saachi prepping food for dinner when Josh was hit, anyway?"

Miri flinched. She shook her head with force. "No. That's the thing. That's why I'm worried about him confronting her and her snapping. When I came out to check on things, she

71

was coming up from the orchard toward the barn. We passed each other on the way. She was acting weird, too. I didn't pick up on it at the time. I mean, I thought she was being short with me because that's how she is, but now I realize it's because she had probably just smacked Josh over the head and was trying to flee the scene of the crime before she got caught."

My head hurt trying to piece everything together. Something was missing from the story. I just couldn't figure out what. Each of the Confluence team members had told me variations of the same tale, but with their own twist. I wasn't sure who was lying or if this was all a big misunderstanding and an example of management gone wrong.

It didn't make sense that Saachi would attack Josh. She might be frustrated with his lack of work ethic or bitter about the fact that he was making more money than she was. But why take that out on him? It seemed more likely that she would confront Ben and Chase, who owned the brewery, not one of the young interns.

Could there be another layer that I was missing?

Could Saachi and Josh be romantically linked? They weren't that far apart in age. Maybe seven years. It wasn't impossible that they could have had a fling that resulted in a bad breakup. I had to stay open to any possibility.

Plus, there was the issue of the condition of the tasting room last night and the missing cash, which was news to me. Chase hadn't mentioned that in his rush to flee the space. Out of everyone on staff, Saachi seemed the most motivated to steal. If she felt like she wasn't getting paid what she was worth and deserved and had learned that Josh and Miri were not only being paid for their services but being paid more, that could easily explain why she was taking the cash.

But it still didn't give her a clear motive for hitting Josh.

Miri tossed the leaf she had mangled in her hand on the

ground. "We should go up to the guest house and check on Josh." Her foot bounced as she spoke. "I hope he's not doing anything stupid."

"Sure, I'll come with you."

I followed behind her, thinking through a variety of scenarios in my mind.

There was no sign of Josh at the guest house. However, people were up and savoring coffee and tea in the dining room. Garrett was seated at a table by the window.

Miri raced into the kitchen while I joined him.

"I was going to offer you coffee, but it looks like you've already been up and out, huh?" Garrett wrapped his hands around his mug.

"You have no idea." I peered over his shoulder, trying to get a look at Miri and Saachi in the kitchen. They were talking in low whispers. I couldn't make out anything they were saying.

"More drama, I'm guessing from the intense look on your face," Garrett noted.

"Yep." I gave him a recap of my morning.

He whistled. "Geez, Sloan. I'm not even halfway through my first cup of Joe, and you're already on the case."

"I don't know what the case is, though. None of it adds up. Chase wants Saachi gone. Ben refused. Josh thinks Saachi attacked him, and Miri is all over the place. I can't decide if she's got an overactive imagination or if she's spinning a web of lies."

"Or both."

"Right." I sighed.

"Can I get you another cup of coffee in the meantime?" Garrett motioned to the buffet. "Saachi came out and announced that breakfast would be ready in a few minutes, right before you showed up."

"More caffeine can't hurt."

Garrett stood to get me a coffee. I stared out the window. The barn was a few hundred feet away. I watched with surprise as Miri, Josh, Ben, and Chase all went inside together.

Saachi came into the dining room carrying a tray of gooey caramel rolls. Her gaze drifted to the window. She must have seen what I had witnessed because she practically dropped the tray of rolls on the buffet and raced outside to the barn.

CHAPTER
NINE

"I LEFT the table for two minutes and clearly missed something." Garrett handed me a steaming mug of coffee. "Saachi almost knocked me over while setting the rolls on the buffet and fled out the door. What did I miss?"

"Everyone on staff went into the barn." I pointed outside. "Saachi noticed and ran off to join them. I don't get it. I'm stumped. I cannot figure out what's going on."

"Hopefully, coffee will help." Garrett stood again. "And sugar. We shouldn't let hot-from-the-oven rolls go to waste." He went to serve us breakfast. Saachi must already have prepped the rest of the meal because he returned with plates filled with fresh fruit salad, rolls, and a sausage and egg scramble.

"Thanks." I smiled at him. "You know this is supposed to be a getaway, and I've been spending this entire weekend spinning my wheels on what's happening with the Confluence staff. Maybe we need to forget about it and enjoy the day."

Garrett scowled. "Are you feeling okay, Sloan?"

"Yeah, why?" I wrinkled my brow.

"Forget about it?" He squinted and not because of the light coming in through the window. "Come on. I think I know you better than that. Like there's any chance that's going to happen."

"Am I that obvious?"

"No. Hardly." He chuckled. "It's not like I can, either. I'm afraid we're the same when it comes to mysteries. I'm all for enjoying the day with you, but I'm not going to be satisfied until we get to the bottom of this. Don't you think it's our duty as fellow craft brewers to make sure everything is on the up and up before heading home?"

I wanted to lean across the table and kiss him. Garrett and I had partnered on some previous cases in Leavenworth before, but his openness gave me an entirely new appreciation of him and how different he was from Mac.

Mac would have made the weekend about himself. Garrett was content to go with the flow and see where things led us. It felt like a true partnership in every way.

Garrett stabbed a piece of pineapple with his fork. "So what do you say, Sloan? After breakfast, I think we should take a walk before the bus shows up for our hop field tour and put our heads together. We're two relatively intelligent people. We should be able to figure this out."

I smiled. "Count me in."

We ate our breakfast, keeping a careful watch on any activity in the barn. Saachi's rolls had baked to a golden brown on the outside. They were smothered with her handmade caramel sauce and toasted pecans. They were soft and slightly gooey like she had intentionally underbaked them. I wasn't sure what her involvement was with Josh's injury and whatever else was going on with Confluence, but she clearly had a talent for baking. Between last night's feast and the breakfast spread she had put together, I was impressed with her skills as an amateur chef.

Garrett and I talked through everything we had witnessed since arriving at Confluence while enjoying our breakfast. No one emerged from the tasting room while we finished our meal.

We took our dishes to the kitchen. "What do you think about taking a look around the brewery?" I suggested. "It seems too obvious to barge into the barn, but Ben did ask for advice about upgrading their equipment."

"I like the way you think, Sloan Krause."

We headed outside. Even in the short time we'd spent savoring breakfast and coffee, the temperature had warmed. The heat of the rising sun felt good on my skin as we walked to the large outbuilding that housed Confluence's brewing equipment. This building had not received the same kind of makeover as the barn and farmhouse. The corrugated metal roof looked like it could collapse at any minute. The siding was cracked and faded, with huge chunks of paint missing.

The doors to the dilapidated building were unlocked, so Garrett and I peered inside.

"Hello, is anyone around?" Garrett asked.

No one answered.

He looked at me and raised an eyebrow. "What do you think? Should we check it out?"

I nodded and stepped inside. I couldn't believe my eyes. This was a professional brewery?

It didn't look as if the place had been updated in the past hundred years. The beams on the ceiling bowed in the middle like they could give way at any moment. Light streamed through huge gaps in the siding. There were broken windows and dusty folding tables stacked with rusted tools and old metal buckets.

The brew setup was in similar condition. It consisted of used kegs welded together on a stand made of a mishmash of pipes and tubing. The most shocking thing was that the brew stand was propped against the wall and sitting on a dirt floor.

A dirt floor? I blinked twice, wondering if my eyes were playing tricks on me.

But no.

How was Confluence operating under these conditions?

I gave the space another scan. Stacks of garbage bags? A makeshift homebrew setup?

There was no possible way the beer we sampled last night had been brewed here. Nor was it possible that Confluence could have passed health and safety inspections. No brewery with a dirt floor would ever get a passing grade.

"What the hell?" Garrett's mouth hung open.

The space was a dump.

Confluence's system was smaller than our setup at Nitro. It was basically a step up from a homebrew system. I wondered how they were able to keep up with any demand brewing with such amateur equipment. Not that I had anything against hobby brewing. That was how many of the best craft brewers in the industry got their start—dabbling in homebrew equipment, tinkering like scientists with hop ratios and flavor combinations. But a system this small wasn't sustainable.

With what had been consumed at dinner alone and the extensive taps in the tasting room, Confluence would have to brew around the clock to have enough to keep the beer flowing.

"This is their setup?" Garrett scrunched his forehead.

"It's like you read my mind. How can they be offering beer getaways and weekly orchard dinners? It doesn't add up."

"Nothing around here adds up," Garrett agreed.

I took a closer look at bags of grain propped against a stack of rickety wooden crates. Grain needs to be stored properly, especially in an orchard where it is likely that furry creatures like rats or mice could tunnel into the bags and have a nice feast. Grain had spilled onto the dirt floor. I wondered if Confluence had a rodent problem or if someone on staff had gotten sloppy.

Sloppy was the perfect description for the state of the nanobrewery. At least seventy percent of brewing is the cleaning and sanitizing. Any reputable brewer will tell you that they spend the vast majority of their day hosing down the floors and scrubbing tanks.

"Garrett, I don't think Confluence is brewing their own beer. There's no way that what we tried last night was produced here."

He looked at me with wide eyes. "I was just going to say the same thing."

I reached down and picked up a handful of grain. "Look at this. There's grain all over the floor. Everything is completely disorganized. It's filthy. There is no way that the beer we sampled last night is being made here. No way."

His mouth hung slightly open. His eyes drifted from a pallet of empty twelve-ounce bottles to a pile of dirty rags crumpled next to a bucket and mop. "Sloan, I'm with you, but I don't get it. What *did* we drink last night, and what's on tap in the tasting room?"

"They have to be getting their beer from someone else." I paused for a second. "That's it. Remember, last night at dinner, how we both commented that the beer tasted familiar? They must be outsourcing it from another brewery in the region."

Garrett gasped. "Enchantment! I remember that honey flavor. It's Enchantment's IPA."

"Yes." Enchantment Brewing was another Wenatchee brewery named after The Enchantments, a nearby hiking region known for its alpine lakes and steep peaks. In the summer, intrepid hikers would pack in gear and trek out into over twenty miles of untouched wilderness.

"That's it, isn't it?" Garrett's head moved from side to side like he was trying to connect dots in his mind.

"It has to be, but why?" I brushed grain from my hands. "It's already been confirmed that Ben doesn't brew, nor does Chase. So are Miri and Josh experimenting with recipes here?"

"If so, their professors at school should have failed them."

"Agreed." I nodded. "Why have a brewery without brewing your own beer?" It didn't make sense. Collaborating with another brewery? Sure. Offering a guest tap? Also commonplace. But passing off another brewery's beer as your own was unheard of. It also had to be costly.

"What if all of this is a front for something else?" Garrett swept his hand in front of him.

"A front?"

"Yeah, what if there's something much shadier going down at Confluence?"

"Like what?"

He shrugged. "I don't know. Ben and Chase working on opening a second pub in Seattle makes me wonder if it's connected. They could be transporting stuff between here and Seattle, which, as you know, is a port city."

"Are you thinking drugs?"

He threw his hands up. "I don't know. Maybe. It's possible, right?"

I nodded, taking another glance around the messy space. "Okay, let's go with that theory. Maybe Ben and Chase are paying off Miri and Josh to keep quiet. If Saachi found out, that could give her motive. Of course, she could also just go to the police."

Garrett scowled. "Retail cannabis sales have skyrocketed

since pot became legal, but that's made the black market even more intense. What if Ben and Chase have an illegal grow operation? The tasting room and brewery are a perfect front. Remember how Ben warned us not to venture out of the main orchard. What if the reason is that there are other crops out there he doesn't want us to see?"

My mind spun with possibilities. Visions of the massive fencing came to my mind. "It makes sense. It would explain a lot."

"There's one way to find out." Garrett looked at his watch. "We've got time. What do you say, should we go take a longer walk?"

"Count me in." I was already halfway to the door. If Ben and Chase really had an illegal grow operation, then things could get dangerous.

CHAPTER
TEN

GARRETT and I checked our surroundings before heading to the outer edges of the orchard that Ben had deemed "off limits." The other event guests were still at the main house lingering over breakfast, I guessed because they were recovering from consuming one too many pints last night. There was no movement in the barn when we scurried past. I felt like a kid about to get caught ditching class. Garrett stifled a laugh as we kept our heads low and darted between trees so as not to be seen.

"We probably look ridiculous," I said when we were far enough away from the barn to be heard.

"I know." Garrett pulled his Nitro baseball cap lower on his brow. "Hey, I promised you an adventure, right? This wasn't exactly what I was envisioning, but I don't feel like we have a choice, and it's not so bad to spend time with you no matter what we're doing."

I felt the same. Despite the bizarre string of events, I didn't want the weekend to end. Not yet.

The rows of trees became thinner. In the distance, the

twelve-foot cedar fence that stretched as far as I could see came into view. "There it is," I pointed.

"Woah." Garrett stopped in mid-stride. "That is not a friendly-neighborhood fence."

"Are those cameras mounted every few feet?" The sun was in my eyes. I had to squint to get a better look, but unless I was seeing things, cameras appeared to be positioned strategically on the fenceposts.

"Yeah." Garrett frowned. "I'd love to get a closer look. I could probably have you step on my hands in order to see over the top of the fence, but I think it's a bad idea. They have gone to a lot of work to make sure that no one gets in, and I don't want to risk one of us getting shot, either."

I breathed in slowly. "Do you smell that?"

He sniffed like a bunny rabbit. "It's a pretty distinctive aroma, isn't it?"

"Yeah." The smell of pot was intense. I supposed it could also be hemp. Both grew well in this region. However, hemp farms rarely had perimeter fencing and cameras. "I wonder if we're on camera now. We should probably head back and let the authorities take it from here. I think a call to Chief Meyers is in order." I knew that Wenatchee wasn't in her jurisdiction, but she could alert her colleagues and would know what next steps to take.

"One hundred percent." Garrett repositioned his hat. It had our Nitro logo that used hop cones in place of the elements of an atom. Mixing science and art was our goal at the brewery. "I don't like this at all. We definitely need to get some help."

Luckily, my phone had service. I called the Chief and left her a detailed message asking her to call me back or to pass on my information and number to the local authorities. I had known Chief Meyers for over twenty years. She had been Leavenworth's active police chief for the duration of time that I'd been in the village. I appreciated her direct yet caring approach to community policing. She often joked that her job was like herding cats, especially during festival weekends when she had to sober up drunk frat partiers. Otherwise, Leavenworth was a fairly sleepy community. Most neighbors kept their doors unlocked, and everyone knew each other by name. It was hard not to feel safe nestled between the mountains and knowing that Chief Meyers was on watch.

"She didn't answer," I said to Garrett after hanging up. "I'm sure you heard my message."

"Yeah. I feel better having Meyers looped in." He stood on his toes to try and see over the fence. "It's too high for me. I think we should head back to the farmhouse. Who knows if someone is watching us right now?"

We retraced our steps. The tour van had arrived in our absence. Guests had begun gathering in front of the house, but we still had some time to spare. I wanted to take another look at the brewery. Maybe there was evidence stashed amongst the chaos that would help prove our theory.

"You want to take one more quick peek inside?" I pointed to the decrepit outbuilding.

"Let's do it." Garrett wafted his hands under his nose. "I recognize that smell."

"Someone started a brew now?" I asked as we cut through the grass. The smell was an aroma I knew well. Steeping grains always reminded me of the smell of Grape Nuts cereal.

Garrett pushed the creaky door open.

We were immediately hit by another smell—smoke.

"Oh, my God, there's a fire," Garrett yelled. "They left the boil going!" He raced over to a rusted stainless-steel kettle. "This is a natural gas system. Is someone trying to blow this place up?"

I coughed and waved smoke from my face.

Smoke was billowing from beneath the keg. The fire had spread to the sacks of grain and flames were starting to lap up the side of the barn.

"Be careful," I called, covering my mouth with my shirt to try and block the smoke.

"Go get help, Sloan," Garrett crouched dangerously close to the fire. "I'll see if I can at least get the gas turned off."

I turned around, choking on the thick fumes. Garrett was right—if he couldn't turn the gas off, the entire building was going to blow. I reached for the door handle. It wouldn't budge. I yanked harder.

"Garrett, it's stuck." I shook the door handle with both hands. The old wooden slats rattled, but the door wouldn't shake free. "I think it's locked."

Smoke continued to billow. My eyes and throat burned.

Garrett ignored the brew stand and ran over to help me. He coughed and gasped for air as he threw his entire body weight into the door again and again. The door refused to open.

"Sloan, someone locked us in here."

Panic pulsed through my veins. I pounded on the door and yelled, "Help!"

Garrett did the same.

It was getting hard to see as the smoke thickened.

"Sloan, keep yelling. I've got to try and turn the gas off." Garrett's voice sounded scratchy.

As he ran toward the flames again, I heard voices outside.

A minute later the door swung open, allowing some of the smoke to escape. Ben stood in front of me holding a fire extinguisher. "What happened?"

"Someone left the boil on." I pointed through the haze to Garrett.

Ben sprayed the flames while Garrett managed to turn the gas off.

I stepped outside of the building and gulped the fresh air. Once the fire had been put out, Ben and Garrett joined me. Garrett blinked repeatedly. I wondered if his eyes felt as gritty as mine.

"Guys, I'm so sorry about that. What happened?" Ben sounded concerned, but I didn't know who to trust at this point. "These old buildings are the worst. This door does that all the time. I'm just glad I heard you..." he trailed off.

"Who would leave a boil going over an open flame?" Garrett coughed twice.

Leaving a brew unattended was something no self-respecting brewer would ever do.

Ben shook his head. "It had to be one of the interns. You'd think they'd teach them better in school."

I shook my head in disbelief. "That has to be brewing 101. I remember my first week of training at Der Keller. Otto made it crystal clear that never, *ever* should a brew be left alone, and even back then, we were working on much more sophisticated systems."

"I'll have a talk with them, don't you worry. You guys go get on the bus. Enjoy the tour. We'll take it from here." Ben practically pushed us in the direction of the farmhouse.

"We can't go on the tour now," I said. "Your entire brew operation almost just blew up."

A solemn look spread across Ben's face. "And trust me, I'm in your debt. I don't know what would have happened if you guys hadn't found the fire. That's why I want you to go enjoy the rest of the weekend. You've already done enough." He gave me a two-fingered salute.

"How did you know we were here?" Garrett asked.

"I heard you had a morning stroll. Sacchi was looking for you," Ben answered. "I told her I would go hunt you down and then I noticed smoke coming from the building and heard your screams."

There was something in his tone that I didn't like. Was he hinting that he'd seen us?

He adjusted his position, shielding his gaze with his hand. "You guys be careful, okay? Enjoy the day, but no more danger for my two favorite brewers."

Was something deeper behind his words?

He returned back inside the building to assess the damage. Garrett and I headed for the farmhouse. I wasn't sure if Ben was being sincere, but I did know for sure that the fire hadn't been an accident.

CHAPTER
ELEVEN

"ARE YOU OKAY, SLOAN?" Garrett asked as we cut through the grass on our way to the farmhouse.

"Yeah, I think so. My eyes and throat burn a little and I smell like smoke, but otherwise, I'm fine. What about you?"

"Same." He cleared his throat. "That was close. Really close. We need to be much more careful for the rest of the day."

My heart rate had calmed down a bit, but the adrenaline from being locked inside a burning building made my entire body feel tingly like I was buzzing from too much caffeine. "Yeah. The door didn't get jammed. Someone locked us in. The question is who?"

"Let's keep alert and see if we can figure it out." Garrett looked to the farmhouse where the rest of the guests had gathered. "And let's keep this between us. At this point everyone connected to Confluence has the potential to harm us. Let's stick together and keep our eyes and ears open."

"For sure." I nodded as Saachi waved us closer.

She tapped her watch. "Where have you been? We're waiting on you."

Garrett pointed behind us. "Did you not see that there was a fire in the brewery?"

He was playing it cool. I wondered if his heart was racing in his chest like mine. Had someone seen us on the fence cameras? Did Saachi know we'd been snooping around? Had she alerted Ben or Chase? I didn't want to jump to conclusions, but if Confluence had an illegal grow on the property, we could definitely be in danger. People had been killed for venturing onto grow sites. It seemed highly unlikely that the door had gotten jammed. What if Sacchi had started the fire and locked us inside?

"The van is here, and everyone else is ready," Saachi snapped.

"Can you give us a minute to freshen up?" I gave her an apologetic smile, glad for once that I had a decent poker face. "I want to go change so my clothes don't smell like smoke."

They couldn't be in too much of a hurry to leave because, aside from maybe half the other guests, Saachi was the only staff member around. There was no sign of Ben, Chase, Miri, or Josh.

"Hurry, please," Saachi said with irritation. "We're on a tight schedule today."

Or were they in a hurry for another reason? Did they want us off the property so that they could work on their secret crops? Did she know that there was a huge marijuana grow on the other side of the orchard?

I went to my room to freshen up and grab my bag. I couldn't stop wondering who was in the know when it came to Confluence's staff. Everyone? Only Ben and Chase? Who was monitoring the cameras? Who had been in the brewery before us?

A new theory began to form. What if Josh knew what Confluence's real cash crop was, either because he'd been brought in from the beginning or because it didn't take a genius to figure out that something more than apples was being grown behind that massive fence? He and Miri were living in the orchard, so they could have easily wandered out to the perimeter to get a close-up look for themselves, or they simply could have smelled pot wafting into their RVs at night. Either way, maybe he had decided to confront Ben and Chase. He could have demanded more money in exchange for not reporting the illegal grow operation to the police. Or he could have threatened to go to the police.

That would explain why someone knocked him out last night. It might also explain why Miri had changed her tune. Perhaps she was scared. If she felt threatened, that made her erratic behavior much more understandable.

I hoped that Chief Meyers would call me back soon. In the meantime, I planned to keep a careful eye on the staff for the remainder of the day.

When I returned outside, Josh, Miri, and Ben had shown up. Chase was the only Confluence team member missing in action. I wondered if that meant anything.

Before Ben could say anything else, Saachi clapped twice. "Okay, people. Let's get loaded up. Josh and Miri will be your guides this afternoon. I've prepared packed lunches that you'll enjoy after you tour the hop farm. We'll see you here later for the bonfire and cookout."

So she and Ben were staying behind.

I was disappointed that they wouldn't be joining us, but on the flip side, that would give Garrett and me a chance to talk to Miri and Josh alone.

The drive to the hop fields was like a scene from *The Sound of Music*. Lush fields of green grasses, blooming flowers, majestic mountains jutting up all around us. Garrett placed his arm around me like he had last night, and I let myself drift into a dream-like state, taking in the scenery and the warmth of his touch.

This was supposed to be a romantic weekend.

It felt like we were taking the next step forward when he gently brushed strands of hair from my face and held my gaze for a moment. "I could get lost for a long time in those golden-brown eyes of yours, Sloan."

The fluttery feeling returned to my chest. It was weird and awkward and strangely comfortable to be wrapped in Garrett's arms. I hadn't dated since Mac and I first met, and quite honestly, I had barely dated before Mac and I had fallen for each other. This was new territory for me. Mac had always been overly effusive and one for showy gestures and expensive gifts.

Garrett was different. When he said something like he could get lost in my eyes, I knew that he meant it. It wasn't a toss-away pickup line. And yet I still wasn't sure what to do with my growing attachment to him. I had made a commitment to myself not to jump into a brand-new relationship after breaking up with Mac. In part because I had morphed into what I thought Mac had wanted me to be, I had never stepped fully into myself in our relationship. I didn't want to make the same mistakes again.

Not that I could. I was a completely different person than I'd been the day I married Mac. I had been so desperate to find stability and have a family of my own that I hadn't paid attention to the red flags early on. His insatiable need to flirt with every woman he met. His tendency to get caught up in himself and in painting a picture of perfection.

I wasn't that same young woman anymore. I had made a family. I had established roots. I had a community. I knew who I was and what I wanted for the future. The only thing holding me back was my own fear.

The irony was that if I had this conversation with Mac, he would likely tell me to go for it. To get out of my own head.

I hoped that I could follow that advice because things with Garrett were easy and comfortable.

"A penny for your thoughts, Sloan." Garrett interrupted my internal monologue.

"I was just thinking about this," I answered truthfully.

"This?"

"Us. This." I smiled and met his gaze, which sent another round of flutters through my stomach. "This feels good. It's easy. I guess I'm kind of waiting for it to feel hard or for the bottom to drop out. That's a pattern that I'm trying to break— to stop the cycle of constantly spinning on worst-case scenarios and just enjoying the moment."

He massaged my arm. "I'm enjoying this moment, too. Everything is easy with you. I'm taking that as a sign that we're onto something good here, but I'll follow your lead. I don't want to rush anything. There's no need. We've got all the time we need." He kissed the top of my head.

I let out a contented sigh.

A couple of years ago, I couldn't have imagined this outcome, but I was ready to let myself savor the now and release my past.

We arrived at the hop fields shortly. Miri and Josh got out to talk to the hop farmer and then directed us to follow them. The fields were perfectly lined with hop trellises. The vines twisted around twenty-foot posts, stretching toward the sky. The calming smell of hops immediately enveloped me.

Miri introduced the farmer, who gave us a lengthy explanation of how the hops were grown and cultivated before launching into a discussion about this region of the world, and how the hops produced here were used in breweries on every continent.

None of it was new information for Garrett or me, but it was still interesting to listen to the hop farmer's perspective on the growing climate and new trends in hop development. I focused my attention on Miri and Josh as the farmer answered questions.

They had stepped away from our group and were talking in hushed voices. I scooted to the edge of the circle to see if I could catch anything they were saying to each other. I could tell by the intense looks on their faces they were discussing something serious.

I shifted my head in their direction, pretending to be stretching my neck. I couldn't make out everything they were saying, but then Miri stopped Josh and raised her voice. "The police, Josh. The police are getting involved. We're dead."

CHAPTER
TWELVE

I STOLE AWAY from the rest of the group. "Miri, I'm sorry to interrupt, but I overheard you say that the police are getting involved. I assume you mean with Confluence."

She clapped a hand over her mouth and stared at Josh in horror.

"How did you hear that?" Josh anchored his elbows to his waist in a protective stance.

"Does it matter?" I gave him my best "mom" look. "Listen, I think I understand the situation and what kind of a position you're both in. Like I said last night, I'm here to help if you'll let me."

Miri blinked hard to fight back tears. She couldn't contain them. They streamed down her face as her shoulders heaved.

I caught Garrett's eye and motioned for him to come and join us. Then I moved them farther away from everyone else. There was a rustic trellis with a wooden bench nearby that I guessed the farm used for weddings. "Let's go have a seat."

Miri's sobs shifted, making her suck air in through her nose and causing her shoulders to quiver. Josh took her arm.

Garrett caught up with us. He quickly assessed the situation and stayed quiet.

Josh helped Miri sit down. Garrett leaned on one side of the trellis. I sat next to Miri. "I know you're upset, but I've found that talking about your problems always helps. It's too much of a burden to carry that weight alone." That was the truth.

Miri brushed her tears away with the back of her wrist. It was dotted with freckles and tanned from the early summer sun. "I don't know what we're going to do. We're going to be in so much trouble."

"Does this have to do with other crops being grown in the Confluence orchards?" I prodded.

"You know?" Miri's eyes were bloodshot.

"It didn't take a genius to figure it out," Garrett added. "The smell alone is a dead giveaway."

"That's what we tried to tell Ben," Josh spoke for the first time. "He wouldn't listen. He said the grow site was far enough away from the tasting room and main orchard that guests wouldn't be able to smell anything. At least not now. His plan was to close the tasting room during pot harvest. I guess that's when the smell is really intense. He told us one of the nearby schools complained that students and teachers got sick from the smell of one of the neighboring hemp fields during harvest, so they had industrial fans installed. But when the wind blows the right direction, it's impossible not to catch a whiff."

"He worked out a story for us to tell guests about a neighboring hemp field," Miri agreed.

"Is there a neighboring hemp field?" I reached into my bag to find a tissue for her.

"Yeah, that's their cover." She took the tissue and dabbed her cheeks.

"How do you two play into this?" I asked, hoping for some clarity.

"We knew what was really going on at Confluence from the beginning," Miri started.

"Not the beginning, beginning," Josh interrupted. "When we met Ben at school, he seemed like he was a professional."

"What changed?" I caught Garrett's eye. He had one arm propped against the hop trellis. I could tell from his stance that he was listening without trying to look like he was interfering.

"The first day when we showed up, we were excited to brew and learn everything there was to know about a real brewery, but those dreams got dashed right away." Miri sniffled. "We never should have agreed to Ben's plan. We were stupid to go along with it. We knew it, too. Didn't we, Josh? We should have trusted our instincts." She fanned her face with one hand and stared at Josh. She didn't wait for him to respond before she continued. "Ben came to us with what he claimed was an amazing business opportunity. A chance to make some serious cash to pay off our student loans. He explained that the tasting room and brewing equipment were just a front for the real operation—pot. But, and this is the truth, we didn't know it was an illegal grow. Honestly." She made a cross over her heart.

"We knew at some level," Josh replied. His response was subdued. He sounded remorseful. "We just didn't want to admit it."

"No, I didn't. I swear I didn't," Miri insisted, shaking her finger at him. "When Ben talked about paying us cash under the table, I thought that was the way the industry worked. It's a state-by-state thing. It's not like the federal government is taking taxes out. I thought all the money in pot was paid in cash and under the table."

She wasn't entirely misinformed. There was truth to both of her points. Washington State had generated one billion dollars in tax revenue from legal cannabis sales the prior year.

Due to federal regulations, though, most banks didn't want to deal with marijuana growers, which made paying employees more challenging. Some dispensaries and growers resorted to paying their employees in cash, but that had changed as the industry continued to expand. Employees were often paid as independent contractors, and an entirely new crop of cannabis-friendly banking alternatives had popped up in the last few years.

"Anyway, my gut from the beginning wasn't sure it was a good idea. I don't have anything against pot, but I want to be a head brewer, and I wanted the practice," Miri continued.

"But the money was too good," Josh said.

"So Ben was upfront with you about Confluence not producing its own beer?" Garrett asked.

"He gave us the green light to do what we wanted with the old junky homebrew equipment he got, but we never even have time. I think I've spent a total of an hour in there. I started to try and clean it up one day, but all of our time is spent in the pot fields." Miri dabbed her eyes.

That made me feel better about the kind of training they had received in their collegiate brewing program.

"What about Saachi?" I asked. "I'm assuming Chase and Ben started the operation together, but did Saachi know?"

"Yeah, of course Saachi knows." Josh looked at me like I had started speaking German. "Saachi runs the show."

That was a twist I hadn't seen coming. "All three of them are in on it?"

"Yep. Saachi orders the beer; she manages everything at the tasting room and guest house so that Ben and Chase can focus on the cannabis."

"What about the rest of the orchard?" Garrett asked. "Do they harvest the apples?"

"For sure." Josh nodded. "They hire special crews to come

in for that and then sell the apples to a cider producer in Yakima."

"How did you hear that the police are getting involved?" I asked.

Miri patted her pocket. "I got a text from Saachi. The cops are there now. They're raiding the place. When we get back, I'm sure we'll be arrested along with Ben, Chase, and Saachi."

I wasn't so sure about that. But then again, I had no idea what the legal ramifications of working for an illegal grow operation would be. I had to assume that, given Josh and Miri's age, a judge would likely be more lenient with them, but I could be wrong. I wasn't about to promise them anything.

"Did either of you have something to do with the police involvement?" Garrett asked, raising his eyebrows at me.

Miri shook her head. "No. We couldn't tell the cops. Not without ruining our own futures. We had to buy our time. Do the work. Get through harvest season and get the hell out, right, Josh?"

Josh stared at the ground.

"Right, Josh?" Miri's voice was louder. "Josh?"

"Look, I caved, okay?" Josh threw his hands in the air. "I'm sorry. I'm not as strong as you. I told you that. You wouldn't listen. This isn't worth it for me. I don't want to go to jail."

Suddenly, everything seemed much clearer. The realization of what had happened last night in the orchard dawned on me. I think it was from the way Josh was drawing circles in the dirt with his shoe and not meeting Miri's eyes. He massaged the back of his head.

"Miri, did you hit Josh?" I asked, keeping my gaze on him.

She gulped and reeled backward like I had punched her. "What?"

I noticed Josh's shoulders crumple. "Josh, did you tell Miri you were going to the police?"

He covered the goose egg on his head completely with one hand. Then his eyes filled with rage as he put it together. "Wait, *you* hit me?"

Miri pinched the bridge of her nose and closed her eyes. "I thought we had a deal that we were going to see it out and then never speak of Confluence again." She tried to move closer, but Josh held up an arm to stop her. "I'm so sorry. I didn't mean to hurt you. I just wanted to stop you from making the call. I knew you would be too busy with the dinner last night, so I figured we could talk about it again today. When did you call?"

"Last night." He looked at her with shock. "I can't believe it was you. I thought it was Saachi. That's why I finally decided to make the call. I thought we were in real danger, Miri."

"We are now. At least I am. You're going to be fine, and I'm going to go to jail." She covered her face as she rocked back and forth on the bench.

"No, I told them the truth. I explained the entire situation and how we had no way out. They know that you didn't want to be part of it, either," Josh insisted.

Josh had alerted the authorities, and I had called Chief Meyers, so it was no wonder that police were swarming the orchard, as Miri had said.

"Listen, I think the best thing we can do is get you both back to Confluence. The police are going to want to take your statements and speak with you." I used my most calming voice to de-escalate the situation.

"We can't leave." Miri pointed to the rest of our group. "We're supposed to serve lunch."

"I think the team here can handle that. There are more pressing matters. I'll talk to the farm staff and call an Uber. Garrett and I will come back with you and give our statements, too."

Miri sniffled again. "Okay, that sounds good."

I left them and went to speak to the farm staff and order an Uber. So much for my romantic afternoon with Garrett, but I was relieved that we finally had answers about what was really happening at Confluence, and I wanted to do everything in my power to make sure that Miri and Josh didn't take the brunt of the fall.

CHAPTER
THIRTEEN

THE REST of the day passed in a blur. As expected, a handful of police cars lined the gravel drive when we arrived at the brewery. Teams of local law enforcement officers and drug enforcement agents swept out in every direction. There were flashing lights and a swarm of activity.

Chief Meyers spotted us and waved us over. "Sloan, Garrett, thanks for the intel."

"This is quite the response." I blinked hard. Between the afternoon sun and the swirling lights, my eyes couldn't take it all in.

"Things were already in motion when I got your call," she said, adjusting the walkie-talkie on her belt. She was wearing her standard khaki uniform and a wide-brimmed hat. "My colleagues with drug enforcement are going to need to take your statements."

"Of course." I glanced over to Josh and Miri, who had been immediately separated and were being questioned by drug enforcement agents. "We learned that Josh came forward. Do you know what will happen to them? I feel bad for them.

They're not much older than Alex. I think they got in over their heads."

The chief nodded. "I'm sure that will be taken into consideration. I do know that the other three adults have been arrested and taken into custody. It's too soon to have firm numbers, but at first pass, the federal agents are estimating that there must be at least four thousand pounds of marijuana here. Super high-octane product can fetch five to seven thousand dollars a pound. I don't know if what they're growing behind those military-style fences is of that kind of value, but either way, we're talking big money."

"Man, Sloan, I think we're in the wrong business," Garrett teased, intentionally bringing some levity to the moment.

"Don't even think about it, Strong," Chief Meyers shot back. "I like my Nitro pints just the way they are, thank you very much."

"What about the fire? Did you hear about that?" I asked, steering the conversation back to Confluence. "It wasn't an accident, was it?"

"Nope. It was an attempted murder," Chief Meyers replied in a tone that could be interpreted as stoicism. I knew it as her simply reporting the facts. "Chase confessed to everything. He and Ben got in a scuffle—his word, not mine—in the tasting room last night. Ben caught him stealing cash."

"Ahh, so that's what we walked into." Garrett's mouth opened slightly in realization.

"Chase admitted that he was going to bail, again his word." She made a funny face. "He realized that Josh and Miri weren't going to keep quiet, and then noticed that you two were suspicious. He emptied the cash register and was going to take all of the cash they had stashed out in the greenhouses, but Ben happened to come into the tasting room right as Chase was stuffing money into a duffel bag. Fortuitous, isn't it?"

"That explains the tables and his bizarre reaction when we found him in the barn last night," I agreed. "But what about the fire this morning? Was that Chase, too?"

The Chief gave her head a half shake. "No. That was Ben. He spotted you on the cameras and decided that if you had an unfortunate accident, no one would be the wiser. Except Chase was wiser."

"Huh?" I scrunched my forehead. "Chase wasn't even around."

"He was." Meyers snapped and motioned to the barn with her finger. "According to Chase, he and Ben got into it again after everyone went to bed."

"That matches what Sacchi told me," I interrupted.

"Good. We'll be confirming his statement with her, too." She waited for one of her fellow officers to pass by before continuing. "The second argument led to a physical altercation. Ben threatened to pin everything on Chase and Chase claims that he realized that Ben was not afraid of escalating things or resorting to violence. He was at the grow site this morning when Ben saw you on the camera monitors. He was worried that Ben was going to do something rash, so he followed Ben. He watched Ben start the fire and lock you in. If his statement checks out, we have Ben on attempted murder, arson, and assault, in addition to the drug charges."

"Whew." Garrett blew out a long breath.

Everything made so much more sense. It had been Ben the entire time. There was one last thing nagging me. "Why did Ben let us out, then? If he wanted us dead, he was succeeding."

"He's not talking at the moment. We'll see if that changes, but I suspect he realized that there were too many people around. Someone else would have come to help you. The buildings aren't that far away." She looked from the brewing outbuilding to the farmhouse. "Maybe he figured that if he played the part of your rescuer, that would help sell his story."

"Right." I let everything sink in as she excused herself to go check in with her colleagues.

We spent the next few hours answering questions and waiting around for further instructions. When we finally got the green light to pack our things and return to Leavenworth, it was long past lunch. My stomach grumbled.

Garrett laughed. "Your stomach is in line with mine. Sorry that the rest of this day is a bust—literally."

"Oh, no, not more puns." I rolled my eyes.

"Sorry. I couldn't pass up the opportunity." His eyes twinkled. "What do you say we grab some lunch in town and then take the long way home? Maybe we can stop for a short hike at the Enchantments. I was looking forward to the bonfire tonight, so I think once we're in the village, we light a fire on your back deck and cozy up with a growler from Nitro. The beer's free."

"That sounds like perfection."

It did. Our relationship was shifting but in its own sweet, easy time. Maybe this weekend had gone exactly as it was supposed to. We had gotten to spend time away and, in the process, had helped shut down an illegal grow operation. Not bad for a first date. I only hoped there were many more to come.

A BREW TO A KILL

ELLIE ALEXANDER

AUTHOR OF BEER AND LOATHING

To you, this cozy community, where it's perfectly okay and acceptable to be warm, kind, and welcoming.

We need more of this in the world. Thanks for spreading the book love.

CHAPTER
ONE

THE AROMA of mosaic hops and rose petals wafted from the brewery. April was in full bloom in Leavenworth, Washington, where Garrett Strong, my brewing partner at Nitro, and I were putting the finishing touches on our spring line of Pacific Northwest-style beers. The first was a cold aged cream ale with aromas of sweet corn. Our rosehips and lemon lager was an update from a beer we had brewed last year, while our pear and apple IPA was a new addition. The fruit-forward brew was layered with local, organic produce, Yakima Valley hops, and a touch of vanilla for a hint of a sweet finish.

"Sloan, how are we doing for time?" Garrett asked as he climbed down from the ladder attached to one of the brite tanks. The vessels were used to clarify, carbonate, and store our beer prior to packaging.

"We should head over to the Festhall soon." I checked my watch. "Maybe twenty minutes."

Garrett tugged a pair of chemistry goggles from his head, causing his wavy hair to fall over one eye. "Perfect. That gives me time to change and steal two of your white velvet cookies before we go."

"You're taking to thievery, I better tell Kat to guard the cookies," I teased. "No, seriously, I'll check in with her to make sure everything is good with the tasting room and meet you in the kitchen to load up in a few." I left him to get ready and went to the front.

A long distressed-wood bar with dozens of taps divided the brewing area, commercial kitchen, and our shared office in the back of the building from the tasting room in the front. Every time I walked into the bright space with its exposed ceilings and bright windows that looked out onto Leavenworth's cobblestone streets, I couldn't help but smile. I was so lucky to be living my dream.

"Hey, Sloan," Kat said from behind the bar, greeting me with a dimpled grin as she pointed to the window. "Can you believe how gorgeous it is this morning? It's going to be perfect weather for the farmers market."

Tangerine light spilled through the rustic, wood-pane windows. Steep-pitched rooflines and Bavarian façades painted in a range of cheerful colors, vibrant blues, warm yellows, and Kelly greens stretched as far as I could see.

Today was the official kickoff festival for the return of the farmers market season. During the winter months, the market went on hiatus, but now that the hills were lush with emerald green grass and rows and rows of dainty pink cherry and apple blossoms, I couldn't wait to get back in the swing of market weekends.

We had decided to set up a booth for the kickoff festivities where we would share samples of our spring beers and sweet pairings. Leavenworth loves a festival weekend. It's kind of our thing. And there was no better way to welcome spring than a polka band and party in the streets.

Kat and I had baked batches of white velvet cookies in the shape of hop cones and frosted them with a citrus royal icing with a super secret ingredient—a splash of our signature citrus IPA. In addition to the ode-to-beer cookies, we opted for rhubarb-filled crumbles and chocolate shortbread.

"I know. The weather gods are on our side this weekend," I said to Kat. "How are things going with prep for the day? Do you need anything before we take off?"

"Nope. I'm all set. It should be pretty chill today since everyone will be at the market. Look at this, though." She reached for her phone and held her screen for me to see. "I posted our daily special and the fact that we'll have a booth at the market on social a little while ago, and we got a message from a travel influencer who's in town. He's huge. He has over a million followers. A Brew with a View, do you know him?"

I glanced at her screen and shook my head.

"Well, that's not a surprise. He's probably not on your radar. I think he's in his early twenties. His name is Josh, and he does these insane hikes and then shoots videos and pics of beer—hence, A Brew with a View. He slid into our DMs to ask if we could give him some cans. He's going to hike Icicle Ridge tomorrow and wants to feature Nitro on the summit."

"Sure. Yeah. That sounds great."

"This could be huge for us. A lot of Josh's posts and videos go viral." Kat clicked off her phone. "The chance of a couple of million beer lovers seeing Nitro at the top of a peak is worth a six-pack or two, right?"

"Without a doubt. I trust you completely when it comes to partnerships like this, so it's a solid yes for me." I was thrilled that Kat had happened upon Leavenworth while on a personal quest to meet her idol during Oktoberfest a few years ago. The meetup with her celebrity crush hadn't gone as she had planned, but sometimes fate has a way of putting the right person in your path at the right time. That was true for Kat. She may not have found love, but she found us. She had become an integral part of Nitro's team and part of my extended family.

Kat's dimples creased as she smiled at me. "Great. I'll hook him up. You'll probably see him at the market. He has the kind of personality that's hard to miss. Big. Expressive. Bold."

"As long as he's not an April." I chuckled and made a funny face. April Ablin was a real estate agent and the self-appointed queen of the village and all things German. She took it upon herself to make sure that everyone in town adhered to her strict vision of kitschy décor. Not a day went by when she didn't pop into the tasting room to insist we hang cheap plastic red, yellow, and black flags from the windows or that we swap our jeans and Nitro hoodies for skimpy barmaid dresses and lederhosen.

"One April is enough." Kat stuck out her tongue. "But, hey, if Josh and his A Brew with a View bring more beer tourists to the village, why not?"

"Why not," I agreed.

Garrett entered the tasting room, pushing a cart with cases of our beers. "Ready to go sling some spring ales, Sloan?"

"That's a mouthful, but yes."

"Love the shirt," Kat said.

Garrett posed for us so that we could get a closer look at his punny T-shirt. The retro design featured mountain ranges and a twist on a familiar saying: THE BREWERIES ARE CALLING, AND I MUST GO.

We said goodbye to Kat and made our way along Front Street. The village looked like a watercolor painting with pink and yellow geraniums cascading from window boxes on the half-timbered buildings. Blue gingham-checked bunting wrapped around the gazebo, fluttering in the slight breeze.

Sunlight drenched the cobblestone streets and kissed Icicle Ridge.

The Festhall was located at the far end of Front Street across from Der Keller Brewing. In any other town of two thousand residents, multiple breweries would probably saturate the market, but that wasn't true in Leavenworth, thanks to the steady stream of tourists who visited the village for one of our many festivals—Maifest, Oktoberfest, Icefest, and so many more. Der Keller was synonymous with Leavenworth and craft beer. Otto and Ursula Krause (my chosen family) had started the brewery in the 1970s and had grown it from a two-person operation to one of the largest microbreweries on the West Coast.

The Der Keller empire continued to expand. My ex-husband Mac had recently taken over operations, a move I had been nervous about. Not because he was dangerous, but because Mac tended to overspend, overcommit, over-embellish, over everything. Otto and Ursula, Mac's parents, had divided shares of their beloved business to Mac, his brother Hans, and me, so they could scale back and enjoy their retirement years. At first, I was convinced we were headed for disaster, but to my surprise and delight, Mac had focused on personal growth since our split. He had stepped into his new role with a focus and determination I had never experienced when we were married.

Der Keller was thriving under his leadership, allowing Hans and me the freedom to offer insight into the brewery's future without constantly having to rein Mac in.

"Wow, it's already hopping," Garrett noted as we approached the empty lot across from the Festhall, where the market setup was in full swing.

White vendor tents in neat rows stretched from one end of the lot to the other. It looked as if every farmer, grower, and crafter from the entire Wenatchee Valley was ready to kick off the season. There was something for everyone—produce, flowers, honey, candles, pastries, bread, wine, food trucks, and more.

"It's going to be a full market. It looks like we're next to Weber and Annabelle." I pointed to a farm stand a few booths away.

Garrett maneuvered the beer cart past a flower vendor unpacking truckloads of tulips, heather, camellias, and snow-drops. Then he went straight to work setting up our Nitro booth with his usual efficiency, unpacking crates of our new spring ales and tasting glasses. We'd been doing the market and festival circuit for the last year, so we had setup down to a science. Garrett hung a large banner with our Nitro atomic hop logo from the back of the tent and strung hop lights around the front.

I set out platters of my cookies with little tasting notes Kat had designed. The white velvet, rhubarb crumbles, and choco-late shortbread cookies were meant to be paired with each of our beers to pull out the spring flavors. Beer tasting was serious business. Mac had trained for years to become a cicerone, the beer equivalent of a sommelier. For me, homing in on a beer's sweetness, acidity, mouthfeel, carbonation, and body came naturally, but one of the things that Garrett and I felt passionate about was making beer tasting accessible and fun. I loved educating beer novices on how the white velvet cookies would balance the smooth, buttery feel of the cream ale, whereas the tangy rhubarb would marry with the rosehips and lemon lager, and the chocolate shortbread would pull out the fruit-forward flavors in the IPA.

Once I finished arranging our cookie display, I unpacked our beer merch, stickers, hoodies, hats, and coasters. Canning our beer was a relatively new option. Since we only produced small batches, we didn't have much extra to spare, but Garrett had scored an inexpensive canning system at a beer convention a few months ago, and we decided to take the plunge. We had taken advantage of the slower winter months to ramp up canning to sell six-packs at the market and to guests who wanted to bring home a taste of Leavenworth. I was excited to see how the community responded to our latest endeavor and had a feeling that today's stock might not last long.

By the time our booth was prepped and ready to serve thirsty shoppers, a polka band paraded through the tents announcing the market's official opening. The mayor followed them, complete in Kelly green lederhosen with black suspenders and matching felt hat. After his short welcome speech, he turned the microphone over to my nemesis April Ablin. In true April fashion, she was dressed in a cotton candy-pink dirndl, with two milkmaid-style braids and hot pink lipstick, which clashed with her dyed orange hair. "Gluten, oh, oh, sorry, I meant Guten Morgan."

She waited for applause.

Someone offered a tepid clap.

"Thank you, thank you." April bowed and then fanned her face. "I'm so touched by your warm welcome and thrilled to be the guest of honor to cut the ribbon for this year's farmers market."

"Doesn't she cut it every year?" Garrett whispered.

"I'm sure she buys the ribbon herself."

He laughed.

April prattled on about Leavenworth's rich history, our Bavarian culture, and the upcoming Maifest. I wasn't sure who she thought her target audience, was because aside from a handful of tourists, everyone else had lived in the village longer than April.

I tuned her out and scanned the crowd of familiar faces. A

group of young backpackers congregated at The Bountiful Basket, Weber and Annabelle's farm booth. The booth was decorated with red and white gingham tablecloths, checkered bunting, and dozens of baskets overflowing with organic strawberries, rhubarb, sugar snap peas, asparagus, herbs, and jars of homemade jams, jellies, and sauces.

The backpackers didn't look much older than Alex, my soon-to-be college student son. And one of them, whom I assumed must be Josh, the beer influencer, given his A Brew with a View logo hat, T-shirt, and backpack, looked like he was about to go head-to-head with Weber.

Annabelle yanked Weber's flannel to hold him back as Josh took a swing.

What was going on?

"Get out of here. I don't want to see you anywhere near my booth, my farm, or my *wife*," Weber practically spat in Josh's face. "That's an order."

"It's a free world, man. Chill out." Josh glanced at his friends for moral support. "We're here to climb and spend money in your town. Your energy is not matching the vibe."

Weber lunged at him. "Get out of here—now."

"It's cool. It's cool. We were only trying to help you out, man. Take a few produce pics and post them on social. Your wife has a perfect, wholesome aesthetic. That's all. No need for you to go all patriarchy on us." Josh shrugged in a way that made it clear he was trying to maintain a casual appearance about the argument, but I could tell from his balled-up fists and clenched jaw that there was more going on.

"This is your last chance. Walk away now." Weber clutched a strawberry in one hand and pointed toward the end of the market with the other.

"Okay, relax." Josh pressed his hands out in an attempt to calm Weber down.

It didn't work.

Weber squeezed the strawberry so tight it smashed in his hand and dripped juice down his flannel like a trickle of blood. He dropped the squished berry on the ground and went after Josh, who took off in a sprint. "That's right, you better run. Stay far away from me because if I see you here again, you will get what's coming."

Chatter stopped. People turned to see what was causing the commotion as Josh ran past Der Keller with his friends following him. Even April paused her un-commissioned speech.

"Keep running," Weber hollered.

Annabelle shrank behind him, her cheeks flaming as red as their baskets of strawberries. Her mortification was palpable. She tried whispering and tugging on Weber's sleeve, but his fierce gaze was focused solely on Josh.

I didn't know Weber well, but he and Annabelle had been coming to the farmers market with their organic produce for years. They were always personable and eager to talk about what was in season on their farm. It seemed out of character for him to threaten and attempt to attack Josh. But then again, I wasn't going to jump to any conclusions. I had no idea what had transpired between them before their altercation.

"Attentionion, attentionion." April made up a word that didn't even sound German as she tapped the microphone. "Let's keep our focus, friends. This is a celebration, and it's time for our ribbon cutting. If you would be so kind as to count down from ten with me, I'll cut the ribbon, and the market will officially be open for business."

She signaled the band to continue and wielded a massive pair of scissors.

The sound of the polka music echoed through the village as April sliced the ribbon. Real applause broke out, and the crowd began to mingle. I was eager to check out the other vendors and share Nitro samples. The start of the market was supposed to be a fun and festive occasion. I agreed with April on that. But I couldn't shake the feeling that something was off. Despite the fragrant scents of caramel corn, roasting almonds, and spring blooms wafting from the booths, my stomach bubbled with nervous energy, like something was about to go very wrong.

CHAPTER
TWO

I PUSHED my irrational worries aside as a queue formed at our booth. The next few hours were a blur of passing out beer tasters, selling packages of cookies and six-packs, and chatting with friends and tourists. We sold out of everything before closing, so I took the opportunity to wander through the vendor booths. Annabelle stopped me as I passed by their farm stand.

"Sloan, do you have a minute?" She shot a wary glance at Weber, who was wrapped up in a conversation with a customer about the best ways to prune cherry trees.

"Of course. How's the market going?"

"Busy, but that's good, right?" She fiddled with her dark curls, twisting them around her index finger in a tight spiral. Then she motioned to the van parked at the back of their booth. "Can you help me with a couple of the last crates of strawberries?"

"Sure." I followed after her. Her red gingham dress and apron matched The Bountiful Basket's color scheme and April's dream Bavarian aesthetic. Annabelle looked natural in the dress, like a perfect advertisement for Leavenworth's healthy, fresh outdoor style.

When we reached the van, she stole another nervous look in the direction of her husband before lowering her voice and leaning in close. "Sloan, I'm really worried about Weber. I don't know what to do."

"What's going on?" I assumed she was referring to the argument earlier, but I didn't want to make any assumptions.

"Something is going on with him. Did you see him snap at the backpackers earlier?"

"Yeah, it seemed unlike him."

"It is." She dragged her teeth across her bottom lip. "He's been jumpy for the past few weeks, and I have no idea why. Josh, the backpacker, asked if I would pose with our products for his social media, and Weber flipped out. He accused Josh of hitting on me. It's ridiculous. Josh and his friends have to be ten years younger than us. I don't think there was anything more to his request than wanting to feature our farm, but Weber's been like this with everything. One wrong word, and he snaps." She snapped her fingers to prove her point.

The tiny hairs on my arm stood at attention. "Annabelle, you're not worried about being in a dangerous situation, are you?"

"No, no, it's not like that." She waved me off. "Weber is a big softie. He's a teddy bear. I mean, sometimes he can have a gruff exterior, but that's his personality. He's one of the kindest men I've ever met, which is why I'm worried. He's obviously stressed about something, but he won't tell me what, and I don't know how to help him if I don't know why he's on edge."

Annabelle lifted one of the strawberry crates. I grabbed the other. "Is everything okay with the farm? Could Weber be worried about finances?"

She shook her head. "The farm is great. He's excited to be

"No. But I'm not very connected on social media, so I'm probably the wrong person to ask."

She proceeded to pull up her Instagram page. "Look, my following isn't as big as Josh's, but it's very active, engaged, and targeted. I'm not just trying to get free stuff from you. I'm going to livestream and be super excited to share about Nitro and take a celebratory sip from the summit."

"Okay, I wasn't implying that we weren't willing to give you some product. I was confused, that's all." I brushed away a bee buzzing near us. It was probably attracted to Harper's shirt.

"Right. Yeah, it happens whenever Josh is around." She gritted her teeth, trying to keep her frustration in check. "He blew up, and suddenly because he has like a trillion followers, everyone wants to partner with him, but I can assure you that I've been a professional travel influencer for years now, and this is what I do. I partner with brands and small businesses, like your brewery, and share your product with a very targeted niche audience."

"That sounds great," I answered truthfully. For everything she had mentioned about Josh and not being in competition with him, her body language, whenever she uttered his name, said otherwise.

"Really? Sweet. Excellent." She bobbed her head like she was surprised that I had agreed. "Uh, what do we do next?"

I pointed to the Nitro table. "We're about to finish packing up for the night. Why don't you pick out a hoodie or hat and then swing by the pub and ask Kat to grab you a couple of six-packs."

"Awesome. You're so cool. You're not going to regret partnering with me. Harper Climbs Hills is going all in for Nitro on tomorrow's climb." She grinned and gave me two enthusiastic thumbs up.

"How did you get into this line of work?" I asked as we walked to the table together.

"I kind of stumbled into it. I actually studied travel in college. I thought I would end up in the industry, maybe working as an event director for a hotel, resort, or cruise ship, but after I graduated, I couldn't get a job. Not as an event lead, anyway. You have to pay your dues and work your way up the ladder, so I worked a hostess job and spent my free time hiking and backpacking. People on social media started taking notice and asking me for recommendations, and then brands began reaching out. It wasn't the path I had planned, but I'm so glad I'm here."

"It sounds like you're following your purpose and combining your passion with your career. You can't ask for any more than that." I had been trying to impart the same advice to Alex. I didn't care what he ended up doing for a career or college pathway as long as whatever he picked brought him joy.

"Sometimes, I have to pinch myself." Harper nodded. "I don't make the kind of money that Josh does on his partnerships. I should be making double what he makes by now." Her tone turned icy at the mention of his name, but she caught herself and plastered on a bright, toothy smile as she continued. "I guess that's the nature of being an influencer these days. Big follower numbers equal big cash, but hey, at least I'm making a living, right?"

"You can't put a value on doing what you love," I replied in my gentlest "mom" voice.

"Tell that to Josh," Harper muttered under her breath. She picked a hop green hoodie and six-pack. "Thanks again for this. I promise to do justice to Nitro and I'll tag you in my post and livestream."

"Great. Happy hiking."

I watched her saunter down Front Street. I didn't care how many followers she had. Any exposure for our nano brewery was great and well worth sharing some of our merch and beer. However, she wasn't doing a good job of hiding her animosity toward Josh. It was more than evident that Harper was envious of his following and considered him competition. I hoped that wouldn't put them at odds on their backpacking trip tomorrow. I was a believer in abundance. Leavenworth had taught me that there was plenty to share and enough for everyone. Hopefully, some time in our Northern Cascade Alps would show Harper that, too.

CHAPTER
THREE

THE NEXT MORNING, I woke to the sound of songbirds and my phone buzzing. The birds were reminding me that it was time to refill the feeders hanging on my deck, and my phone was vibrating with social media notifications.

Josh and Harper had both posted sunrise photos from the top of Icicle Ridge. They had tagged Nitro in their posts, creating a swell of new interest in the Instagram account Kat had set up for us. I dragged myself out of bed and went to the kitchen to make a pot of coffee so I could be semi-coherent in my responses to the flurry of comments on our page.

While I waited for the coffee to brew, I scrolled through Josh and Harper's profiles. As Harper had mentioned, Josh's photos of our Obsidian Stout and Hoppy IPA were beautifully backlit, with the rising amber sun acting as a halo and the snowcapped jagged prominences in the foreground. In contrast, Harper had captured the dewy sunrise in her livestream while chatting with her followers from the summit.

I was surprised that they had been able to connect to Wi-Fi. The densely wooded trail that led to the top of Icicle Ridge was known for its steep ascents, rushing streams, and picturesque waterfalls. The payoff for making the three-thousand-foot climb was the breathtaking views of the rugged Cascade Mountain Range that stretched as far as the eye could see, and the blooming sunflower fields below.

I responded to comments as I savored my coffee and went through the weekend agenda. Garrett, Kat, and I planned to take shifts at the market today. We had two overnight guests at Nitro, so I needed to make breakfast for them, bake a few more batches of cookies to restock our supply for the market, and start our soup of the day. With that in mind, I tugged on a pair of jeans, a Nitro hoodie, and my tennis shoes and tied my long hair into a ponytail.

The walk from my cottage to the brewery took me past the miniature golf course, where a family of deer nibbled on the manicured lawn. I could hear the Wenatchee River rushing with early spring snowmelt in the distance. Everything smelled of new growth—heady hyacinths, sweet lilacs, and dewy grass.

The village was equally atmospheric. Each building had its own unique character and charm, with intricate patterns etched in the eaves, colorful shutters, and beautifully carved wooden doors. As the morning wore on, villagers would gather for coffee and slices of cake at outdoor cafés and soak up the mountain views, but for the moment, I enjoyed the stillness and the melody of birdsong.

At Nitro, things were also quiet and dark, so I tiptoed into the kitchen and warmed the ovens. For breakfast, I wanted to make our signature French toast with the bread I had purchased last night. I started by whisking eggs, heavy cream, a splash of our IPA, vanilla, lemon, and a touch of brown sugar. I cut thick slices of the bread and soaked them in the egg mixture. Then I added a pat of butter to a sauté pan and grilled each side just to crisp it up. I would finish the toast in the oven while I made a strawberry compote.

After I had repeated the process with the rest of the loaf, I placed the slightly browned slices on to a parchment-lined baking sheet and set it in the oven to warm. Next, I washed and sliced strawberries that Annabelle had given me and added them to the pan along with more butter, brown sugar, fresh lemon juice, vanilla, and another splash of IPA. The strawberries would simmer on low until they were soft and tender, and a thick sauce had formed.

I would finish the German-style breakfast with grilled sausages, fresh fruit and yogurt, and hand-whipped cream to top the French toast.

While the strawberries were simmering, I made a large pot of coffee and boiled water for tea. When Garrett and I had renovated the upstairs guest rooms, we had created a cozy breakfast nook with a long shared table, bookshelves, and a coffee and tea cart. We served meals family-style so that guests could get to know one another over a leisurely cup of strong coffee and German pastries.

Now I just needed to bring everything upstairs once I heard movement. Since there still wasn't any sound of footsteps overhead, I made a triple batch of white velvet cookies. We would take half to the market and save the other half for the tasting room.

Garrett had hired me without ever meeting me when he inherited his Great-Aunt Tess's diner and boarding house. He had transformed the dated space, gutting the back area and installing brewing equipment, as well as refurbishing the diner by tearing out the retro booths and replacing them with sleek high-top bar tables and stools and the wooden bar that divided the tasting room and brewery operations. His beer was some of the best I had ever tasted, so I didn't hesitate when it came to taking the job. Well, if I were being honest with myself, I would have taken any job, given that I had discovered Mac shagging the beer wench at Der Keller shortly before Garrett's offer. But aside from that, I had been impressed with Garrett from the first day.

His only flaw in Nitro's grand-opening plan had been a lack of warmth or any pub food on the menu. Fortunately, that's where I came in. We made a good team. Garrett allowed me autonomy and complete freedom with our daily soup and food offerings. He also gave me free rein with design. I had blended his passion for the science of brewing with the history of the inn and Leavenworth to create a welcoming vibe with personal touches, like framed black and white family photos and menus illustrated by Alex.

I sighed contentedly as I rolled out the cookie dough. Not only was I lucky to live in Leavenworth, but I was so lucky to be surrounded by so many people I loved and adored.

Reminiscing about our early days reminded me that I needed to make a soup for today's menu. I surveyed the walk-in fridge to see what we had on hand. I found roasted artichokes left over from a dip I'd made and decided on a chicken artichoke stew.

I drizzled olive oil in a large pot, placed it on the stove, and turned the burner to medium. Then I added diced onions, carrots, and celery. Once the veggies had begun to sweat, I added chopped garlic, red pepper flakes, salt, and pepper. Then I covered them with chicken broth and tossed in the artichokes and chicken breasts. I would let the soup simmer until the chicken was tender. Right before we served it, I would finish it with heavy cream, spinach, and a trio of Italian cheeses.

The sound of the water pipe rattling alerted me that our guests were up and showering. I plated the French toast and had started to assemble trays to take upstairs when Kat bounced into the kitchen, waving her phone.

"Have you seen social this morning, Sloan?" Her eyes sparkled with excitement she grinned and poured herself a cup of coffee. "We've gained over five hundred new followers already."

"I woke up to my phone buzzing," I said, spreading the strawberry compote on the toasted eggy bread. "Great work."

"It's not me. I didn't do anything. Josh slid into our DMs, and I don't know the other person who tagged us, Harper Baum. She must be a friend of Josh's." She walked to the refrigerator and returned with three kinds of coffee creamers. We kept a variety of dairy and alternative milk options on hand for guests.

"I met Harper last night." I placed a generous dollop of lemon-infused whipped cream on the French toast and told her about how Harper had approached me at the market.

"Hey, we'll take it." Kat stirred oat milk into her coffee. "I'm going to have to start pitching more influencers. It's not just followers, but thanks to so much social media activity, the beer suites are booked through June. People love the beer & B concept."

She helped me carry everything upstairs and set up breakfast. Once our guests were happily enjoying a hearty farm-style meal, I checked in with Garrett and agreed to take the first shift at the farmers market. Since it was Saturday, the market would run from nine until two. I wasn't sure how many beer tasters we'd have this early, but if nothing else, I could give out cookies and sell six-packs and Nitro merch.

It didn't take long to pack since most of our supplies were already set up from last night. I was glad for my hoodie on the short walk from Nitro. Spring mornings tended to hold a chill that would burn off by midday, when the sun would warm our cobblestone streets and send locals to Front Street Park to enjoy lunch in the gazebo or on the grassy hillside.

I passed The Gasthaus, a cheap hostel popular with backpackers. The worn and shabby building had seen better days. Missing tiles and chipped paint on the exterior and a collection of dead flowers in the garden boxes made me wonder if the hostel was having financial trouble. As far as I knew, it seemed like The Gasthaus was always booked, but it had been years since I'd been inside.

I waved hello to Klaus Schmidt, the owner. He didn't notice me because he was deep in conversation with Weber. I wondered if Weber was supplying Klaus with local produce and their jellies and jams. Annabelle had mentioned that they were branching out and selling to more merchants in the village. I made a mental note to touch base with her about the possibility of partnering with Nitro. We already had established relationships with regional farmers and growers, but having another wouldn't hurt.

I didn't have a chance to talk to Annabelle because the market was packed. Last night's crowd paled in comparison. By the time I finished setting up, a line stretched across the street. I spent the next few hours slinging pints and chatting with friends and neighbors.

The morning flew by. When Kat came to relieve me at noon, I couldn't believe it was already lunchtime, although my stomach disagreed. I decided to stop and grab some brats at the Bavarian Grill on the way back to Nitro. The walk-up German grill was right across the street from The Gasthaus.

To my surprise, Klaus was still outside. For a second, I wondered if he'd been on the porch all morning. Not that it mattered.

What did matter was that the hostel's owner was nose-to-nose with none other than Josh from A Brew with a View.

"You insult my food and my accommodations, and you're out on the street. It's that simple," Klaus shouted. He towered over the young social media influencer.

Josh puffed out his chest in self-importance. "Look, man, I'm all about authenticity. My followers know when I'm trying to feed them a line that's not true, and that is literally the worst breakfast I've ever had in my entire life. I'm not taking the post down. I wouldn't recommend The Gasthaus to my worst enemy. It's filthy, rundown, and disgusting. I stand by what I said." He placed his hands on his hips in a show of power.

Klaus pounded Josh's chest with his index finger. "Get off my property. Don't come back, you little entitled ass."

"You can't kick me out," Josh countered. "We had a deal. Where am I going to go?"

Like last night at the farmers market, Josh was causing a scene. People passing by stopped to see what was going on.

"Off my property." Klaus shot his finger toward the street.

"I don't think you understand who you're dealing with. I could go live right now and absolutely destroy you. With over a million faithful followers, you'll be canceled, and good luck getting any future business," Josh threatened.

Klaus fumed. "Get out now, and if you know what's good for you, kid, get out of the village and never come back." He stormed into the hostel and slammed the door shut.

Josh yanked his phone from his pocket and started livestreaming.

I made a beeline for the Bavarian Grill. I appreciated Josh's posts about Nitro, but given that he had basically had the same argument with Weber last night, I sensed a pattern forming. Stirring up trouble seemed to be his thing, and I didn't want any part of it.

FOUR

THE NEXT DAY on my way to Nitro, I walked with a spring in my step. Our market opening had been a success, and there was a promise of a Sachertorte at the bakery later in the day. Sunday was the only day they made the chocolate, almond, and apricot cake, and I wanted to pick up slices to share with Garrett and Kat as thanks for their hard work getting everything ready for the season.

However, the happy buzz faded as I entered the village to find The Gasthaus roped off with yellow caution tape, police cars barricading the walkway, and two police officers posted at the front porch.

I hope nothing bad happened.

I sucked in a breath through my nose and placed my hand on my stomach.

The thought was short-lived because a voice called out to me.

"Sloan, do you have a minute?" It was Chief Meyers, Leavenworth's head detective and a longtime friend.

"What's going on?" I asked as I approached the front entrance.

Chief Meyers motioned to a bench near the wood-carved nutcracker in the center of the square. "Walk with me for a minute, would you?"

I followed after her, picking up on her cue that she didn't want to talk until we were somewhere more private. The village was still relatively quiet, except for a handful of business owners who had come out from their shops to get a look at the reason for the squad cars and flashing lights.

She sat and clicked off the walkie-talkie attached to the belt around her waist. "I take it you haven't heard yet?"

I shook my head. "No, what?"

"There's been a death." Her dark, intelligent eyes darted toward The Gasthaus. "A backpacker was killed last night."

"On a hike?" I couldn't process why the hostel would have such a police presence. Maybe they were staying at the hostel. Then I gasped. Was it Harper?

Chief Meyers raised a bushy eyebrow, picking up on my shock. "Do you know something?"

"I'm not sure. Maybe. Were they killed on the trail?"

"No, at the hostel." She studied my face as I took in the information.

"Was it Harper?"

Her lips pressed into a frown as she shook her head. "Josh. Apparently, he's some kind of an influencer, whatever that means."

"Josh?" I let the news sink in, feeling a wave of nausea ripple through my stomach.

Josh was dead?

I clutched my throat and forced myself to swallow. "Wait, but Klaus kicked him out yesterday."

"Did he?" She took out a pen and a yellow legal pad and scribbled a note. "What else can you tell me?"

I told her everything, from Josh reaching out to partner with us to his fight with Weber at the Friday night market and the confrontation I'd witnessed between him and Klaus yesterday.

"It sounds like he really made an impression, doesn't it?" She tapped her pen on the top of the page. "I was informed that Josh was in the village because of an exclusive partnership with Nitro. Can you explain that any further?"

"What? Who told you that?" I blinked in part because of the way the sun was glinting off the stained glass windows across the street, but also because her words were news to me.

"I'm not at liberty to share, but I can say that the source was less than reliable." She cleared her throat.

It didn't take much to read between the lines—April Ablin.

"The first I heard of Josh was on Friday afternoon when he reached out to us on social media." I handed her my phone. "You can see the thread in our direct messages. If he came to Leavenworth because of a partnership with us, it was a risky move given that he didn't even get in contact with us until after he was here."

She made another note. "Tell me more about this argument he had with Klaus."

"I didn't stick around long enough to hear everything, but the gist was that Klaus accused Josh of trying to ruin his reputation on social media, and Josh claimed that the hostel was dirty and in disrepair. It got ugly pretty fast."

She flipped through her notes until she found the page she wanted. "According to witnesses, it sounds like there was quite a scene. Klaus is reported to have physically assaulted Josh. Can you confirm that?"

I replayed what I had seen yesterday. "Technically speaking, yes. I saw Klaus tap Josh on the chest. Not that I condone any kind of unwanted touch, but I'm not sure I would go as far as to use the word assault. That feels a bit strong."

"You observed him lay hands on Josh's body?" Chief Meyers asked, maintaining eye contact.

"Yes. When you put it like that, yes." I paused. "You should probably speak with Weber Rails, too." I told her about the argument at the farmers market.

"Thanks for the suggestion. He's on my list." She gave me a brisk nod and made another note. "We take every threat of violence seriously. Particularly when the victim ends up dead in his hostel room hours later."

"Can I ask, how did he die?"

"He was hit on the head with a blunt force object. My team is searching the hostel for the murder weapon as we speak." Her eyes drifted to the slanted roofline of The Gasthaus, where dozens of shingles were missing, and a blue plastic tarp was secured over the chimney. "Hopefully, we'll be able to recover hard evidence connecting the killer to the crime." She paused and checked around us to make sure no one was nearby. "This stays with us, but my gut feeling is that the crime wasn't premeditated. I suspect that the killer and Josh were involved in an argument that escalated. We'll have to wait for the autopsy and any evidence to prove or disprove my theory, but I've been in the business long enough to know that this likely isn't the work of an experienced or well-thought-out killer."

A wave of sadness came over me. Josh might have been brash, but he was young and enthusiastic. He had his entire life ahead of him. He didn't deserve to die.

"Is there anything else I can do to help?"

She licked her index finger and used it to free two pages stuck together in her notebook. "You mentioned Harper when I told you about the crime. I assume you meant Harper Baum."

"Uh, yes. Harper, of Harper Hikes Hills. She was a friend of his."

"Tell me what you know about Ms. Baum."

"She approached me at the market on Friday night about partnering with Nitro to do a livestream on the summit of Icicle Ridge. I thought she and Josh were partners, but she made it very clear that they were running their own unique businesses. She got pretty upset about it."

"Upset how?"

"Like Josh, she's a social media influencer. She livestreams her hikes on Harper Hikes Hills, but when I made the mistake of connecting her and Josh, she got visibly angry. She told me that she's been a professional influencer for years and has been hustling to get more followers on social media. Every time Josh's name came up, she would flinch. She seemed envious and bitter that Josh had amassed a huge following by going viral."

"Noted."

"I'm not implying that I think she killed him, though."

"I never would suggest as much, but I will certainly have a chat with her." She tipped her wide-brimmed hat. "Thank you for your insight. It's been most helpful. One last question before I return to the crime scene."

"Sure." I laced my fingers together, trying to maintain my composure. I still couldn't believe that Josh was dead and he'd been killed only a few feet away.

"Why did you think Harper died?"

"Oh, because I figured that Josh wasn't staying at The Gasthaus because Klaus had kicked him out."

"Got it. That helps paint a picture. I appreciate your time, Sloan. I'll be in touch, and let me know if you hear anything." She gave me a curt nod and walked toward the hostel.

I stood in the park for a minute, trying to collect my

thoughts. Josh was dead. He had gotten into two very public arguments with Klaus and Weber. Did that give either of them a motive to kill him? And what about Harper? She hadn't been successful in her attempts to disguise her animosity toward Josh. In my mind she had the most likely motive—killing her rival would pave the way for her to take over his following.

I wasn't sure who the killer was, but I knew that I was going to do everything I could to help Chief Meyers bring them to justice and restore peace in my cozy Bavarian village.

CHAPTER
FIVE

I RETURNED TO NITRO, still trying to process the fact that Josh was dead. Who could have killed him, and why? The irony that he climbed treacherously steep mountains and cliffsides but had died in our sweet village wasn't lost on me. Did that mean that someone I knew had done this? The only other explanation was that a stranger or someone from out of town had killed the young influencer.

Speaking of strangers, I bumped directly into a woman studying a map that looked like it had been submerged in water, tumbled dry, and stuffed into the bottom of her backpack for days. She tried to smooth out the crinkled edges by placing the map on a bench and stretching it between her hands. Her rainbow-colored pack made her look top-heavy. She yanked the pack off and set it on the corner of the map to try and hold it down.

"Can I help you? It looks like you might be lost," I offered. It was commonplace amongst villagers to offer tourists directions, restaurant recommendations, or stop to take photos. They were the lifeblood of our economy, and we all took it upon ourselves to make guests feel welcome during their stay. Of course, April Ablin took our welcoming spirit one or two thousand steps further with her aggressive need to greet anyone and everyone with a never-ending perfumed hand-shake, a fake German curtsy, and cloyingly sweet and conde-scending diatribes about the Bavarian history of our fair city.

"Huh? What?" the woman asked, squinting and shielding her face with her hand. "Sorry, I didn't hear you walk up."

"No worries. I didn't mean to startle you. I've lived in the village for years, and I noticed you battling with the map and thought I might offer my assistance. If you need help, I'm happy to point you in the right direction."

"Oh, wonderful. How thoughtful." She sounded breathless. She wiped her forehead with the sleeve of her rainbow-striped shirt. "I'm a bit turned around. I've been backpacking in the Enchantments for a few days, and I'm very eager for a hot shower and a real bed, but I can't seem to figure out where my hostel is on the map."

"Are you staying at The Gasthaus?"

"Yes, yes. That's it." She smiled with relief and apprecia-tion, highlighting her deep-set brown eyes and a scattering of freckles.

"The good news is that you're very close." I pointed across the street to the hostel. "The bad news is that you might not be able to check in right away. I'm afraid there was an incident earlier that the police are investigating." I didn't want to tell her the incident was a murder. Not only because I didn't want to scare her, but also because I wasn't sure how much Chief Meyers had shared publicly.

"Oh, that's the hostel." She picked up the map and stared from it to The Gasthaus. "Maybe I couldn't see the name on the sign because of the police. I swear, when I walked by earlier, I thought it was something else. But then again, I also thought it was on that end of town." She pointed toward Der Keller. "I guess I'm more sleep deprived than I realized."

"Well, I'm glad we figured it out." I smiled.

She folded the map and tucked it into her bright rainbow pack. I was impressed that she could even lift the heavy pack. It looked like her pack was about half as big as her. "What happened? Do you think the police will be long? Should I find another place in town to stay tonight?" she asked.

"I don't know. I'm sure Chief Meyers can answer those questions. She's in the khaki uniform and hat right over there."

The young woman gulped and rocked back on her heels as she positioned the pack over her shoulders. "Oh, no, I don't need to speak with the police. Maybe I'll figure out another place to crash. Come to think of it, I might continue on to Wenatchee. It's not that far, is it?"

"No, it's about a thirty-minute drive from here."

"Yeah, okay. Maybe I'll cancel the hostel and head to Wenatchee. I saw that there's a bus that looks pretty reasonable, and I heard there are some lovely spots along the river where you can camp. I've been wanting to check out their indoor market, and a lot of the other hotels in Leavenworth are out of my budget." She cinched her shoulder straps. "Thanks again for your help. Have a nice day." With that, she took off at a good pace in the opposite direction.

I watched her dart to the far side of the sidewalk as she passed The Gasthaus.

That was a quick shift. She had gone from wanting a hot shower and bed to driving to Wenatchee to camp on the river.

Why the change of heart?

I didn't want to jump to conclusions, but her demeanor had changed when I mentioned Chief Meyers. Was she skittish about talking to the police because she knew something about Josh's murder? She had been backpacking in the same area where Josh and Harper had hiked yesterday. Was there a chance that they had had an encounter that had gone wrong? Could she have followed him into town, killed him, and now was trying to make a quick exit?

Possibilities swirled in my mind.

I wished I had asked the young hiker more or at least gotten her name.

Josh's murder had definitely rattled me. The more likely scenario was that she was tired from days of logging long mileage on the trails and didn't want to wait around for the police activity to clear. She wasn't wrong about the cost of hotels in the village. Since we were in the shoulder season, prices were lower than they would be in the summer or fall, but being a year-round tourist destination made prices remain high. That was one of the reasons that the hostel was constantly booked to capacity and a reason that Garrett and I opted to keep our rates at Nitro as low as possible. The Gasthaus was one of the only other places in town where younger or more budget-conscious travelers could stay and not break the bank.

However, I couldn't rule out the mysterious backpacker as having some kind of involvement in the crime. If she had already booked her stay, her sudden change of heart seemed even more surprising.

I sighed and turned to cross the street, but stopped mid-stride when I caught a flash of her colorful pack in front of the Nutcracker Shop.

This was my one chance to ask her a few follow-up questions. I didn't want to let a potential suspect get away, and I had the perfect excuse—the bus schedule. I could tell her about the express bus that would save her money and time.

Or that's the story you're telling yourself, Sloan.

I was probably overreacting, but I crossed the street

anyway. It shouldn't have taken me long to catch up with her, but as I hurried along the cobblestone streets, there was no sign of her. She had vanished.

It was hard to disappear in the village, but she had. I went to the bus stop in hopes of finding her waiting for a ride, but she wasn't there. I checked the Nutcracker Museum, the Gingerbread Haus, the hat shop, and the bookstore. No one had seen a backpacker fitting her description all morning.

I tried the hotels next. She couldn't have gotten far. She only had a few minute head start on me. Had she ducked down a side alleyway? Could she be hiding out in a basement in one of the Bavarian buildings?

It didn't make sense unless my hunch had been right.

Had I spooked her when I mentioned the incident at The Gasthaus and Chief Meyers? Could she have hitched a ride on Highway 2? There were plenty of cars and trucks that traversed the highway. Since she had taken off at a sprinter's pace at the end of our brief conversation, it was feasible that she could have grabbed a ride and was already long gone.

I sucked in a long breath and surveyed the village, which normally would be sleepy on a Sunday morning. Police lights lit up the gazebo and Maipole. Villagers just waking for brunch and coffee milled about around The Gasthaus. Rumors of Josh's murder were probably running wild. But where did that leave me?

I had to tell Chief Meyers about the mysterious backpacker. If there was even a tiny chance she was connected to Josh's death, I could never forgive myself for not sharing what I knew.

I retraced my steps past the gazebo, keeping an eye out for any sign of the woman.

When I made it to the hostel, Chief Meyers was questioning Harper. I waited for her to finish before waving her over.

"Sloan, long time no see. What can I do for you?"

"I may have another lead for you." I glanced around, wishing the backpacker might appear. I told Chief Meyers about my encounter with the stranger and how she had basically vanished in plain sight.

"Interesting. I've had two similar reports of a woman spotted in the village." Chief Meyers scrunched her brow in thought. "Can you provide any additional details about her appearance or her gear that might give us some ability to identify her?"

I frowned. "I should have asked her more questions. I didn't even get her name. At the time I just thought she was a lost tourist, but as soon as I mentioned talking to you, everything about her body language changed and then she took off."

"I understand, but you got a good look at her, right? Can you describe her?"

"Yeah. She was about five and a half feet tall with short, bobbed brown hair, and dark brown eyes. I'm not great at placing ages, but I would guess that she's in her early twenties. She said she had been backpacking in the Enchantments for a few days. The only other distinguishing thing was her pack. It was rainbow-colored with blocks of red, yellow, orange, and blue in each section. I commented on how cute it was."

"That's helpful." Chief Meyers made a note. "A rainbow pack shouldn't be hard to miss. I'll put the word out to my team and if you happen to see her again, please alert me immediately."

"I will."

She moved on to another conversation. I needed to get to Nitro. Kat was covering breakfast for our overnight guests, but I wanted to get a head start on the afternoon menu and make sure the tasting room was in good shape. I had a feeling that we might have a big crowd later in the day. Once word spread of Josh's murder, villagers were likely to congregate at the pub over pints to rehash what had happened. I was glad that Nitro was a gathering place for our community, and maybe someone would have more answers than I did.

CHAPTER
SIX

As EXPECTED, the tasting room filled up within an hour of opening. Villagers lingered over frothy pints and bowls of my chicken artichoke soup while swapping theories and rumors about what might have happened to Josh. I kept an ear open as I delivered drinks and food, but there didn't seem to be any news that I hadn't already heard.

When Harper strolled in looking like she had had a run-in with a wild animal on the trail and found an empty spot at the end of the bar, I took the chance to see if I could learn anything from her.

"How are you doing?" I asked, handing her a coaster but internally wondering if I should pour her a cup of strong coffee instead. Her hair was disheveled, deep purple rings circled the bottom of her eyes, and I recognized the scoop neck sweatshirt and hiking leggings from her livestream yesterday. Had she slept in her clothes?

She blew out a breath, intentionally causing her lips to motorboat. "I don't even know how to answer that." She tossed her backpack on the floor. "I can't believe this nightmare. I didn't want to leave my stuff at the hostel because the police aren't telling us when they're going to let us back in and honestly, I'm scared. I don't know if it's a good idea to stay there. I thought Leavenworth was super safe, but now Josh is dead." Her voice rose in a sharp pitch. "I just saw him yesterday, and now he's dead. Dead? I can't wrap my head around it."

"I can only imagine how you must be feeling. I didn't know him well, and I'm in shock, too, but I can promise you that Leavenworth is safe, and the police are doing everything they can to ensure all of our safety."

She massaged her temples with force as she clenched her jaw. Then she stared at her hands as if they weren't real. "I don't know. I'm not saying that I don't believe you, but I don't know how I can sleep there tonight. Josh was staying in the room next to mine. His stuff is going to be there, but he won't. And then I can't stop thinking about what's going to happen once news of his death gets out to his followers. Social media is going to implode."

Harper's body language made me want to trust that she was genuinely shaken up by Josh's death, but her last comment raised a red flag. Was she concerned about her social media accounts?

She gnawed on her dirty thumbnail. "It doesn't make sense. Who would want to kill Josh? No one here knew him, and if anything, everyone in the village should have been happy to have him here. He brought so much attention to Leavenworth by deciding to hike here and feature you and the rest of the town. I don't get it. Unless it was that farmer from the other night."

"You mean Weber?" I tried to keep my face passive. Did she know something about what had transpired between him and Josh at the farmers market?

"Maybe. I don't know his name. I just know that Josh was

going to feature his produce on his social account, and the guy freaked out on him."

That matched what I had witnessed.

Harper leaned closer and rested her elbows on the wooden bar. "You know, I think I saw him last night."

"Weber?"

"I can't be sure. It was dark, but I was coming back from dinner late. Josh was supposed to come. At the last minute, he changed his mind and stayed behind because he said that his stomach was still hurting. He got sick after breakfast. In fact, he got pretty pissed at Klaus, the hostel owner, because he was convinced that breakfast made him sick. I can't help thinking that if he'd only come with us, then maybe he'd still be alive..." She trailed off.

"It's not your fault."

She nodded in agreement but didn't look convinced. "I guess I feel bad because I was envious of Josh. He struck social media gold. Going viral like that doesn't happen often, and like I told you the other night, I've been on the grind trying to consistently grow for years. It was hard not to be jealous, but at the end of the day, Josh was a decent guy."

"You mentioned seeing something last night," I nudged.

She sucked in air and shot a nervous glance around us before dropping her voice. "Yeah, when I came back to the hostel. It was after quiet hours but not super late. Quiet hours start at ten. It was probably eleven-thirty, maybe closer to twelve. We stayed out listening to a band at this cool bar, the Underground. We didn't want to wake anyone, so we went in through the back entrance. As we were heading upstairs, a guy wearing all black flew down the stairs, ran past us, and took off outside. At the time, I thought it was weird, but I had had a few drinks and I was exhausted from the early hike, so I didn't give it any attention. Now I can't stop replaying it. He might have been Josh's killer."

This was big news.

Her face turned as white as the walls. "That's another reason I'm not sure I can stay there another night."

Harper was revealing much more than I had expected, which was good, but it also had me creating a new list of questions in my mind. First, had the police officially announced that Josh had been murdered? And if not, how did Harper know?

Also, could she have an ulterior motive for being so forthcoming? Was this her strategy to shift suspicion away from herself? I wasn't sure, but I knew I had to take this chance to see what else I could extract from her.

"Hey, you know, I just realized that I haven't offered to get you a drink. Do you want a pint? Something to eat?" I motioned to the whiteboard menu behind us.

"Uh, yeah, a beer might help take the edge off." She squinted to read the descriptions. "I loved both the beers you gave me for the livestream yesterday, but is there anything a little lighter you recommend?"

"Our spring Pilsner is lovely, with notes of strawberry and lemon."

"That sounds great." Harper shifted in her seat.

I went to get her beer. Garrett was pouring a Pilsner for another guest.

"Can you do an extra?" I asked, subtly motioning to Harper. "I want to keep her talking."

"Your wish is my command, Sloan Krause." He winked. Then he gave a nod to the far end of the bar. "I noticed you've been deep in conversation with Harper. Any big revelations?"

"Yes, actually, a couple."

He tilted the edge of a long, narrow Pilsner glass beneath

the tap handle. "I'm glad you're having luck because no one else in the pub seems to know much." He handed me the golden-colored ale. "Take this one and report back."

"Will do."

I returned to Harper and set the beer on her coaster. "Tell me what you think. If you don't like it, I can get you something else."

"No, I'm sure it will be great." She took a small taste. "Yep, it's delicious."

"Can I ask you why you thought the person you saw fleeing the hostel last night was Weber and whether you've told this to the police? It could be important." I was glad that most of the crowd had moved outside to the patio. We had the bar to ourselves, which I hoped would help Harper continue to feel comfortable opening up to me.

"Yes, of course. I told the detective everything." She sat up with newfound importance. "Like I said, I'm not sure it was Weber. He was the same height and build, but it was really dark, and the guy was dressed in black, which seems suspicious, don't you think?"

I nodded, but I also wondered if Weber were a distraction. It would be quite convenient for Harper to claim that she saw him. She knew about the argument between Weber and Josh. If she were the killer, it would be a clever move.

"You mentioned going out with other friends," I said. "Were these other backpackers or people you met at the hostel?"

Harper's back stiffened as she clutched the beer glass and took a long drink. "Yeah, some of both, why?"

"I bumped into a woman earlier this morning who was hiking Icicle Ridge yesterday. She had a rainbow pack. Did you see her on the trail, by chance?"

"No." Harper looked to the ceiling as she thought for a

minute. "She had a rainbow pack, like rainbow stripes or like a Cotopaxi colorful pack?"

"The latter. I don't know the brand name, but it was chunks of color."

Harper's mouth hung open as she set her beer on the bar. "You're sure? Oh, my God. This changes everything." She stood up and reached for her backpack. "I have to go find the police. Forget everything else I said. I think I know who killed Josh."

"Who?"

"Serena." She held her arms up like she couldn't believe I wasn't following.

That didn't help me.

"Who's Serena?" I wrinkled my brow, trying to remember if I had ever heard that name.

"Josh's ex-girlfriend. She's been trolling him on social for weeks. She said she's the one who shot the videos that made him go viral, and she wants a cut of his partnership money."

"And she came on this backpacking trip?" I couldn't mask my confusion.

"No. No way. Josh wouldn't let her come within ten feet of him. It got pretty ugly. He was talking about taking out a restraining order because she was stalking him. She kept showing up everywhere he went and harassing him about money. I didn't know she was in Leavenworth. But that back-pack you described—that's her signature pack. I think Serena's in town, and I think she killed him."

CHAPTER

SEVEN

"WHAT DO I owe you for the beer?" Harper asked as she flung her pack over her shoulder and stumbled over her own feet, tripping herself. She caught the edge of the bar.

"Careful," I cautioned.

"I'm fine. I really have to go." She shifted from side to side like she couldn't stand still. "How much is the beer?"

"Don't worry about it. On the house."

"Thanks so much." She smiled. This time it didn't look forced. Since hearing about the rainbow backpack, her entire demeanor had shifted, which made me wonder if she was telling the truth. If she had seen someone in black sneaking out of the hostel last night and then Josh was discovered in his room this morning, it made sense that she was worried about her personal safety.

"Come back later, and I'll pour you a fresh beer." I motioned to her full glass. "You didn't get a chance to finish your drink."

"That's okay. I have to find the police right away and tell

them about Serena." She took a final swig. "For courage. Wish me luck."

I watched her go. Wondering how much of her story I should believe, I picked up her pint glass and took it to the sink.

"Well, what's the scoop?" Garrett asked as I dumped Harper's Pilsner into the sink. "Have you closed the case?"

"Ha, I wish." I filled him in on everything Harper told me.

He listened intently while filling bowls with Doritos and peanuts, our classic pub snacks that were always complimentary for guests. When I finished, he twisted his lips in contemplation. "Does Serena's physical description match the woman you saw this morning?"

"No, that's the thing. Literally, the minute I mentioned the backpack, Harper was a changed woman. She went from being skittish to confident in a matter of seconds, but she didn't ask any follow-up questions. As soon as I said rainbow pack, she was out of here."

"Are you inclined to believe her?" He helped himself to a chip.

"I'm not sure. Her behavior when she came to the conclusion that Serena must be in town certainly seemed believable. She appeared relieved, which makes me think that maybe she really was spooked about staying at the hostel. If she killed Josh, why would she be scared to sleep there?"

"Good point." He offered me the bowl of chips. "Want one?"

"No, thanks." I shook my head. "Then again, is the mystery woman with the rainbow pack another easy way for her to deflect suspicion away from herself? Why wouldn't she have asked for more details, like did I get a name, what did the woman look like, how old was she?"

"Also good points." Garrett wiped Dorito dust from his hands.

"The woman was in Josh's age range, and I still can't explain why she took off so quickly when I mentioned the police."

"And where she vanished." Garrett wiped down a tap handle with a dry cloth.

"Exactly." I snapped twice.

"The good news is that Harper is going to find Chief Meyers," Garrett said, as he angled another glass underneath the tap. "I have a feeling that the police are going to ramp up their search for rainbow backpack."

"I like that. That's how we'll refer to her from now on." I chuckled. "I agree, although I also don't think we can rule out Weber. If Harper is telling the truth and she saw him at the hostel last night, that doesn't look good for him. What explanation could he have for lurking in the youth hostel after quiet hours?"

"Late-night fruit delivery?" Garrett suggested but immediately shook his head. "No way. No one's buying that."

"Harper did back up what we witnessed at the market. She said that Josh wanted to feature the farm, and that set Weber off. I don't want to believe it, but there is a possibility that Weber snuck into the hostel, killed Josh, and just by luck happened to be seen making a getaway by Harper and her other friends."

"Or not so lucky, depending on your perspective," Garrett added. "I guess Chief Meyers can check with Harper's friends. They might be able to back up her story and provide her with an alibi."

"That would be great. I would love to start eliminating possible suspects at this point, but instead, we're adding them." I paused for a minute and looked around the tasting room. "Where's Kat?"

Garrett nodded toward the back. "In the kitchen. She's putting together meat and cheese plates. Why? Your eyes have that look."

"What look?" I widened my eyes.

"Like you've had an ah-ha moment."

"Maybe. Your point about Harper not bothering to ask me for a description gave me a thought. What if we can find a picture of Serena? I got a good look at her. I can easily identify her if she's on Josh's social media. I gave his Instagram page a quick glance when he posted, but I know Kat will be game to help me scroll through his content—there's a lot of it."

"Good plan." Garrett topped the IPA with a foamy head. "I've got things under control here if you want to go sleuth out social with Kat."

"Yell if you need us." I went to the kitchen, where Kat was arranging plates with hunks of cheese, grapes, strawberries, apple slices, crackers, and dips. "Ohhh, these look delish."

"You like?" She swept her hand over the counter and posed with her other hand beneath her chin. "My stellar chef skills, I can put cheese and crackers on a plate."

"Hey, don't knock it. It's an art form. They really do look delicious, and we eat with our eyes first, you know."

"What does it mean if your eyes want to eat everything they see, always?" Kat scrunched her dimpled cheeks into a silly grin.

"That is called being a foodie." I laughed. "While we're on the topic of vision, I'm hoping to recruit you for a mission."

She arched her shoulders and saluted. "At your service, Sloan."

I pulled Josh's account up on my phone. "Here's the goal. Let's see if we can find a photo of a young woman. She's about your age with dark brown hair that's cut in an angled bob and brown eyes. She might be Josh's ex-girlfriend, so I'm hoping we might be able to..."

"Get hard evidence of her on social," Kat exclaimed with delight, cutting me off.

"Exactly."

She hurried to the sink to wash her hands. Then she scooted next to me and got out her phone. "Do you know when they broke up? If it's a while ago we might need to scroll back before they ended things. The other problem is he could have wiped her clean from his feed if it was nasty."

"I don't have any details, other than according to Harper, Serena, his ex, apparently had been stalking him and posting negative comments on social."

Kat ran her tongue over her teeth as she thought. "That could be problematic. He might have blocked her."

We spent the next half hour scouring Josh's public profiles.

"He wiped any evidence of her existence clean," Kat declared, reaching for a handful of grapes.

"Oh, well, it was worth a shot, right? I haven't found anything either." I sighed and blinked. My eyes were dry from staring at the screen and scrolling through hundreds of photos.

"Wait, wait." Kat popped a grape between her teeth. "We're not done. I've got another idea—discord. I'm going to search for any posts hating on Josh. If Serena were angry enough to get blocked from his social, then there's no way that she didn't post somewhere else."

I made myself a cup of coffee while Kat continued to try and trace Serena's digital footprint.

"Got it!" She clapped twice and waved me over. "Look, here she is."

I stared at her phone. The image on the screen was of a woman at the top of a snow-capped peak posing with Josh and sporting a rainbow pack. She was the spitting image of the woman I'd bumped into this morning.

"That's her."

"Serena Bradley." Kat tapped the screen. "Look at the text under the photo."

I nearly dropped the phone when I read the caption: WHEN YOUR EX STABS YOU IN THE BACK, THE ONLY OPTION IS TO PUSH HIM OFF THE CLIFF, AGREED?

Kat's eyes widened as she watched my response. "It's right there in print. She threatened to kill him. She must have followed through on her threat. Sloan, I think we found the killer."

CHAPTER
EIGHT

I STARED at Kat in disbelief. My hunch was right. Serena was Josh's ex-girlfriend. Suddenly our run-in earlier made much more sense. "We need to let Chief Meyers know. This information will likely change the scope of her investigation."

"Yeah, you should go right now." Kat motioned to the door. "I can finish the rest of the prep, but you have to promise to tell me what Chief Meyers says."

"Deal." I gave her a thumbs up. "Thanks so much for your help. What would we do without you?"

"Are you kidding? Now I can add social media detective to my résumé. I'm basically a pro now. Maybe I should offer up my services as Chief Inspector."

"It's a skill." I grinned and left the kitchen. Hopefully, Chief Meyers was still at the hostel or at her office near Front Street Park. Nervous energy buzzed through my body as I gave Garrett the update and went outside. The aroma of cherry blossoms and jasmine wafted through the warm afternoon air. Their intoxicatingly sweet scent reminded me to breathe deeper.

I checked The Gasthaus, but the officer stationed at the hostel reported that Chief Meyers had left to follow up on some leads about thirty minutes earlier. I didn't have any luck at the station either, so I left her a detailed voicemail and texted her links to the threatening post Kat had found.

I would have preferred to speak directly with Chief Meyers, but there wasn't much more I could do until I heard back from her, so I crossed the street and had started to make the short return trip to Nitro when I noticed a familiar face coming out of the pretzel shop—Annabelle.

Was she trying to be incognito in a pair of black jeans and a black hoodie tucked over her head? I almost turned the other way, but she caught my eye, glanced around her, and then motioned to the park.

I watched her skittish movements like she was worried that she was being watched as I met up with her at the gazebo.

Annabelle sank onto one of the benches and opened a bag of pretzels. "Would you like one?"

"No, thanks. I'm fine," I said, sitting next to her. "But, as always, they smell amazing."

"Do you care if I eat while we chat? I'm a comfort eater, and my stress level is off the charts right now." She lifted six pretzels, each bigger than her face, from the bag. "I went overboard, but I couldn't decide on a flavor, so I got one of everything they had."

"That sounds like the perfect plan to me. Plus, pretzels keep." My gaze drifted toward the pretzel shop across the street. Was Annabelle in danger? Was she telling me the truth about Weber being a teddy bear, or could she be running from him?

"They might not today." She returned the stack to the bag and sank her teeth into a cinnamon and sugar-coated pretzel.

"I'm teetering on the edge, Sloan. In fact, I'm really glad I saw you because I really need some advice."

"I don't know what advice I'll be able to offer, but I can lend you a listening ear."

Annabelle ripped off a chunk of the pretzel and blinked back tears. "Thanks, you're so wise and grounded. I wish I could be more like you, but I'm a mess. I don't know what to do. I think I probably need to go to Chief Meyers. I can't believe I'm saying this, but I'm worried that Weber might have had something to do with the kid's death." Her voice was so low, it was like she was concerned that someone would hear us, even though there was no one within earshot.

"What?" I tried not to overreact, but it was no wonder she was stress-eating.

"Sloan, he left the house last night." She scooted closer and took a huge breath like she was trying to keep her nerves from getting the best of her. "He was gone from a little after ten until midnight." She tore a section of the sugary pretzel off with her teeth.

That was in the window of time that Harper had seen the man in black fleeing the scene. I wish I knew from Chief Meyers when Josh had been killed.

"After news broke of the murder, Weber told me to tell the police that he was out in the field." Her voice cracked.

"In the dark?"

She chewed a huge bite of the pretzel and swallowed. "It's ridiculous. Who is going to believe it?"

"Do you know where he was? Could he have been in the field? Is that common?" I certainly wasn't a professional farmer, but Mac and I had managed a large garden and small hop field on our property on the outskirts of town, and I'd never had a reason to check the sleeping vegetables at night.

"I don't know." She choked on the bite.

"Are you okay?" I reached out to help her.

"Yeah." She clutched her chest, coughed twice, and then set the half-eaten doughy treat on top of the bag. "It's not common. That's for sure. He told me there was a problem with the irrigation system. He has everything connected to his phone. He uses tracking apps and has cameras installed to be able to check on the fields remotely."

"Okay, that sounds logical."

She brushed cinnamon crumbs from her hands. "Maybe. I went to bed to read. He got an alert on the app and said he was going to go check outside. I didn't think anything of it at the time. I mean, I thought it was unusual that there was an issue with the irrigation system, but that's why he has the apps. I must have fallen asleep. When I woke up, my book was on top of my face, and Weber wasn't back. So I went to check and noticed that his car was gone. This was at eleven-thirty. He didn't get home until after midnight. Where did he go?"

"Could he have gone to get a part to fix the system?" I asked, even though it was highly unlikely any hardware shops would have been open in the village.

"That's what he told me. He said he drove to Wenatchee thinking one of the big box stores might be open late."

"It sounds like you don't believe that," I said gently.

She shook her head. "I checked. Everything closed at ten. He would have looked at store hours before making the drive to Wenatchee. He's lying. I just don't know why. I can't believe he would hurt anyone, but I'm really having a hard time coming up with what other reason he would have been gone last night."

I knew how terrible it felt to lose trust in your spouse. When Mac cheated on me, it made me question everything and eroded my trust in myself. It had taken years to rebuild my confidence, and even now, I still had flashes where I drifted into self-doubt.

"Why would he kill Josh? I know he freaked out when he thought Josh was flirting with me, but Weber's not the jealous type. He's not like the slightest bit possessive. We're usually great partners in business and marriage. Something is going on with him, and I refuse to believe that he could be a killer, but am I fooling myself?"

I placed my hand on her arm. "You know Weber better than anyone. If at your core you don't think he's a killer, I would trust that, but your instinct about telling Chief Meyers what happened last night is right. Weber probably has a logical explanation for where he was and what he was doing. Maybe the cameras in the fields will serve as his alibi."

Annabelle gasped. "I didn't think of that. Yes, good point. You're right. I need to tell Chief Meyers. I could never live with myself if..." She didn't finish her thought.

"Are you sure that you're safe? You're welcome to stay with me."

"No, honestly, thank you, that's very kind, but you know Weber. He and Hans are best friends. Weber is one of the kindest men I know. Something is up with him, but I'm not worried about my personal safety. I just want to figure out what's wrong and help him. Do you think you could talk to Hans? They bike twice a week. Maybe Weber has opened up to him."

"Of course. I can swing by his workshop now."

"That would be so helpful. I'll go to the police station." She folded the pretzel bag. "Thanks again for listening; you're a good friend, Sloan."

"Anytime, and don't hesitate to call if you need anything. I'm here, no matter the time of day. You can call me at four a.m. if you need to." I couldn't help falling into a mothering role. My years in the foster care system hadn't prepared me for adulthood. There was no one to guide or nurture me. I had been rudderless, adrift. It was one of the reasons I had fallen so hard for Mac. He had given me a lifeboat—a family, a connection, a home. Those experiences of learning to rely only on myself had given me a valuable perspective now. Whenever I could, I wanted to offer the support, understanding, and nurturing I needed when I was young to anyone I could.

"Hopefully, I'll be fast asleep by then, but I appreciate it." She picked up the pretzel bag and moved with purpose toward the police station.

I considered everything Annabelle had told me on the walk to Hans's woodshop. Like her, I wanted to believe Weber, but there was no denying that there were some gaping holes in his story. Hopefully Hans could shed some light on the situation, but for the moment, Weber was back on top of my suspect list.

CHAPTER

NINE

HANS'S WOODSHOP was located a few blocks off Front Street. It was equal parts a lush garden, a working studio, and a gallery. His talent and creativity were evident in the wooden trellis that snaked along the perimeter of the property. The cedar wood was wrapped with fragrant early-blooming jasmine and Amarillo hops. There were large outdoor pieces like hand-carved seating, upcycled water fountains, birdhouses, and fire pits. Wandering through the grounds always made me feel like I was stepping into the pages of *The Secret Garden*.

I stopped to admire an iridescent hummingbird sipping from a feeder hanging on the scalloped eaves; I knew Hans had meticulously beveled each piece of the wood section by section before securing the intricate filigree pattern to the roofline.

I opened the side gate that led to the gallery and almost turned around at the sound of voices coming from the studio. If Hans were with a client, I didn't want to disturb him.

I stopped to admire a fledgling pear tree that Hans was training to grow in a "T."

Maybe I should come back later, I thought, inhaling the

fragrant scent of the blossoms, but before I had a chance to change my mind, a shadow appeared in front of me.

It was Weber.

He looked like he'd been running a marathon. His cheeks were flushed, deep burgundy like the heirloom tomatoes planted along the fence. Sweat poured from his brow. He tried to mop it with his shirt sleeve, which was already drenched.

"Sloan, you scared me." He froze and recoiled slightly.

"Sorry, I was on my way to see Hans. I didn't realize you were here, and I certainly didn't mean to startle you."

"Nah, it's cool. It's on me." He tried to laugh, but it sounded forced and strained.

"Is everything okay?"

Weber twisted his head behind him as if he'd seen a ghost. Then he clenched both hands into tight fists. "I'm fine. Fine. I gotta go, though. I'm late for... for something." He didn't elaborate or wait for me to respond. Instead, he raced toward the front gate.

I understood why Annabelle was upset. Weber's behavior was erratic and unhinged. Was it because he had killed Josh in a fit of passion and now was riddled with guilt? I didn't want to believe that the gentle farmer was a killer, but everything about his actions over the past few days made me question whether he had turned violent.

"Well, if it isn't my favorite Krause family member." Hans's voice shook me from my thoughts.

I looked up to see him walking toward me with a pair of gardening shears.

Hans was tall and trim, yet muscular from all the heavy lifting he did. His shaggy hair had a reddish tint and his skin was naturally tanned due to working outdoors.

"I'm glad you showed up, Sloan. You're giving me a reprieve from having to tackle that creeping ivy that apparently has decided my roofline is the best spot in the village to plant roots."

"Ivy is the worst."

"You're telling me." Hans motioned to Adirondack chairs near the firepit. "You want to sit for a minute?"

"That would be great."

Hans waited for me to get situated. The sun had warmed the wooden seat. I leaned back and tilted my head.

"Can I get you a lemonade? Iced tea?" Hans offered, brushing sawdust from his pants.

"No, don't go to any trouble. I came to see you because I want to get your opinion on the murder investigation."

"Way to cut to the point." Hans set his shears on the grass next to him. "Yeah, what's going on? I heard the news but not any details."

I gave him an overview of everything I knew.

"Let me guess; you're here because of Weber?" Hans picked a piece of grass and rubbed it between his fingers.

"You know me too well." I paused for a second, allowing the fruity smells of the garden to wash over me. "I don't want to put you in the middle of this or make you uncomfortable, so please don't feel obligated to talk about this if you don't want to, okay?"

Hans scowled and tossed the blade of grass on the ground. "Sloan, come on, it's me."

"I know, but I want to talk about Weber. You two have been friends for years, and it's okay if you want to stay out of it."

"You know about Weber?" Hans sounded surprised.

"What do you mean?"

Hans rested his chin on his hand and crossed his legs. "Weber's been going through some stuff."

"Annabelle said as much."

"Wait, stop. Annabelle is aware of what's going on?"

"Uh, I don't know. She mentioned that he's been on edge. She's worried about him, and then last night."

"That's so weird. Why did he come to talk to me about last night? He said that he had been keeping it from Annabelle. I encouraged him to be honest with her. The truth can be painful, but it's the only thing that ultimately sets you free."

"So he admitted to it?" My stomach dropped.

Hans held up a hand. "Let's go back to the beginning. I feel like we might not be on the same page here."

"Me, too." I shook my head, trying to refocus. "Okay, Annabelle is going to the police because Weber lied to her about where he was last night. She thinks he could have snuck out to kill Josh."

Hans opened his mouth in shock. Then he put out a hand to stop me from continuing. "Stop right there. We are definitely talking about two different things. I wouldn't share this normally, but these are extenuating circumstances, and you'll keep this between us until Weber has a chance to talk to Annabelle, right?"

"Of course."

"I know. I just have to say it for myself." Hans shook his head. "I can't believe Annabelle thinks Weber killed Josh."

"She doesn't." I hesitated. "Well, at least she doesn't want to, but she can't explain his behavior and then he lied to her about disappearing last night."

"I can see how that would be confusing." Hans nodded. "That's why I told him he needs to be honest with her. Weber had an accident on the farm a few months ago that he didn't tell her about."

"What kind of an accident?"

"He tipped the tractor when it was operating and came within inches of being crushed."

"That's terrible. Was he injured?"

"Not physically." Hans raised an eyebrow. "But mentally. He's been having panic attacks ever since. He keeps replaying the accident in his head because he could have died. But he didn't, which I've reminded him of. I've been encouraging him to speak with a therapist. Until the last couple of days, he's refused and tried to muscle through it. I don't think that's working. He hasn't been sleeping, which has made him short and on edge with everyone. It's gotten much worse. Did you notice that he was red and sweaty? He's in a cycle of constant anxiety. He was sharing that his heart rate has been spiking, and he's lightheaded and dizzy all the time."

"That's terrible." I instinctively put my hand over my heart. "Why hasn't he talked to Annabelle about this?"

"It started initially because he didn't want to tell her about the tractor. He thought she would be upset because she had warned him a few times that he was too cavalier with how he was operating it." He paused and exhaled slowly. "Then too much time had passed, and the anxiety got out of control. Hence, why communication is key."

"Good point."

Panic attacks could explain Weber's emotional state. I experienced anxiety to varying degrees throughout my child-hood and well into my adult life. I was grateful to Marianne, my foster care case worker and trained therapist. She had given me a variety of tools to employ when panic started to threaten to devour me—meditation, tapping, deep breathing, journaling, connecting with nature, and more. As a parent, I passed on those tools to Alex and had many conversations with him about the importance of caring for our mental health. I'm sure he was tired of hearing it, but I never wanted him to feel a stigma or concern about going to therapy.

"I'm sorry that Weber's been having a rough time, although I'm glad he has a friend like you to talk to, but that doesn't explain where he was last night. And why he lied to Annabelle. I'm worried that if he doesn't have an alibi, Chief Meyers might not have any other option but to arrest him."

"He has an alibi," Hans said, focusing his gaze on me. "He came here last night. I'm his alibi."

CHAPTER
TEN

"Weber came here last night," I repeated to Hans as I tried to make sense of it myself.

Hans nodded slowly. "He had a bad panic attack. He tried to go outside and do some deep breathing to calm down. It didn't work, so he came here. I told him we needed to go to the emergency room."

"Did you?"

"Yeah. They checked his heart just in case and confirmed that it was anxiety. They gave him a mild sedative to help him relax, demonstrated some other breathing techniques, and wrote a referral for therapy."

"Why was he here just now?" I looked toward the front gate as if expecting to see Weber standing there.

Hans uncrossed his legs and sat up taller. "Because he's going to his first counseling session this afternoon, and he still hasn't told Annabelle. Not telling her is exacerbating his anxiety. He's in a vicious loop."

"She's going to be relieved to know that he wasn't sneaking

out to kill Josh, and I'm sure that she'll completely support him."

"That's exactly what I said. He's on his way to find her now. I suggested it might be a good idea for them to go to the appointment together."

This news changed everything.

"And you're sure Weber was here last night?"

"He showed up about ten-fifteen. I sat with him for another ten minutes before I drove him to the hospital."

"How long was he there?" I asked, wondering if there were a possibility that Weber had killed Josh after he had seen Hans.

"At least twelve-thirty. I stayed with him until they were done running tests. Then we walked back here together. I wanted to make sure he was in good enough shape to drive home." Hans pressed his fingers together. "Between the medication and confirmation from the tests that the doctors ran, he was much calmer. He told me that he was going straight home and tell Annabelle everything."

Again I wished I knew the exact time that Josh had been killed, but it seemed highly unlikely that Weber could have had an opportunity to sneak into the hostel while dealing with a personal health crisis. And Hans was with him the entire night. There wasn't a single person on the planet I trusted more than Hans.

"You look like Alex, studying for the SATs," Hans said with a half smile and one eye closed, like he was trying to read my mind.

"I feel like I'm missing something, but this has been very helpful. I think we can cross Weber off the list of suspects. I'm still not sure who the guy in black was that Harper saw running out of the hostel. Knowing that Weber was with you definitely changes things."

"Good. I'm glad, because there's no way he did it," Hans said with complete confidence.

"From the first night when he freaked out at Josh at the farmers market, I didn't want to believe that he could be a killer, but then the evidence kept mounting. I'm glad you cleared things up and I'm really glad that Weber has a friend like you. Connecting him with support is so important. Even more so, normalizing therapy. You're one of the good ones, Hans Krause."

"As are you, Sloan *Krause*." He wrapped his arm around my shoulder. "Are you sure I can't get you something to drink? Or what about one of Mom's springerle cookies? She just dropped off a fresh batch yesterday."

"Thanks, but I'll take a rain check. I need to go relay this to Chief Meyers and follow up on another lead."

"Fine. That means more sugar for me." Hans patted his waist. "I'll walk you out. I need to check the sprinkler system before I go head-to-head with this old-growth ivy."

I chuckled. "Hey, have you heard from Leah lately?" Leah was Garrett's younger sister who was finishing her medical residency in Portland. She and Hans had hit it off during ski week. Leah was considering taking a position at the Leavenworth Community Hospital, and she and Hans had been emailing and talking regularly ever since.

"Yeah, she's coming up next week. She has two extra days off, so she is going to do an official interview at the hospital, and we're going to do some hiking. She mentioned that she was planning to check in with Garrett to see if you guys want to join us for one of the hikes, or at least meet up for dinner."

"Sure." I tried to temper my excitement about the possibility that Leah could be seriously considering a move to the village. "Only as long as you two want company. I know that you're still in the early stages of dating, and I can speak for

Garrett too, when I say we would not want to crash your party."

"It's not a party. It's just a hike." Hans sounded casual. Maybe too casual.

"Okay. Great. Keep us posted. We're around next week."

We stopped at the gate. I gave Hans a hug. "Good luck with the ivy, and thanks for everything."

I wasn't sure where to go first, but I decided the police station was probably the best choice. Hopefully, Chief Meyers was back by now. I wanted to ask her about the time of death and fill her in on my conversation with Hans.

I hurried through the village until I reached the station. A wooden carved sign reading POLIZEI hung above the office. Window boxes bursting with red and yellow geraniums and a kiosk with hiking, mountain biking, and river rafting brochures made the station seem more like a travel center.

Inside there were more posters touting Leavenworth's abundance of outdoor recreation opportunities, as well as educational materials about the importance of staying vigilant in the backcountry, like how to respond in a bear or cougar encounter and how to keep Washington's forests safe from wildfires.

"Is Chief Meyers back yet?" I asked the officer at the front desk. He had been a few years older than Alex in school and had played on the soccer team. That was the thing about living in a town of two thousand people. It was fairly impossible to go anywhere in the village and not know everyone.

"No. Last I heard, she was over at the hostel. Have you tried her cell?"

"Not recently. I can swing by the hostel on the way back to Nitro. If I happen to miss her in passing, can you let her know that I have some new information about the case to share with her?"

The officer made a note. "I'll make sure to pass it on."

I thanked him and left.

There wasn't much more I could do until I spoke with Chief Meyers. She needed to know about Serena and that Weber had a rock-solid alibi in Hans.

Harper was pacing in front of the station. She looked like she was trying to decide whether or not to go in from the way she would tentatively place a foot on the bottom stair and then quickly pull it back again.

"Hey, Harper."

She jumped from the bottom rung and threw her hand over her mouth. "Oh, my God! I think my heart just stopped. I wasn't expecting to see you."

"Sorry. I didn't mean to startle you." Startling people seemed to be a theme for me lately. Did I need to get better about announcing my presence, or was everyone in the village on edge because of Josh's murder?

Harper fiddled with a brochure that she had balled up in one hand. "It's not your fault. I've been trying to work up the courage to go inside. I'm just so scared."

"Scared. Why?"

"Because I'm fairly sure that the police are going to arrest me for killing Josh."

CHAPTER
ELEVEN

I COULDN'T CONTAIN my shock. Was Harper confessing to the crime? Every cell in my body fired like it was on high alert. I wasn't worried that I was in danger. It was broad daylight in the middle of Front Street. The odds were good that Harper wasn't going to attack me, but I was still stunned that she could have killed Josh.

She wadded the brochure tighter. "I guess it's better if I go in there on my own instead of being handcuffed and dragged away. But do I need a lawyer?"

Was she asking me?

I paused, trying to buy myself a minute to process.

She continued. "In the movies, they always ask for a lawyer, but how does it work in real life?"

"Are you planning on confessing?"

"Confessing?" Harper stuck out her tongue and shook her head like she was sickened by the thought. "No, why would I confess?"

I held up one hand. "Wait, slow down. You said the police were going to arrest you for Josh's murder."

"Yeah, because they think I did. I didn't kill him. I can't even kill a spider if I find one in my apartment, and I hate spiders."

"Why do you need a lawyer, then?"

She stuffed the wrinkled brochure in her pocket. "Because, according to Klaus, he saw me going into Josh's room shortly before he was killed, but I swear I didn't do it." She made an "x" over her heart. "You believe me, right? I swear on my life that I didn't kill him."

"I thought you were out having beers in the village when Josh was killed."

"I was, but I did go see him when I got back." She hung her head and stared at the wooden slats.

"Did you tell the police this?"

"No." Her voice wavered with emotion like she was holding back tears. "I realize how bad this looks now. I should have been honest, but I was worried that they were going to think I did it, so I just left that part out. Everything else is true. I did go out for drinks, and I did see a guy in black running away from the hostel when we got back. But I didn't go straight to bed. I went to Josh's room to confront him."

"Confront him about what?" This was very different than the story she'd told me just a while ago at Nitro.

"Him stealing my content. He's been doing it forever, but recently he hasn't even been subtle about it. He takes my captions and hashtags and copies them word for word. He isn't even trying to hide it. Or I guess I should say wasn't." She grimaced. "I should have left it alone and just let it go, but I had a few drinks, and I guess I felt bold, so I decided to confront him."

"Did you?"

"Not exactly. I banged on Josh's door. I guess I must have been louder than I realized. That's probably when Klaus spotted me. Anyway, the room wasn't locked, so I went inside. Josh was passed out on his bunk. It was dark. I don't even remember what I said to him. I probably wasn't very coherent, but I told him to stop plagiarizing my content. I warned him that I was going to call him out on social media if he kept doing it. I thought I heard him mumble an apology, but that could be wishful thinking. He mumbled something. I felt better, and it sounded like someone was coming down the hall, so I went to my room and passed out. You know the rest. I woke up to learn that he was dead. Now the police think I did it, and they're going to arrest me for murder. This is the worst day of my life." Her knees buckled like she was going to collapse.

"You need to tell the police everything you shared with me," I said, hearing the "mom" tone creeping in again. "Chief Meyers is an astute detective. I'm sure she'll listen without judgment to everything you have to say."

"Maybe, but you have to admit it looks pretty bad for me. I was the last person to see him alive, and Klaus must have seen me leaving Josh's room. That's the thing, though. Why would I have called attention to myself? If I had wanted to kill him, I would have been much more stealthy about it. I was drunk. I was pounding on the door and shouting. I'm sure I woke Klaus and half the hostel up. Does that sound like something a killer would do?"

"No." She had a good point. "Do you remember what time this was? It could be very critical in determining the time of death."

"Uh, not exactly. As I mentioned, I had a few drinks at the Underground, so I was a bit out of it. It wasn't long after we all returned to the hostel. I went straight to Josh's room, so maybe eleven forty-five?"

I made a mental note. A new thought had begun to surface, but I wasn't going to share it with her.

"Before you go talk to the police, can I ask you about Josh's ex-girlfriend?"

"Serena? Yeah, what about her?" Harper twisted her neck like she was holding a yoga pose.

"Do you think there's a chance that she could have been the person you saw running down the stairs?"

Harper scowled. "Hmmm. I'm not sure. I could have sworn that it was a man. He seemed tall and big. I've only seen Serena in photos and videos online, but she's tiny. Unless it was a trick of the camera or a special angle, she always looked like she barely came up to Josh's shoulders. The person I saw seemed much taller, but..."

"But what?"

She scrunched her face. "I was under the influence of some strong beers. It was dark. I was on a mission to confront Josh after getting hyped by my friends about how crummy it was that he was stealing my content, so maybe. Yeah, maybe." She sounded surer of herself as she continued. "It could have been Serena. That makes so much more sense. Who here would want to kill Josh? No one has a motive. I thought maybe that farmer guy because he seemed irritated by Josh trying to hit on his wife, but that seems like a big stretch to go from that to murdering a stranger."

And now I knew that Weber couldn't have been the person she had seen in the stairwell that night. However, I kept that information to myself.

"Serena has been unhinged since Josh broke up with her. That's a motive for murder, right?"

"Potentially," I agreed.

"That has to be it." Her mouth fell open. "Serena must have followed him up here. I bet she was out on the trail with us when we were hiking Icicle. She could have been watching his every move from afar and trying to figure out the best time to strike. What if she were waiting for him to go to sleep? The rest of us went out and left him there like a sitting duck."

Harper's words began to mash together as she talked through this new potential theory. "She could have attacked him while he was sleeping." She froze and clapped her hand over her mouth again. "Oh, my God. What if Josh was already dead—or dying when I went into his room?"

"Already dead. I thought you said that he mumbled an apology to you."

"I *thought* that he mumbled something, but now that I'm thinking about it, it sounded more like a moan or a muffled cry for help. What if Serena hit him and knocked him out right before I got there? What if he wasn't apologizing? What if he was begging me for help, and I was a little buzzed so I didn't even realize it?" She took the stairs two at a time. "I don't care about a lawyer anymore. It's all falling into place. Serena must have killed him. I have to go tell the police this now. Thanks for talking it through with me."

She yanked the wooden door open and vanished inside.

I was glad that she was going to the police, although I didn't envy Chief Meyers's position. She was going to have a lot to sort out. But I did agree with Harper that it seemed like we were closing in on the real killer.

CHAPTER
TWELVE

"Sloan, we were about to send a search party out for you," Garrett teased when I returned to Nitro, where he was wiping down the front patio tables and setting out new flower arrangements in beer bottle vases. They were customer favorites. We used recycled Der Keller bottles and filled them with roses, sprigs of rosemary and lavender, and sent them home with anyone who wanted one.

"Whew, you are not going to believe everything I've learned."

He tossed the towel on one of the tables and pulled out a chair. "Have a seat. You can fill me in, and I could use a little hint of sun before it's back to the brew cave."

I didn't resist. I sank into the chair and let my body relax in the late afternoon heat. The sun had warmed the iron table tops and chairs, making them feel like the heated seats in my car. After a long, cold winter, the bright rays felt like a gift from Mother Nature. Our dark snowy winters held their own kind of magic, but there was nothing that compared with our Bavarian village in the spring.

I loved that Garrett recognized that, too.

He craned his neck to the sky, soaking in the warmth before letting out an audible sigh and turning his attention to me. "That feels good, doesn't it?"

"Yeah, especially with the aroma of hops, grilled brats, and sweet blooming roses." I sucked in a deep breath. "Thanks for reminding me to take a moment to drink this in."

He reached for my hand and laced his fingers through mine. "Thanks for slowing down with me."

"Always." I squeezed his hand, instantly calmed by his comforting touch. "Okay, but I do want to fill you in while we have a second."

I told him about my conversations with Hans and Harper. He listened carefully, nodding along and stopping me every once in a while to ask for clarification. When I finished, he puckered his lips and shook his head.

"That's like a week's worth of information in a couple of hours, Sloan."

"I know. It's a lot to process, but it does feel like we're getting closer. We know that Weber didn't kill Josh. I don't think Harper did, either. She was physically distraught when she came to the conclusion that Josh might have been begging her for help. She doesn't seem like the type, and she did raise a very good point that it wouldn't have made any sense for her to cause a scene and then kill him."

"Agreed," Garrett said. "A scorned lover certainly fits the bill for a motive if Serena killed him."

"It's logical. I mean, it's irrational and terrible, but if Serena and Josh's breakup was as nasty as everything seems to be leading us to believe, it certainly is possible that she could have killed him. And that would explain why she was so skittish when I mentioned the police."

Garrett nodded. "It could be why she took off and you

couldn't find her. If she realized that she had slipped up when talking to you, it's no surprise she tried to get out of the village as fast as possible before someone else caught on." He glanced toward Front Street. "I wonder if Klaus could have made a mistake. Maybe he saw Serena leaving Josh's room, not Harper."

"Good thinking. Harper said she never saw him. She assumed that he heard her banging on the door, but, yeah, it might have been Serena. They're about the same height and if it were dark it would be hard to tell. He probably assumed it was Harper since she's a guest at the hostel."

The more I thought about it, Serena was the most likely suspect. She had the motive, she had been in the village, and now she was nowhere to be seen. I wondered if that's why Chief Meyers had been gone all day. Had she come to the same conclusion and was trying to track Serena down?

"You know, things are under control around here. We could leave Kat in charge for a few minutes and wander over to The Gasthaus and have a little chat with Klaus. I've been meaning to swing by, anyway. He had reached out about the possibility of doing a branding partnership where we brew a special beer for him to serve at the hostel."

"Good idea. Should I go grab a couple of six-packs?"

"Sure." Garrett stood. "I'll wipe down the last of the tables and set out these flowers while you do that. Can you let Kat know we'll be back shortly?"

"I'm on it." I hurried into the tasting room for sample beers to share with Klaus and to inform Kat of our plans.

"Good luck and be careful," she cautioned, twisting her face into a grimace. "The hostel creeps me out."

I set the beer on the bar. "It does? Why?"

She shuddered. "It just has a super creepy vibe. There's bad energy there."

"Really? Tell me more." This was news. I didn't know Kat had spent any time at The Gasthaus.

"Remember when my friends came up to ski last month?"

I nodded.

"They stayed at the hostel and all of them said it was terrible. Run down, sketchy cleaning and maintenance. I met them for a drink one night and everything was so overpriced and gross. Klaus served microwaved mini corndogs, Costco fries, and cheap beer which probably cost him nothing, but he charged us twenty dollars."

"You never said anything."

"I know, I felt bad. I knew you and Garrett would have tried to work something out, but we were booked here and everywhere else in town is so expensive."

"Next time, tell me." I put my hand over my heart. "I would have had them come stay at my place."

"That's nice, Sloan. It's not a big deal. I'm just not a fan of the hostel or Klaus. He seems like he's taking advantage of young travelers. He charged my friends massive cleaning fees even though they brought their own sleeping bags and used the shared bathrooms, which they said were super disgusting, like totally gross, by the way."

"Thanks for letting me know. I haven't been inside the hostel for a few years. I'll keep a careful eye out when we talk to Klaus."

"Cool. See you in a while." Kat returned to stacking pint glasses.

I took the six-packs and returned to meet Garrett. "When did Klaus ask you about doing a collaboration?"

"The other night at the farmers market kickoff. He stopped by the booth when you were over talking to Annabelle. Why?"

"Kat just told me that when her friends were visiting last

month, they stayed at The Gasthaus, and the hostel was in bad shape."

"That checks out." Garrett's forehead creased with worry lines. "Klaus mentioned that he's got a new investor and is getting ready to start a major renovation on the property. He is going to overhaul the hostel, give it a facelift, update the guest rooms, and expand the dining options."

"Maybe that explains it."

We walked two short blocks to the hostel. The police tape and any evidence that a crime had occurred were gone. I wasn't sure if that made me feel better or worse.

Garrett knocked on the front door, which required a key code for entry.

It took a few minutes before Klaus peered out the small window. His cloudy eyes narrowed as he scoffed and muttered something under his breath before proceeding to let us in.

"I wasn't expecting anyone," he said, shuffling to make space for us in the cramped and dingy entryway that smelled distinctively of mold.

"We thought we would bring you a couple of tasting options." Garrett handed him the beer. "If it's not a good time, we can come back later."

"Nah, it's fine. This way." Klaus took the beer and headed for the kitchen.

I took note of the fading and torn wallpaper in the hallway, the threadbare rugs, and scuffed floors. Dust as thick as a fluffy cat lined the floorboards and the overhead fluorescent lighting flicked on and off. The shared kitchen and dining space weren't much better. Dishes were piled in the sink. A sign reading BROKEN was posted on the dishwasher and the countertops were stained with coffee rings.

"Take a seat." Klaus motioned to the mismatched rickety chairs and scratched table.

My chair was coated in a thick film of grime. I hesitated before I sat down, wishing I had brought along a towel. I had a feeling I was going to stick to the chair and didn't want to know the last time it had been cleaned or the root cause of the stickiness, especially because the moldy smell permeated the kitchen, too.

Brewing and cleaning are synonymous. We spent at least double the amount of time cleaning the tanks and mopping the floors in the brewery as we did on the actual brewing process. It was good that Klaus had plans to revamp and refresh the hostel, because given its current condition, I was surprised that it hadn't been shut down by the State Board of Health. Kat wasn't exaggerating. I knew from the exterior that the hostel needed a fresh coat of paint and new gutters, but I had no idea how bad it was inside. How was Klaus getting away with charging guests any amount of money to stay?

Garrett caught my eye and made a face as he sat across from me.

"What have you got for me?" Klaus asked, cracking open a can of IPA.

"That's our signature IPA with notes of lemon and orange," Garrett started to say, but Klaus cut him off.

"It's fine. That's what I need. These kids are so demanding these days. It used to be that I could stick out some bananas, granola bars, and cans of Coors Light, but no, now they want avocado toast and fancy craft beer."

Garrett cleared his throat and kicked me under the table. "I don't know if I would call what we produce fancy, but craft, yes."

I jumped in. "It sounds like you're getting ready for a big remodel."

"I don't know. I think I might sell. I'm too old for this game."

"Really?" Garrett sat up taller. "I thought you mentioned that you had an investor at the farmers market the other night."

"That fell through." Klaus chugged his beer. "It's fine. I'm done. I'm going to sell, take the cash, and retire on a sunny island somewhere. It's too much stress trying to compete with the ritzy hotels and glamping tourists these days. Whatever happened to a good old-fashioned hostel? I give you a bed, a bunk, a hot shower, and a place to make your coffee in the morning. What else do you need? These hikers today are weaklings. They want Wi-Fi and to livestream from our mountains. It's ridiculous."

"You mean Josh?" I asked. "I heard you asked him to leave."

"I didn't ask him to leave. I told him he wasn't welcome anywhere near my property, and if he showed up again, I'd get the cops involved." Klaus bristled and sloshed beer on his stained shirt. He wiped it with the back of his hand. "It wasn't just him. It's all of them. They are an entitled bunch."

Garrett seized the opportunity to shift the conversation to Josh's murder. "Did you see anything that night? It must be so upsetting to have had a murder occur under your roof."

Klaus took a long drink of his beer, gulping it like he was trying to hydrate. "Yep. I saw everything."

"Everything?" I nudged.

"That young woman, Harper. I'm waiting for Chief Meyers to show up and arrest her so I can stick a FOR SALE sign out in front and get out of the village for good."

"Are you sure you saw Harper?" I took out my phone to show him a photo of Serena. "Could you have seen this woman instead?"

He didn't bother to look at the picture. "It was Harper. I saw her kill him with my own two eyes."

CHAPTER
THIRTEEN

"You saw her kill Josh?" Garett sounded incredulous.

"That's what I said. Why are you two so interested? Isn't this a matter for the police?" Klaus chugged the rest of his beer and opened another.

Had he already been drinking? His words slurred, and his speech was muddled and almost incoherent.

"I bumped into Serena earlier and then learned that she and Josh used to date before having a nasty breakup," I explained, trying to ignore the constant drip of the leaky sink faucet. "It seemed plausible that she could have been involved."

"Nope. Not her. It was the other one—Harper." Klaus's cheeks flushed with a rosy hue. Was it from the beer or anger?

His eyes glazed as he balled one hand into a fist and smacked the table. "She pounded in his head, and I saw her do it."

I flinched.

Without raising his voice or making any sudden movements, Garrett placed his open palms on the table as if trying to keep Klaus calm. "Does Chief Meyers know this?"

"You guys are asking a lot of questions." Klaus took another huge swig of his beer. "Are you working with the police? I thought you were here to talk beer."

"We are," I insisted. "Everyone in the village is talking about the murder, so I guess we're caught up in it, too."

Klaus had shifted in his chair, arching his back to make his shoulders appear broader. There was something off-putting about his body language and reaction to our questions. A prickly feeling ran up my spine. It was a feeling I had learned never to ignore. My internal compass had always steered me correctly, and I wasn't about to dismiss it now.

"We should probably get back to the pub," I said to Garrett, hoping he would pick up on my cue that it was time to leave.

"Right." Garrett pushed back his chair and started to stand. "Why don't you let us know what you think of these beers? We can brew something lighter, too. But it sounds like you've got some decisions to make about the hostel before we move forward."

"Fine." Klaus didn't move. "You can see yourselves out, right?"

"Sure." Garrett smiled.

I got up and followed him to the front, but instead of leaving, Garrett put a finger to his lips and pointed to the stairs.

"What?" I whispered.

"Let's go take a quick look at the guest rooms." He gestured again and peered over my shoulder to make sure Klaus was still in the kitchen.

"You think?" I wasn't sure it was the best idea, but I had to admit that our conversation with Klaus had me wondering if we were wrong about Serena or Harper. Could it have been him this whole time?

Garrett nodded but didn't speak. He was careful with each foot placement so as not to make any extra noise as we tiptoed upstairs. When we reached the landing, he lowered his voice and started down the hallway. There were handwritten, fading signs pointing to a shared bathroom to our left and a storage area for backpacks and gear to our right.

Like the main floor, the upstairs had seen plenty of foot traffic. The floors were worn and patchy. Sections of the ceiling had big chunks cut out, probably from water damage. The roof had obviously leaked at some point from the water stains that trailed down the dingy walls.

"This way." Garrett continued down the hall until we reached the bunk rooms. The doors to each of the rooms were open.

I guessed that was likely because Chief Meyers and her team had searched the property extensively after Josh's murder.

Garrett stepped into the first bunk room.

A foreboding sense of doom flooded my body. I wasn't sure if this had been the room Josh was staying in, but the thought that he had been killed here or nearby made me want to reconsider our decision to snoop around.

"How could Klaus have seen Harper kill him?" Garrett asked, his voice still barely above a whisper.

"What do you mean?" I squinted in the shadowy room.

"Look how tight the quarters are." Garrett extended his arms. His fingertips touched either side of the bunks. "If Josh was on one of the bunks and Harper standing here, there's no way Klaus, or anyone else for that matter, could have been in the room, too. Or if he was, why didn't he stop her? How could she have gotten out? He would have blocked the doorway."

I glanced behind us. "Or the hallway. It's not very wide either."

"Exactly." Garrett bobbed his head in agreement. "I think he's lying."

"You don't think he saw her?"

"I don't know, but I don't think he's telling us the truth."

I was about to ask if he had a theory as to why Klaus might be lying. I was starting to form my own, but before either of us could get another word out, a deep voice sounded behind us.

"Don't move a muscle."

Garrett and I both slowly swiveled in the direction of the sound.

Klaus stood, bracing himself in the door frame with both feet. He held a baseball bat in his arms like he was ready to swing.

"Wait." Garrett threw his arms up in surrender. "I can explain."

"What are you doing in here?"

"We were looking for any additional clues that might help us understand who killed Josh," I answered truthfully, hoping that being honest would pay off.

"Get out." Klaus pointed the bat toward the hall. "No one is supposed to be up here."

"Sorry, we didn't realize that." Garrett moved to the door with his hands still raised.

"What kind of evidence are you looking for?" Klaus raised a bushy eyebrow.

"Maybe something the police left behind or overlooked," I suggested. I wasn't about to admit that he was the reason we had come upstairs.

Klaus's eyes bulged in his head. They darted in every direction like he was trying to piece together whether he should believe my story or not.

"Get out of here," he repeated.

Garrett squeezed past him first. I followed next, raising my hands up, too. The last thing we needed was for Klaus to perceive us as a threat. I wanted to get out of the hostel as quickly as possible. I didn't like the wild look in Klaus's eyes or the feeling of fear bubbling up in my stomach.

This had been a bad idea.

I considered our options. We could make a break for the main stairs, but Klaus was too big to get around. His body took up most of the hallway. There was no chance of escaping down the back stairwell.

Was I overreacting?

Why was I planning my exit route?

Technically we weren't in danger.

The truth was that Klaus was in the right. We were trespassing on his property. He hadn't given us permission to come upstairs. He was well within his rights to tell us to get out.

But I couldn't ignore my gut feeling.

Sweat pooled on the back of my neck. My mouth felt gummy, and the hallway felt like it was closing in.

The flickering rust-yellow fluorescent lighting and moldy aroma didn't help.

"Seriously, sorry about that," Garrett said in a calm and steady voice. "I guess the thought of helping to solve the crime got the better of us. Sloan and I shouldn't have come up here."

For a minute I thought everything was going to be fine. That Klaus would laugh it off with us, but instead, he narrowed his dark eyes at Garrett and snarled, "No. You shouldn't have come up here. Now I'm going to have to figure out what to do with you."

FOURTEEN

WHAT TO DO WITH US? I didn't like the sound of that.

"Get moving. Head down the hallway," Klaus commanded.

Garrett shot a brief look of support my way before following Klaus's orders.

"You don't need to do anything with us," Garrett said, keeping his face forward as we marched down the hallway. "Sloan and I will leave right now, and that's the end of this."

"That ship sailed when you decided to come snoop around up here. You should have left when you had a chance." Klaus smacked the bat between his hands.

I gulped. My heart thudded against my chest.

Did Garrett have a plan?

Because mine was to hurl myself down the stairs once we got to the end of the hallway. There was a chance that Klaus could take a swing at me, but I trusted my agility. I was in good shape and quick on my feet. I couldn't say the same for him.

The only thing he had on his side was bulk. Well, that and probably nothing left to lose. He had killed once. What would stop him from doing it again?

I moved faster at that realization.

His lumbering presence might have intimidated me under different circumstances, but there were two of us. He couldn't kill us both and get away with it.

I wished there were a way to signal Garrett without alerting Klaus, but I couldn't come up with anything.

My stomach flopped more as we approached the crest of the stairs.

I could feel Klaus's hot breath on the back of my neck.

I couldn't wait. I had to take my chance—now.

"Go, Garrett," I yelled as I ducked and nearly fell down the stairs. Thankfully my hand made contact with the wall at the last second. I steadied myself just as I caught Klaus swinging wildly out of the corner of my eye.

"Get help, Sloan!" Garrett yelled.

The distraction had bought him enough time to grab a hiking pole from the gear rack. Klaus was winding up again for another swing. I hesitated. I didn't want to abandon Garrett, but we needed help.

I raced downstairs and out the front door; at the very last minute, I remembered the lock and bent down to stick a book in the frame.

"Help!" I shouted as loud as I could. "We need help!"

The sounds of shuffling feet and loud thuds echoed through the ceiling, followed by a sharp cry of pain. The thuds turned into a full-on scuffle with groans and grunts, with an occasional crash like one of them was being slammed into a wall.

I couldn't tell who was winning.

Should I go back up?

Should I find a weapon?

I was about to make a run for the police station when Chief Meyers appeared like magic. She didn't ask a single question, rather grabbed the door, put her hand on her holster for her gun, and took charge of the situation.

The next thing I knew, she was escorting a handcuffed Klaus down the stairs. Garrett came behind her, with one hand pinching his nose to stop it from bleeding.

Chief Meyers took Klaus outside while I went to check on Garrett. "Are you okay? You're bleeding."

He kept his head down and pressure on his nose. "It's just a bloody nose and a few bumps and bruises, but I'll be fine."

"Let me get you some tissues." I hurried to the kitchen to find Garrett something to help stop the bleeding and returned with a roll of paper towels. "Did he actually hit you?" I tore off a paper towel and handed it to him.

Garrett sat on the bottom step and soaked up the blood. "Yeah, but fortunately, he has terrible aim, so he just nicked me."

I sat next to him and put my hand on his knee. "I can't believe Klaus killed Josh. I wonder why. Do you think he was finally fed up with hikers like Josh?"

"I can answer that," Chief Meyers said, stepping inside. She assessed Garrett first. "Do you need medical attention?"

"No, it's stopping." He lifted his head to prove his point.

"Stay sitting and keep pressure on it," Chief Meyers directed. "How are you holding up, Sloan?"

"Fine. A little shaken, but fine."

"Good." She gave me a curt nod. "I suppose you two would like to hear what I know?"

"Yeah, I don't understand. We heard that Klaus kicked Josh out and they got in an argument. Was he fed up with the young tourists? Did Klaus snap?"

"It's more than that," Chief Meyers said. "That's where I've been all day. We were able to track Serena down. She's in Wenatchee. Speaking with her gave me a full picture. She shared a text exchange between her and Josh that he sent the night he was killed."

"I thought they weren't on speaking terms."

"They weren't, which is why she became concerned. Josh and Klaus were in talks to partner together on a revamp for the hostel. That's the real reason he was in town."

"Josh was the investor Klaus mentioned?" Garrett asked, pinching his nose tighter.

I handed him another paper towel and squeezed his knee tighter in a show of support. I felt terrible that he had gotten hurt, but it could have been much worse.

"Yes." Chief Meyers paced between the entryway and common area as she spoke. "Josh found a listing on a message board about The Gasthaus. He reached out to Klaus about the possibility of partnering. He was looking for more ways to expand his travel brand, and a youth hiking hostel sounded like a good fit. They made plans for Josh to come for the weekend to check out the village, the hiking trails, and the property, but according to the text thread we recovered from Serena's phone, Klaus grossly exaggerated the condition of the hostel. Once Josh saw how much work was going to be required to get the building up to code and up to the standards that aligned with his brand, he opted out. They didn't have a deal. There was nothing in writing. This was simply a visit to see if the partnership was going to be a match."

"And then Klaus lost it?" I asked.

"He had all of his eggs in the Josh basket. Not a wise move." She crossed her arms over her chest and shook her head. "He thought it was a sure thing. According to his bank statements, he had already made a down payment on beachfront property in Cozumel."

"Why would he kill Josh, though? Wouldn't it have been

wiser to try and convince him of The Gasthaus's potential?" Garrett asked.

"*Wiser* is the keyword." She gave Garrett a nod of acknowledgment. "When Josh informed him that he wasn't going to move forward with their partnership, Klaus threatened him. That's why Josh reached out to Serena. She was in Seattle preparing to hike Mount Rainier, but became so concerned that she took a bus to the village to try and find him. Klaus confronted him one last time, and when Josh continued to refuse, he turned violent. I don't think he intended to kill Josh, but that will be for a jury to decide."

"It's so awful and unnecessary."

"It's a real tragedy." Chief Meyers bowed her head. "I'm glad that I was already on my way here and that we have a suspect in custody, but it doesn't change the reality that a life was cut too short."

"So Klaus lied about seeing Harper in order to try and frame her?" I released my grasp on Garrett's leg.

"It's quite an interesting strategy, don't you think?" She shook her head and sighed. "I will need to take official statements from both of you, but for the time being, why don't you go get cleaned up and rest? I'll swing by Nitro later and take your statements there."

Garrett didn't put up a fight. We thanked her and walked hand in hand to the pub in quiet contemplation.

"What do you say, Sloan? Should we embrace the rest of the day? I'm personally feeling grateful to be here, alive with you." He stopped in the middle of the sidewalk, leaned in, and kissed me tenderly.

I kissed him back, lingering in his arms and the late afternoon sun.

Garrett finally pulled away. He tilted his head slightly, still maintaining eye contact, and smirked. Then he pointed to his injured nose. "There was talk of a chocolate torte if I remember correctly, and I'm fairly sure that the only way my face will feel better is with chocolate and a brew."

"I will raise a pint to that." I grinned and laced my hand through his again. When Mac and I were together, I couldn't stand his constant need for PDA, but something had changed with Garrett. I didn't mind his show of affection or stopping to kiss him on the sidewalk in front of the pretzel shop in broad daylight.

Maybe it was a sign of my progression into fully trusting myself. Or maybe it was true love. Either way, I wasn't going to spend any extra time analyzing or overthinking it. I was going to embrace it. Garrett was right. We were in the most charming town in the Pacific Northwest, surrounded by snow-capped mountains, blooming orchards, and a community of friends and family we loved.

Josh's death was a tragedy and served as a reminder that none of us were promised tomorrow.

So for now, I was going to get giant slices of the bakery's chocolate, almond, and apricot torte. Then we'd find a sunny spot on the patio where we'd share cake and frothy beers and celebrate simply being together. Because embracing this beautiful life was exactly what I intended to do.

ACKNOWLEDGMENTS

As always with any story (whether short or long or somewhere in between) I'm so grateful to my bookish circle for providing insight and help to make this novella stronger and for coming along on Sloan's journey. To the Tech Guy for his cover design, formatting, and all around tech expertise, plus those beer brainstorming sessions! To Raina Glazener for her copyediting expertise and fixing those pesky commas. To my ARC team on Patreon for giving this next installment of the Sloan Krause series a first look, with a special shoutout to Courtny Bradley and Lily-Ann Gill for our book chats and your humbling support.

Sloan has a special place in my heart, as do all of you. I'm raising a frothy pint in gratitude.

Cheers,

Ellie

A SLOAN KRAUSE MYSTERY SHORT

Ale
I Want for
Christmas
is a Clue

ELLIE ALEXANDER

AUTHOR OF BEER AND LOATHING

This book is dedicated primarily to you, with a little nod to TikTok. I know, stay with me on the TikTok part.

The truth is I wasn't sure I had time in my publishing schedule this year for the third Sloan Krause mystery short, but I've received so many letters, emails, and direct messages from you asking (sometimes very kindly begging) for another round of Sloan. It warms my heart to know that you love her and the entire Krause family as much as I do.

I've been wanting to set a story during the holiday markets in Leavenworth, and this seemed like the perfect opportunity. However, my writing schedule has been very tight this year, with some new projects debuting in 2024, an upcoming re-release of my first mystery series, and putting on the inaugural Ashland Mystery Fest this past October. I had sketched out a plot for a full-length Sloan Krause Mystery earlier in the year, but sadly, I knew there was no way I could pull it off.

Enter TikTok. I happened to be scrolling and stumbled upon a behind-the-scenes video of Taylor Swift where she talked about how it took her a week from start to finish to put out one of my all-time favorite holiday tunes, Christmas Tree Farm. I thought, hey, if Taylor can write, produce, record, and release a song in a week, I can write a holiday mystery short in six weeks.

I dusted off my original plot sketch, tweaked it for the holidays, and started the mad dash to get a rough draft ready. My fingers flew over the keyboard. Being back in Leavenworth with Sloan for the holiday season was a dream. I played Christmas Tree Farm on constant rotation, lit a Festive Fir candle so my office smelled like a snowy winter pine forest, and nibbled on German marzipans. The result is the story you're about to read. I hope it's a wonderful holiday escape for you.

Hoppy Holidays!
Ellie

CHAPTER
ONE

"Garrett, are you ready? We're going to be late." I hoisted a tub filled with *Zimtsterne*, a popular German Christmas cookie I had baked earlier in the day. The cinnamon stars were made from ground almonds, warming spices, and egg whites. Traditionally, they were topped with a sugary glaze, but I had slightly tweaked the recipe of Ursula, my former mother-in-law', and incorporated a splash of holiday chocolate stout. The result was a nutty cookie with a sweet and spicy finish. I had a feeling they would go fast at the holiday market tonight. But first, we had to get to the park to set up.

As if on cue, Garrett, my brewing partner and owner of Nitro, raced up to the bar, pulling a cable-knit sweater over his head. He smoothed down his wavy hair and shot me a sheepish grin. "Sorry, I lost track of time. The labels for the Merry Brew Year turned out so well." He reached into the back pocket of his jeans and held a label for me to examine.

Our Merry Brew Year was a collaboration with a nearby brewery in Wenatchee. We brewed a winter warmer together with caramel, toffee, cinnamon sticks, cloves, and apricots grown in the region. We were tapping the first keg tonight to kick off the holiday festivities.

The label had a retro vibe with clean mid-century modern artwork and bright pops of color. Garrett sketched a New Year's Eve scene with party hats, sparklers, and frothy pints of ale. Alex, my soon-to-be-college-student, had used Garrett's vision to create a sleek, digital image for the beer bottles and stickers.

"These are fantastic."

"Is Alex bringing stickers tonight?" Garrett tried to smooth down his unruly waves with his fingers.

"Yep. He'll meet us there." I glanced at the clock in the spacious tasting room. I loved everything about Nitro, from the exposed beam ceilings to the frost-coated front windows that looked out onto our village. The brewery was warm and inviting all year, but it was pure magic during the holidays. We had draped evergreen boughs intertwined with dried orange and lemon slices, cranberries, and rosemary sprigs around the long distressed wood bar and wrapped them around the windows and front door. Amber and gold candles sat at each high-top table, along with miniature bunches of winter flowers. But the showpiece was the holiday bottle tree Garrett had constructed from one thousand tawny beer bottles illuminated with fairy lights.

I caught a glimpse of my reflection in the shimmery bottles. My long brown hair was tied in a ponytail, and my olive skin was bright with color.

"We should get moving," I said to Garrett. "Kat's already there."

"After you, Ms. Krause," he replied with a playful wink, opening the door for me.

A blast of icy alpine air hit my face as we stepped outside. The snowplows had already made their way through the village, pushing growing mounds of fresh white powder onto either side of the street. Winter tended to be slower paced than the fall and summer in the high Northern Cascade Mountains, except this weekend—Christkindlmarkt.

Visitors from near and far would venture to our snowy getaway for a long weekend of holiday shopping at the outdoor markets designed to resemble an actual German village. Leavenworth was known for its half-timbered architecture, shingled rooftops, and cobblestone streets. The town that I called home had reinvented itself decades ago. Thanks to the jutting peaks that nestled our little town like a giant hug, every building along Front Street had been renovated in Baroque style. Throughout the year, we hosted full-fledged Bavarian celebrations complete with lederhosen, dirndls, polka bands, and dancing in the streets.

The holiday markets were the most popular events of the year. Attendance outpaced Oktoberfest, which was saying something because the beer-centric fall festival attracted thousands of visitors. Christkindlmarkt was a three-day holiday extravaganza that would begin tonight with the children's lantern parade. Children would decorate paper lanterns and parade down Front Street with their glowing lights, following Santa and Mrs. Claus to the gazebo, where they would greet kids with gingerbread cookies and candy canes. Ever since Alex was a toddler, the event had been my favorite part of the holiday season. The family-friendly weekend would feature authentic Bavarian food and beer, arts and crafts, gifts, music, and entertainment.

The energy was already palpable as Garrett and I navigated the frozen sidewalks and turned onto Front Street. Downtown was a sea of red, green, and gold. Illuminated stars and snowflakes hung from lampposts. Every building was decked out with colorful lights and handmade wreaths.

"Our stall is in Front Street Park, right?" Garrett asked as we crossed the street. The aroma of roasting chestnuts, sizzling sausages, and freshly baked gingerbread cookies wafted through the frigid air.

"Yes, I think we're supposed to be near the food tent." My stomach rumbled at the thought of food. I was suddenly famished. I'd spent the afternoon bouncing back and forth between baking cookies in Nitro's industrial kitchen and helping Kat manage the tasting room.

"First order of business, after we get the stall set up, is dinner, agreed?" Garrett asked, reading my mind.

"Absolutely." I grinned. Garrett and I had been getting closer, and the past few months felt like we were always in sync. He was so different than Mac, my husband of nearly twenty years. I appreciated that our relationship had begun with a friendship and continued to build from there slowly.

Dozens of temporary wooden market stalls had been constructed next to the gazebo in Front Street Park. Garlands and wreaths hung from archways. Red bows and ornaments dangled from the A-frame ski chalets. Everything looked like it was straight from the pages of a storybook.

A tingling spread through my body as I paused to take it all in.

Mulled wine, or *Glühwein*, bubbled in large cauldrons, infusing everything with the intoxicating fragrance of cinnamon and cloves. Each stall offered a dazzling array of unique goods that could never be found at a chain store— handcrafted wooden toys, porcelain ornaments, nutcrackers, pottery, scarves, mittens, wreaths, and winter floral arrangements.

The park was punctuated by a massive spruce Christmas tree adorned with shimmery white twinkle lights. Heart-shaped gingerbread cookies decorated with pink, green, and white icing and tied with ribbons dangled from the bakery stall. Musicians playing traditional carols warmed up their voices in the gazebo.

"Wow, this is something," Garrett said, whistling.

Kids in bright puffy jackets and stocking hats toted sleds up the small hill at the far end of the park where they had created miniature runs. Parents waited nearby with hot chocolate in hand.

"Pure magic," I agreed with a smile that evaporated as quickly as my breath in the cold evening air when I spotted April Ablin approaching us.

April was Leavenworth's welcome ambassador, a title she had given herself. As part of her self-appointed role, she made it her mission to ensure everyone adhered to her vision of the Bavarian aesthetic. Her current aesthetic was a vintage winter fur dress coat. The plush fabric was a deep forest green with furry cream trim with a matching shawl, bowknot, and fluffy pompoms. She looked like she was ready for a North Pole cosplay costume contest.

"Sloan, Garrett, *guten Abend*," she called in her signature nasally tone, sashaying through the crowd to reach us. "I thought you two would never show up. The lantern parade begins in less than thirty minutes. Did you receive my email?"

"Which one?" I asked in all sincerity. April constantly spammed our inboxes with lengthy, unnecessary messages.

She squeezed her candy apple red lips together and furrowed her brow. "Sloan Krause, tonight is not the night for you to take that tone with me. You know what email I'm referring to. The message clearly stated that every stall needs to be set up and ready for business by 5 p.m."

"Oh, that email. Right." I plastered on my most professional smile. Was it wrong that I took slight pleasure in making

April fume? "Well, good thing we have thirty minutes to prepare."

She puffed air from her nose like a racehorse waiting to flee the gate. "There's no need for sarcasm. This is the key event of the holiday season. Thousands of visitors will be in the village this weekend, and I want cheery smiles and a *das Willkommen* attitude. Is that clear?"

As usual, April butchered her German pronunciation and grammar. I didn't bother to correct her or pay any attention to commands. April had zero authority over anything we did. Not that we would be anything less than welcoming to our guests. Garrett and I and our small but mighty team at Nitro were buzzing with excitement, authentic excitement. Not April's superficial kindness. Her attempts to ingratiate herself with visitors were just a ploy for her gain.

Garrett deftly shifted the conversation. "Would you mind showing us where our stall is?"

April scoffed but puffed out her shawl and pointed toward the far end of the park. "Come on, it's this way."

I was tempted to stop at every booth we passed. The Kunst and Kaffee (or Art and Coffee) stall featured three holiday blends, each paired with intricately painted hand-crafted ceramic mugs.

"We're coming back for coffee later," I said to Garrett, inhaling the freshly brewed scent of dark roasts.

I waved to Greta Muller, who owned Botanic Oasis. Not surprisingly, the flower shop's booth was a sensory feast for the eyes. An archway of red roses strung together with euca-lyptus bunches and white heather sprigs invited visitors closer. A red and white striped awning provided shelter from the light snowfall. Wreaths made from winter herbs, twigs, and berries in varying sizes hung from the stall's wooden beams. Crates and barrels overflowed with an array of seasonal flowers and greenery.

"And for a few of those wreaths," Garrett added. "Those would be a nice addition to the windows."

"This way," April called, picking up her pace as we turned onto the second row of stalls.

A woodworking booth sat at the corner. I didn't know the crafter well. His name was Owen Kessler. Rumor had it that he moved to the village after making it big in Seattle's tech world. Hans, my former brother-in-law and found family, hadn't had great things to say about Owen.

Hans had a wood shop in the village where he produced custom furniture and art pieces. He went out of his way to introduce himself to Owen and offered to share any knowledge. Owen dismissed Hans and explained that he was a successful business owner, entrepreneur, and venture capitalist who needed no advice from a local woodworker. According to Owen, his goal was to scale up production of his ornaments and toys. Leavenworth was his testing ground for bigger and better endeavors.

Hans brushed it off, but Owen hadn't exactly endeared himself to the village.

Our stall was next to a pottery booth. It stood out with its natural, earthy designs. A potter's wheel sat in the booth's corner, where Pierce Wagner was molding a lump of clay into a beautiful bowl. "Hey, I hear we're going to be neighbors," he said, looking up without removing his hands from the mound of soft clay. "I hope that means I might get some Nitro samples."

"Count on it," Garrett replied. "Are you going to be demonstrating your pottery techniques tonight?"

"That's the plan." Pierce nodded to his treasure trove of handcrafted ceramics displayed on a long reclaimed-wood table. Vases, bowls, decorative tiles, mugs, plates, and ornaments in a variety of sizes were neatly arranged by design. Some of Pierce's pieces were glazed with deep, rich earth tones, while others were left natural to allow the clay to take center stage. "Everything you see there is for sale, but I thought it would be fun to throw a few pieces."

April cleared her throat loudly to interrupt. "You all can chitchat later, but you must get set up ASAP. We're in the countdown to the lantern parade." She practically pushed us forward.

I shot Pierce an apologetic smile. "Samples soon."

"Can I trust you to take it from here?" April said with an irritated sigh. "Also, is that what you're wearing tonight, Sloan?"

I set the tub of cookies on the table in our booth and pointed to my jacket. I had layered for the evening with thick leggings, my fur-lined boots, a fleece Nitro hoodie, a ski jacket, and gloves. "This, yeah."

She blew air between her lips like a motorboat. "You definitely did *not* read my email. I strictly noted that winter Bavarian attire was recommended."

"This is my winter Bavarian attire," I shot back. I was pouring beer. I certainly wasn't going to freeze my ass off in a barmaid's dress all night. The temp was already in the low thirties, and as soon as the sun sunk entirely behind the mountains, it would plummet even more. What I didn't say out loud is that April would be hard-pressed to find anyone living in Germany today wandering outside in the dead of winter in a skimpy dirndl.

"I suppose you're going to say the same thing, aren't you, Garrett?" April squinted at him, revealing glittery eyeshadow and fake rhinestone gems dotting either corner of her lids. I

212

hoped she used suitable makeup adhesive to stick on the faux jewels. If one slipped into her eye, it would really hurt.

"Yep. We're all about function. It's supposed to dip into the teens tonight. We can't very well pour beer if we can't feel our fingers." He wiggled his gloves and pulled up the edge of his cable-knit sweater to demonstrate his point. "Don't worry, though our Merry Brew Year will give people a true taste of Beervaria."

April rolled her eyes. "Whatever. I don't have time to deal with this. Just be ready for the market to open as soon as the parade is done."

She swept away like a queen getting ready to greet her loyal subjects.

"At least she's predictable," Garrett said after she was out of earshot. "But my God, how much money does that woman spend on fake German dresses?"

"I don't want to know." I chuckled. "I don't think I've ever seen her wear the same dress twice, so it has to be a small fortune."

We got to work setting up our chalet-style structure. I strung dried hops and twinkle lights around the peaked roofline while Garrett turned on the outdoor heaters. We wanted a warm, inviting space where people could linger and sip frothy pints. In addition to the Merry Brew Year, we would pour two Nitro classics—our hoppy Northwest-style IPA and a robust dark chocolate stout.

We would also sell my cookies, Nitro merch, and cans of our most popular ales. Garrett and I had a system down. We had done several festivals and had a permanent booth at the farmers market all summer, so despite April's warning, our space was sparkling and ready to go with plenty of time to spare before the parade commenced.

"That's a new record." Garrett's fist bumped me. "You know what that means? I think we need to tap the first keg."

"You won't get any argument on that from me."

As Garrett poured us samples of our winter collaboration, I spotted a group of familiar faces in the crowd coming toward us.

"Hey, Mom, everything looks great," Alex said, greeting me with a hug and a kiss on the cheek. He was accompanied by Hans, Mac, Ursula, and Otto. "I have stickers for you."

"*Ja*, it is lovely," Ursula agreed. "We wanted to say hi before the parade and bring zis for you both." She offered Garrett and me packages wrapped with pastry paper and tied with red and white string.

"Is this what I think it is?" I bit my bottom lip in anticipation.

Otto beamed with delight at his wife. "*Ja*, she has been baking all week." He rubbed his stomach. "I have been sampling so much I zink I might not need to eat for another week."

Ursula swatted him playfully. "Don't lie. You know you will finish off ze next loaf later tonight."

Garrett looked from me to Ursula. "I have no idea what this is, but my mouth is already watering. Should I open it now?"

"No. Save it for later. It is my Christmas Stollen. You can have it for breakfast in ze morning." She patted Garrett's arm. "I hope you like it. You will have to let me know what you zink, *ja*?"

"Of course, but I'm sure I'll love it."

My heart fluttered watching the interaction between the Krause family and Garrett. When Mac and I separated, losing Ursula, Otto, and Hans was my biggest fear. They had adopted me in my early twenties and made me part of their family. What I had come to realize was that the bonds we built ran deeper than marriage. They were all my family. We were teth-ered together with an invisible string. That was even true of Mac. Although we hadn't worked well as husband and wife, we were great parents to Alex and had started to carve out a genuine friendship in the last year.

My heart swelled. I fought back happy tears.

When I found Mac shagging the barmaid, I never would have imagined that this is where it would lead me. Sometimes, our setbacks and failures crack us open into who we are supposed to be. I couldn't believe it, but lately, I felt grateful to Mac instead of feeling angry or resentful. I had been compla-cent in our relationship, trading living authentically for the comfort and stability of a family. Now I understood I could have both. It was all possible.

"Mom, Mom, did you hear me?" Alex interrupted my thoughts.

I brushed away a tear and turned to him. "Sorry, what?"

"I asked if you wanted to see the sign. I did the digital design, and Uncle Hans carved it out of wood." He nudged Hans. His latest growth spurt had put him on equal eye level with his uncle.

Hans reached behind his back. "Should we do a drum roll, Alex?"

Alex strummed his hands on his jeans.

Hans pulled a sign made from rustic barn wood from behind his back. It was decorated with atomic stars and hop cone garland and read: POURING CUPS OF HOLIDAY CHEER.

"That's perfect." Garrett clapped. "You know how much I love a beer pun."

"Alex gets all the credit." Hans passed the sign to Garrett and ruffled Alex's head. "I think this kid has a future in design."

"Or beer," Mac interjected.

I was about to step in because I could tell Alex was uncomfortable. He'd been quiet about his college decision, and I didn't want to add any extra pressure.

But the sound of shouting and shattering pottery made us all stop and turn toward Pierce's booth.

Owen Kessler towered over the pottery booth, holding a massive vase over his head. He looked like he was auditioning for the role of Sasquatch with his huge black jacket and work boots. "Are you going to tell everyone what you've done, or should I break another?"

"Put that down." Pierce jumped to his feet, sending the wet clay on his wheel flying in every direction.

"I dare you to come closer," Owen said, hoisting the vase higher.

"Put the vase down, or else you will regret it."

"Am I, Pierce? I don't think so. I know your little secret, and soon, this entire town will too." Owen released his grip on the vase. It fell to the ground and smashed into pieces. He swiped something from the table, stuffed it in his pocket, brushed his hands together, and casually strolled away.

"What was that all about?" Garrett asked what I knew we were all wondering.

Pierce ran to the front of his booth and began picking up shards of broken pottery. Alex, Hans, and Mac immediately joined in to help.

"Sorry about that," Hans said, piling pieces in a stack. "I've met with Owen a couple of times, and he can be intense, but I've never seen him do something like this."

"This is nothing," Pierce said, seething with rage. "He's done much worse than break a couple pieces of my pottery, but I'm putting an end to it tonight. Owen Kessler has to be stopped."

My stomach lurched like I'd sampled an overly fermented beer.

"Take a deep breath," Hans suggested, modeling calm breathing for Pierce. "He's trying to get a reaction out of you."

"He got a reaction out of me alright, and he's going to seriously regret that." Pierce wiped wet clay on his apron. "Owen better stay far away from me tonight. Because let me tell you, if he so much as puts a pinky finger on another piece of my pottery, I will kill him."

TWO

IT TOOK a minute to get Pierce to calm down. The vase and bowl Owen had broken were beyond repair. Hans and Alex tossed the fragments into the trash. Mac procured a broom and dustpan and swept up any remaining bits. I felt terrible for Pierce, not just because of his ruined ceramics but also because his exchange with Owen was a terrible way to start an evening of what should be merriment.

Garrett poured tasting samples for everyone. "How about a sample of Merry Brew Year to cleanse our palates?"

Pierce took his glass but declined Garett's attempt at a toast to try and lighten the mood.

Ursula, Otto, and Mac complimented us on flavor profiles and tasting notes but had to get back to Der Keller before the parade began. Alex and Hans hung the sign and helped us finish setting out pint glasses and stickers for purchase.

"Sorry to ditch you all, but I have to get to the train station," Hans said, checking his watch. "Leah gets in shortly. Are you still up for dinner later, though?"

"Any chance to see my sister is a yes," Garrett replied, clapping Hans on the back.

Leah, Garrett's younger sister, and Hans met last winter when she visited the village for a week of skiing and adventure. She and Hans hit it off instantly and had been dating long-distance ever since. Although that was due to change shortly. Leah had been offered a job at Leavenworth Community Hospital and would be permanently moving at the end of the year. She'd been looking at apartments and little cottages for rent, but as she and Hans continued to deepen their connection, I wondered if things might be getting much more serious. I certainly wouldn't be disappointed with a winter Leavenworth wedding. Not that I'd been hinting as much to Hans or anything.

He'd been tight-lipped about his intentions, but it was clear that the two of them were well-matched. They were also both in their forties. They'd had careers and dated previously. While they hadn't known each other long, something about the timing felt synchronistic. They knew what they were looking for and had found that in each other.

"Do you care if I go find my friends?" Alex asked. "I'm off from Der Keller tonight, but I can stay if you need help with the booth."

"No, we're fine. Go have fun," I said, waving him off. "Should I Venmo you dinner money?"

"Mom, I'm a working guy now. I've got plenty of cash." He rubbed his fingers together like he was holding a stack of bills. "Well, technically not cash, because who has cash but money in the bank."

"But you're going to college soon. Here's a tip: let your parents pay whenever they offer." Garrett winked.

"Yeah, good point." Alex laughed. "Venmo me all your money, Mom."

He took off. We listened while April announced that the parade would start in five minutes. Gaggles of youngsters carrying illuminated paper lanterns wound their way toward the Maipole.

"This was always my favorite part when Alex was little," I said to Garrett, hearing the touch of nostalgia in my voice.

He wrapped a protective arm around my shoulder, pulled me closer, and kissed the top of my head. "Time marches on, doesn't it?"

"It does." I felt my throat start to tighten. Alex would be gone in a few months, off to college to carve his own path. I was ready for him, but I wasn't so sure if I was ready for me. "It's so bittersweet. On the one hand, I wouldn't want to be back in the throes of the toddler years. It was exhausting. But on the other hand, I miss it so much."

"Spoken like every parent I know," Garrett replied, massaging my shoulder.

"I'm glad to be here with you now. I know I already said it, but it's magic."

"You're magic, Sloan." Garrett's voice rumbled low with emotion.

I leaned into him, happy to be able to steal a moment together. We stood with our arms wrapped around each other, watching lanterns flicker on Front Street like fireflies. The high school band marched, playing upbeat renditions of holiday classics. Santa and Mrs. Claus led the parade to the Festhalle, where the Christkindl would welcome everyone with a special treat.

The Christkindl is an angel-like creature with blond hair and wings who visits German families on Christmas Eve, bringing them gifts. Much like America's Santa Claus, the Christkindl makes appearances at the holiday markets in

Germany, poses for pictures with children, and receives letters detailing their wish lists.

People began spilling into the market as soon as the parade was underway. The next few hours passed in a blur. Garrett and I poured tasting samples and full pints and packaged gift boxes of six packs and Nitro merch. The atmosphere was lively. Laughter filled the crisp night air as groups congregated by our booth, clinking glasses and sharing memories of holidays long gone. I loved that Nitro was a central hub for those seeking camaraderie and warmth. The beer flowed, and my cookies vanished.

Kat and two of our volunteers came to relieve us. We relied heavily on volunteers for festivals like this. They poured beer for a few hours in exchange for free pints and food at the end of their shift. It was a win-win for everyone.

"Are you ready for a break?" Kat asked, tugging on a pair of red and green fingerless gloves. "Or maybe I should ask if there's any beer left to serve. Everyone seems to have a Nitro stein in their hands."

"I just changed the keg," Garrett said as he twisted the temporary tap handle. "But this is the last one we brought over, so when it blows, that's it for the night."

"Got it." Kat bobbed her bouncy curls, pinned back from her apple-shaped face with two bejeweled barrettes. "You two go have fun. We'll keep the taps flowing."

I grabbed my bag and waited for Garrett. "Text if you need anything. We won't be far. My first stop is going to be for a brat."

"Be sure you try the brown sugar and black currant coffee at Kunst and Kaffee." Kat pressed her fingers to her lips and blew a kiss. "It's amazing—chef's kiss. We should see about doing a partnership with them. It would be the ideal winter coffee for our B and B guests."

"You had me at coffee," I teased. "We'll check it out, and I'll talk to Blake about the potential of wholesaling or doing a special Nitro blend. That's a great idea."

We left the booth in Kat's capable hands. She had become an integral part of our small team, and I appreciated that she was always thinking about ways to expand and partner with the local business community. When Garrett inherited his Great Aunt Tess's historic inn and diner, he tore down most of the original interior, leaving the commercial kitchen intact and ignoring any changes to the second floor until he got the brewery up and running.

Last year, we invested in remodeling four guest rooms upstairs. Each was themed after a key ingredient in hops—water, yeast, grain, and hops. We opened the rooms for overnight beer tourists. They could stay in a working brewery, receive private tours of the facility, special tastings, and a full farm-style breakfast, with a little splash of beer mixed into German pancake batter or chocolate waffles.

"Where to first, Sloan?" Garrett asked, interlacing his fingers between mine. Even though we were both wearing gloves, a shot of electric energy ran up my arm. Garrett majored in chemistry in college. Sometimes, I wondered if he had secretly discovered a way to bottle up the elements because my body constantly wanted to draw close to his, like two super-charged magnets refusing to be torn apart.

"The line for brats looks long," I said, nodding in that direction. "Why don't we try Kat's recommendation and grab a coffee? That way, it will keep our hands warm while we wait in line for food."

"It's a plan." He squeezed my hand tighter.

Kunst and Kaffee was located in a charming wooden kiosk that, like Nitro, resembled a mountain chalet. The façade was decorated with strings of gingerbread garland and fairy lights.

The roof was dusted with a light layer of snow. I could smell the booth from a few feet away. The familiar scent of richly brewed coffee and warming spices made my stomach rumble again.

Blake Schmidt, the owner, stood behind the stall, diligently crafting espressos and *Milchkaffee*, or coffee with milk. She was new to Leavenworth. She opened the art and coffee shop this past summer, blending her love of painting and ceramics with her knowledge of coffee. The shop offered coffee and paint nights and latte art classes. I wasn't great at guessing ages, but Blake was probably in her early thirties. It was nice to see younger entrepreneurs opting to make Leavenworth their home.

"*Frohe Weihnachten!*" Blake greeted us with flawless German. "What can I pour for you?" She used a carving knife to shave ribbons of chocolate from a large block.

"Everyone is raving about your black currant and brown sugar blend," I said, releasing my grasp on Garrett's hand.

Blake topped a hot chocolate with a mound of whipping cream, chocolate shavings, and red and green sprinkles. She handed it to a customer and wiped her hands on her red and white dirndl apron, which matched her cozy après ski sweater. "Oh no, now I hope it lives up to the hype."

A small chalkboard menu listed drink specials—a gingerbread latte, German chocolate mocha, and cinnamon and nutmeg cappuccino.

"Oh, yeah, I should have said we also have specials for the market." Blake noticed me studying the menu. "Would you like one of those instead?"

"No, I'll stick with a cup of your holiday house blend," I replied.

Garrett held up his fingers. "Two, please."

Blake's cheerful smile disappeared as she poured our

drinks. She stared behind us like an animal that had been cornered. Her eyes bulged with fear.

I turned my head in the direction of her gaze and spotted Owen. He propped his back against a candle booth and glared at Blake, making a slicing motion across his neck.

Blake lost focus. Instead of pouring the coffee into mugs, she spilled it on the counter and her arm. "Ouch. Damn. That's hot. I think I burned myself." She dropped the carafe and clutched her arm in pain.

"You should run it under cold water right away," I urged, feeling my first-aid instincts kicking in. Running a nano brewery required being trained in first aid and CPR.

She winced and gnawed on the inside of her cheek. "Uh, yeah, right." She turned on the compartment sink, rolled up her sweater sleeve, and held her arm beneath the stream.

"Keep it there." I turned to Garrett. "Should I run to find the paramedics?"

Blake stole a glance in Owen's direction. I turned in time to see him repeat the same menacing gesture and walk away, keeping his gaze narrowed on Blake.

What was that about?

Was he trying to intimidate her?

Did he have some kind of vendetta against the holidays? First smashing Pierce's pottery, now threatening Blake.

"No, no, I think it will be fine," Blake responded, closing her eyes and biting her tongue.

Obviously, it wasn't fine.

"I think it's smarter to have a professional take a look. A coffee burn is nothing to mess around with." I made an executive decision.

Garrett gave me a nod of approval. "I'll wait here with her."

Blake tried to protest, but I took off before she could say anything else. The coffee was steaming hot. She could end up with a second or third-degree burn, which definitely needed medical attention. I'd seen an emergency services tent listed on the map, except it happened to be on the opposite side of the market. I retraced my steps, but as I passed Botanical Oasis, I stopped in my tracks.

Greta Muller held Owen Kessler by one arm, trying to yank him into her booth. "Owen, please, please. I'm begging you. Don't do it. I'll do anything. *Anything*. Please."

Owen shrugged her off. "It's already done, Greta. Get over it."

Greta crumpled into a ball, her shoulders deflating like the air out of a balloon. "Owen, you're going to ruin the holidays and my entire life."

"Then, I suggest you get a life, Greta." Owen yanked free from her and stormed away to the food tent.

I didn't have time to linger long enough to console Greta, but I tapped the edge of her booth. "Listen, I need to get the paramedics, but then I'll come back. You're going to be okay, right?"

She managed to nod, but it was far from convincing. "Yeah. I mean, my life is over, but sure, I'll be fine."

THREE

It was clear that Greta wasn't okay emotionally, but Blake's injury required immediate attention. "I promise I'll be right back," I told Greta in my most calming mom voice. "Why don't you sit down in the food tent? Maybe have something warm to drink. Take a minute for yourself."

"What about my booth? I can't sell flowers like this." Greta sniffled and wiped her nose on the sleeve of her sweater. Then she balled her hand up into a fist and smashed it into her jaw like she was trying to hurt herself.

Fortunately, there was a lull in the crowd as the mayor took the stage in the gazebo to read a collection of German Christmas tales.

"Put up a sign that says back in a few minutes. Everyone will understand." I couldn't wait around any longer. "There's been an injury. I need to get the paramedics, and then I'll come help with the booth, okay?"

She sucked air through her nose and shook her head in agreement.

That was good enough for me. I sprinted to the EMS tent.

The medical team acted promptly, grabbing first aid supplies and following me back to the coffee stall. Blake was still running water over the burned area. An angry, large red welt appeared on her forearm. I was glad that the professionals were taking over. We waited while they tended the burn, bandaging it and giving Blake strict after-care instructions.

"I can't believe I did that," she said once the paramedics left.

"It is excruciating?" I asked, already guessing the answer.

"It's a little better now." Her eyes creased with pain.

"Should you continue working?" Garrett sounded doubtful.

"They said I'm fine. I need to follow up with my regular doctor if there are any signs of infection; otherwise, it will just need time to heal. They said it's a bad first-degree burn. It could have been much worse if it wasn't for my thick ski sweater." She touched the stained sleeve above her bandage.

"I'm glad to hear that," I said truthfully. I wanted to ask her about the exchange I'd witnessed between her and Owen, but I needed a casual way to bring it up. "Did the coffee pot slip?"

"Huh?" She scrunched her face in confusion.

"I wondered if the pot slipped out of your hand." I pointed to the counter where coffee had splattered everywhere.

"Oh. Um, yeah." She grimaced. She clearly had a limited range of motion as she tried to pick up a dish towel. "It must have. I should have been more careful."

"It must be distracting," I said, hoping to make her comfortable. "There were so many people in line at our stall earlier that I could barely keep up. I'm surprised we're not both covered in beer."

"Better beer than hot coffee," Garrett added.

"Yeah, well, I'm an idiot," Blake said, shaking her head in disgust. "I know better. I don't know how I did that."

I did. She was distracted by Owen making a threatening gesture at her.

Was there a reason she was keeping that part of the story to herself?

She poured two fresh coffees, guarding her injury by holding her arm close to her body. "Sorry about that again, and thanks for your help. I hope you enjoy this one. Like you heard, it's a dark roast with heavy black currant undertones and a brown sugar finish."

Garrett lifted his cup to mine. We both sipped the coffee. It was delicately balanced with a robust and bold jolt followed by a light and sweet finish.

"This is fantastic. No wonder Kat wants to brew this for our B and B guests." Garrett licked his lips.

"Your B and B guests?" Blake perked up. Her skin flushed, and tiny pearls of sweat beaded on her forehead.

"We don't have to go into detail tonight, but we're interested in serving this at Nitro." I took another sip of the coffee.

"That would be amazing. Yes. Count me in." She fidgeted, trying to find a comfortable way to hold her arm. "I've been wanting to expand business partnerships, and to have Nitro as my first would be incredible. I could really use the exposure and extra cash. I didn't realize how much cash I would be bleeding out this first year. They say to expect not to make any money until year three, but I guess I didn't anticipate that I would be losing so much money."

"Running a small business is not for the faint of heart," Garrett replied. "If you ever need help or insight into managing festival season versus the off-season in Leavenworth, please stop by the pub. Sloan and I would be happy to lend any insight."

"Absolutely," I agreed. Otto and Ursula welcomed me into the village nearly two decades ago and taught me everything they knew about brewing. I tried to pay that forward whenever I could.

"Thanks. I should probably get this mess cleaned up," Blake mopped up spilled coffee with a towel.

"Take it easy, and let's touch base soon about a Nitro breakfast blend." I raised my cup in thanks.

"That burn looked bad," Garrett said as we walked away.

"I hope she listens to the paramedics. I know I tend to go into mom mode, but I'm worried about it getting infected and her continuing to work tonight."

"It sounds like maybe she needs the cash," Garrett made room for a group of elves lugging skis and snowboards to pass by. "I didn't realize that she was struggling."

"Neither did I." I waved to a couple of Alex's friends, whom I recognized. The high school was hosting a costume contest at the ski hill later.

"We'll have to make a point to follow up on coffee and see if we can do anything to help her get through winter. I hope she knows how quiet January and February can be."

As a local, I looked forward to the calmer, snowier winter months when the village glowed under thousands of twinkle lights and a swath of stars. Visitors came on the weekends to ski and snowshoe, but the winter crowds paled compared to Maifest or Oktoberfest. The slower season was a time for us to regroup, do basic repairs and maintenance, and have a little reprieve from the constant influx of tourists. However, as a business owner, it was critical to plan for the downturn. Cash flow could quickly become a problem. Over the years, I'd seen too many businesses fail to prepare for the off-season and have to shutter their doors by spring. I didn't want that to happen to Blake.

"So, brats?" Garrett asked.

The line had thinned a little. "Sure, but first, I need to run and check on Greta."

"Greta? From the flower shop? Don't tell me tonight all of the vendors are accident-prone, and she stabbed herself with cutting sheers."

"No, nothing that serious. She was upset with Owen when I ran by her stall to get help for Blake. I promised her I would check in once I knew that Blake was okay." I wrapped my gloves tighter around the coffee cup. The heat was welcome as snowfall began to pick up.

"I'll wait in line while you speak with Greta. If I'm done first, I'll meet you in the food tent."

"Have I told you lately that you're the best?" I met his eyes, feeling a familiar tug pulling me to him.

He raised an eyebrow and gave me a mischievous grin. "No. You should probably tell me again. Or maybe show me later."

"Deal." I kissed him on the cheek and went to find Greta.

When I got to her booth, I found the note explaining she was on a break and would return soon. I was glad that she had taken my advice and opted to take some time to compose herself.

Snow fell in heavy clumps and blew sideways. People took cover under the tents in the park. None of the kids sledding down the hill seemed to mind. They cheered with delight, sticking their tongues out to catch the wet flakes.

I spotted Greta near the stage at a table in the farthest corner of the food tent. She was deep in conversation with Owen again. I couldn't make out what they were saying over the sound of the carolers, the delighted screams on the sledding hill, and the crowd's chatter, but it was evident from their body language that the conversation wasn't going well.

Greta tugged on Owen's jacket, dragging him away from the tent.

Owen yanked free.

She dropped to the ground and latched her arms around his leg like a toddler.

He shook her off and then gave her a gaze as frigid as the night, freezing everything in its path with its glacial indifference.

Greta gave up, releasing her grasp and wailing as Owen strolled toward the stage as if nothing had happened.

What was going on between the two of them?

Greta didn't move. She remained crumpled on the snow-packed ground, rocking back and forth on her knees. Seeing her crying while groups of friends and strangers around her swayed in unison, pint glasses in hand, none the wiser, was a strange juxtaposition. Their movements synchronized to the music gave the impression of a communal dance. Laughter and clinking glasses drowned out the sound of her tears.

I hurried over to her. "Greta, are you okay?"

Her cheeks were puffy and splotched with color like an overly toasted marshmallow. "No, I'm awful. This is the worst night of my life."

The icy snow cut through my leggings as I bent down beside her. "Because of Owen? Do you want to talk about it?"

Her quick, shallow breaths sounded like a car engine struggling to start. "There's nothing to talk about. Owen ruined my life, and now my only choice is to ruin his."

FOUR

I'D SPENT enough time in breweries to have heard it all. A beertender is part beer expert and part therapist. "Why don't we have a seat? I know it might not seem like it in this moment, but talking about our trauma always helps." I was speaking from a place of truth. Growing up in the foster care system forced me to armor up from a young age. I'd learned to conceal my feelings and stuff my emotions as a coping strategy. But over the years, I also knew it was a strategy that didn't serve me.

"Talking about it won't help," Greta sniffled. "Owen did this to me. He's enjoying every minute of seeing me like this."

I didn't mention that Owen had moved over by the Christmas tree, where he was chatting with someone I didn't recognize. Unless he was a gifted actor, he seemed to pay no notice to Greta.

"Would it be better if we went to your booth? I'd be happy to help you close it up for the evening."

"Do you think I should close it?" Her wide, oval eyes filled with more tears. "I guess you're right. How am I going to be functional with customers when I can't stop crying?"

"It's your call. I can also help run the register if you want to keep it open." What I was trying to imply was that shivering on the snowy ground wasn't doing either of us any good.

"Okay, yeah. Let's go to my booth. At least that way, I won't have to lay my eyes on Owen. If I never see Owen Kessler again, that will be fine by me." She clutched her hands into tight fists as she stood up. "In fact, I hope he skis off a cliff this weekend and plummets to his death."

That was a strong reaction, but I chose to ignore it. Greta was in emotional distress and probably didn't realize what she was saying. I stood, too. My coffee had gone cold, and Garrett was probably already heading in this direction with brats hot off the grill, but I didn't want to leave Greta alone. She was obviously in no shape to be alone.

"Thanks for being so nice to me," she said through chattering teeth. "I can't believe this is happening here—now—tonight. This was supposed to be a great evening. I spent the week preparing dozens of wreaths and holiday bouquets. If I don't sell everything, it's all going to go to waste, so I should probably just suck it up and finish the night. Owen is dead to me anyway."

"It's your call. You tell me what you need, and I'll jump in."

She wiped her eyes with her finger, smudging her mascara. "No, forget him. He's an ass. I'm not going to let him ruin the night. This is the holiday market."

Her tone shifted dramatically. It was like I was witnessing her go through the stages of grief instantaneously.

"You know, whatever. Never mind." She stopped in mid-stride. "Thank you for everything, but I don't need any help. I'm fine. I will get back at Owen the best way possible—through my bank account."

"Are you sure?" I didn't think she was being honest with me. Was it because she didn't want to bother me? Given how distraught she'd been, I hated just leaving her alone.

"Yes. Really, thank you, but you should go enjoy your night." She lifted her hands, encouraging me to go.

"Okay." I hesitated. Greta was a grown woman. If she didn't want my help, I wasn't going to force it. "Two things, though. Will you set aside a few of the miniature wreaths for me? We want to hang them at the pub."

"Sure. It's the least I can do." She smiled through her clenched jaw. "What else?"

I touched the base of my eye. "Your mascara is smeared."

"Thank you. I wouldn't want to look like a raccoon for the rest of the evening." She dabbed her finger on her tongue and wiped her eye. "Thanks again, Sloan, and I'll have the wreaths waiting for you."

She continued without me.

I watched her turn down the first row of stalls. I thought about following after her but decided against it. She would figure it out, and it was evident that her sadness about whatever had transpired between her and Owen had morphed into anger. It was better to let her deal with that in whatever way was best for her.

"Sloan, hey, good timing." Garrett caught up with me, balancing a tray of grilled brats, red cabbage, and German potato salad.

"You went for the works." I swiped a bite of potato salad with my fingers.

"I don't know about you, but I'm famished."

"Same." I fell into stride with him.

"How did it go with Greta?"

"She and Owen got into it again. I don't know anything

about their relationship. She didn't want to talk about it, but I think she's calmed down. She went back to her booth. I asked her to hold onto a few wreaths for us. We can pick them up on our way out."

"Perfect." He nodded to an empty table near the back of the tent. "Is this good?"

"Perfect." We enjoyed our meal, demolishing our food in companionable silence. I hadn't realized just how hungry I was or how grateful my feet were for a break at the end of a long day.

"You ready for another round and some dessert?" Garrett asked, resting his fork next to his empty plate and starting to get up.

"Yeah, but you stay. I'll run and grab us a couple of pints."

"I can get us drinks," he protested.

"No, you already got dinner; I'll run over to the Der Keller tent and be right back." The Der Keller beer tent was adjacent to the entertainment stage. Instead of walking around the tent, I took a shortcut through the back. I squeezed past the Christmas tree, stuffing my fingers in my ears as I hurried by the speakers and ducked out behind the stage. There was less light on the back side of the tent, so I pulled out my phone and used my flashlight app to guide me.

I tripped on what I assumed to be a pinecone and nearly landed on the ground. I caught my footing at the last minute, but my phone went flying.

It landed nearby, screen-side up, which was lucky.

As I bent over to pick it up, I noticed what looked like a pair of boots a couple of feet away. I wiped my phone on my jacket sleeve and positioned the light on the boots.

There was a body in the pair of boots.

And a body.

Not just any body, but Owen Kessler.

He lay face up with a carving knife stabbed in the middle of his forehead.

FIVE

I FROZE MOMENTARILY before something instinctual kicked in.

"Owen, are you okay?" I bent down to check for any vital signs. I thought I could feel the faintest hint of a pulse in his neck. Blood oozed from his forehead and dribbled onto the crystalized white snow.

I needed help—now.

Without thinking, I left him on the ground and sprinted to the paramedic tent.

"Do you need a frequent customer punch card?" The paramedic who had assisted Blake earlier teased, sipping a mug of hot chocolate. Her smile quickly turned serious when she saw my face.

"It's Owen Kessler," I gasped, clutching my stomach. "He's been stabbed."

The team abandoned their hot cocoas and gingerbread cookies and sprinted after me. It took less than a minute to get to Owen.

"Should I call 911?" I asked, watching the first responders spring into action.

"Yes. Tell them to send everyone."

The pool of blood near Owen's head spread out like a crimson flower blossoming in the snow.

I spoke to the dispatcher as the emergency crew assessed Owen's condition. They didn't attempt to remove the knife speared in his forehead, but they did start rescue breathing.

"Does he have a pulse?" I asked, repeating questions from dispatch. My fingers were going numb. I tried to wiggle them to keep blood flowing, but I had a feeling it had as much to do with seeing Owen cling to life as it did with the cold.

"Yes, but it's weak. He's not breathing, and he's lost a lot of blood." The paramedics lifted his body onto a gurney. "We need to transport him now. A wound like this can be fatal."

I had expected as much, but hearing it confirmed made my legs feel wobbly. The snowfall that had seemed charming only a while ago suddenly felt ominous and sinister. A pervasive cold came over me. I couldn't stop shivering. My tongue felt gummy, and my extremities stung.

Time crept to a slow crawl.

Garrett would be calling out a search party for me soon.

The wail of sirens cut through the lively music and holiday carols. I wasn't sure how long I'd been gone, but I was relieved to see Chief Meyers approaching us with two police officers. More first responders marched in a neat line behind her, each with their flashlights pointed at us.

I shielded my eyes from the light and tried to stay out of the way while Chief Meyers asked the paramedics for a report as they began transporting Owen to an ambulance waiting nearby.

The sirens and lights must have alerted attendees that something was wrong because a small crowd began to form around us.

Chief Meyers took charge. "Folks, we're going to need you to clear the perimeter. Please give us some privacy."

She had a naturally commanding presence. Chief Meyers had been in Leavenworth as long as me, and I had come to appreciate her direct approach to community policing. She wasn't one for long chats or warm and fuzzy conversations, but she truly cared about keeping the village safe and connected.

After completing her preliminary scan of the crime scene, she approached me. "Sloan, I hear you found him, and you know him. Is that correct?"

"Yes. Although not well. It's Owen Kessler. He moved to the village early last year and opened a wood studio next to the Nutcracker Museum."

"I've heard the name but never met him." She unzipped her brown police jacket that hung almost to her knees and removed a small yellow legal pad. "Can you walk me through exactly what happened? You found him, is that right? What time was that? Anything else of importance."

"Of course." I replayed leaving Garrett in the entertainment tent and exiting out the back.

"Why did you leave through that exit?" She asked, waiting, ready to make a note.

"I guess laziness. I knew it was a shortcut, and had already been a long night."

"Can you elaborate on why it's been a long night?"

I told her about Blake's burn and Greta's breakdown.

"And both women had exchanges with Owen before you discovered him, correct?" Her sheriff's badge glinted as an officer passed us with their flashlight propped on their shoulder.

"Yes. And, actually, even before that, there was another

incident with Pierce Wagner. Owen smashed two of Pierce's pottery pieces."

Chief Meyers had a solid poker face, but I caught a slight raise of her eyebrows. "Here at the market?"

"In front of everyone." I gestured in that direction. "He picked up a large vase and smashed it on the ground."

"Hmm. It seems I'm adding Pierce Wagner to my person of interest list." She motioned to the body. "Do you recognize the knife?"

The knife impaled in his skull?

I wanted to tell her that I'd gone out of my way to avoid getting a close look at the resulting gash, but instead, I shook my head. "No. Although since this is a craft fair, there are several artists with tools like that."

She made another note, then she tucked the notebook into her interior coat pocket. "Thank you for the information, Sloan. It's helpful. I'll be in touch should I have further questions, and since Nitro is likely to be busy over the weekend, do let me know if you hear anything else that you think could be pertinent to the investigation."

"Of course." I nodded solemnly. "Do you have any idea if he's going to make it?"

She frowned and gave her head a slight shake. "He's been grievously wounded, and as I'm sure you noticed, he lost a substantial amount of blood. It's good you found him when you did. If he has a chance of survival, it's thanks to you."

My hand instinctively went to my heart as I let out a sigh. "Hopefully, the emergency room doctors will be able to save him."

"Agreed." She gave me a two-fingered salute. "I'll be in touch."

I took a second to try and center myself before returning to the festivities.

Garrett was waiting for me where I'd left him. He pushed back the bench and stood up, reaching for my hand. "Are you okay? We heard that there was an accident. I was so worried."

"No, it's not me. I'm fine." I stared at my hands, which wouldn't stop shaking.

He blew out a long breath and patted his chest. "That's a huge relief. You left and then didn't come back, and then I heard the police sirens, but they wouldn't let us get any closer. Rumors are flowing faster than an open keg. Someone said there's a body behind the tent, but that can't be true."

My legs quaked. I needed to sit—now.

I slumped onto the bench. "The rumors are true. It's Owen Kessler. They don't know if he's going to make it."

"Sloan, no." Garrett gasped and sat next to me. He removed his glove, then mine, and began caressing my fingers.

His touch was like a grounding force, tethering me to the earth and bringing me back into reality.

"It's all a haze, but I went out the back by the stage to get our beers. It's really dark on that side of the tent since all the activity is in the market." I nodded in the opposite direction. "I dropped my phone and then realized that Owen was lying on the ground."

Garrett held my hand tighter. "You don't need to talk about it right now if you don't want to."

"No, it's good. I've got to move this energy out of my body." I took a sip of air through my nose for courage and continued. "It wasn't pretty. He was stabbed in the head with a carving knife. There was a lot of blood."

"That's awful."

It certainly wasn't the sweet holiday image I wanted replaying in my mind.

"I assume Chief Meyers is here?" Garrett asked.

"Yeah, she's on the scene now. They've secured the area. I

gave her my statement." My eyes drifted to the children's choir taking the stage. This couldn't be happening. How was it possible that Owen had been stabbed?

"Does she have any ideas who did it?"

I shook my head. "No, but I have three potential suspects based on what we've observed tonight—Pierce, Blake, and Greta."

"Doesn't Blake have knives like that for cutting slices of her pastries?"

"Exactly. And I saw her and Owen have an intense interaction before she burned herself. I'm convinced that he's the reason she spilled the coffee."

"Why?" Garrett studied my face with interest.

"He was standing a few feet away from her stall and made a slicing motion across his neck twice. I think he was threatening her, but I have no idea why. Right after that, she was distracted and dumped the coffee on her arm. I don't know what was happening between them, but I think we should try to find out more."

"You think Blake could have attacked him?" Garrett asked what I had wondered since I first spotted Owen sprawled out on the snow.

"I don't know, but it's a possibility."

CHAPTER
SIX

"WHAT ABOUT SOME delicious apple strudel? Would that help?" Garrett asked, waving his hand over a tray of dessert. "Maybe you can try and eat something before we do anything else."

"I'll try a bite, but honestly, I'm not sure I'm going to be able to stomach food yet. I'm pretty shaken up."

"What about a beer?" Garrett asked. "Would a hoppy pint help take the edge off?"

"I'll pass on that too." My hands continued to quiver.

Garrett handed me a slice of the flaky apple strudel. I tried a couple of bites, but my appetite had vanished. I couldn't stop replaying the picture of Owen's bloody body surrounded by the pristine white snow. Who would attack someone at a festive holiday market?

Owen hadn't been the most personable guy, but that didn't mean he deserved to be gravely injured.

Pierce seemed like the most obvious suspect. Owen had caused a scene and ruined Pierce's art in front of a crowd. Pierce had threatened to kill Owen. I hadn't taken it seriously then, but maybe I should have.

Greta was also a viable suspect. She had been hysterical both in trying to force Owen not to leave and then falling apart when he did. I didn't understand the dynamics of their relationship, but her emotional response made me wonder if she could have stabbed him in a fit of rage or passion. Then there was Blake. Whatever had transpired between her and Owen hadn't been positive. The knife that injured him could have come from her booth, but that could also mean that dozens of shoppers at the market could have done it.

"You're barely touching your dessert," Garrett noted.

"I can't eat." I pushed the plate away. "Not now. Could we walk around for a while? I'd like to speak with Blake. Maybe moving will burn some of my adrenaline off."

"Whatever you want to do." Garrett put his gloves back on and stood to bus our table.

I surveyed the tent while I waited for him. Could the attacker have slipped out the back of the tent unnoticed like me?

The last time I'd seen Owen, he'd been standing next to the Christmas tree listening to the band. What if they saw him leave and seized the opportunity? Or could they have been waiting outside? Was it a pre-meditated crime?

A knife to the skull didn't seem very thought out to me.

Greta knew that Owen was in the tent. I had watched her walk away. She easily could have looped around and come back to the tent. Pierce and Blake had been in their booths, but that didn't mean they were out of the clear. Not unless Chief Meyers established alibis for them. Any of the vendors could have left their stalls unattended, snuck behind the tent, stabbed Owen, and returned to business as if nothing had occurred. With so much activity and people around, it would have been easy to blend back in with the crowd.

Slow down, Sloan, I cautioned myself. Jumping to conclusions or coming up with wild theories wouldn't do anyone any good.

"Ready?" Garrett placed his arm around my shoulder. "I'm here for whatever you need. If you change your mind and decide you want to leave, just say the word, and I'll swoop you out of here like your own personal bodyguard."

I laughed. "That's a perfect role for you." His kindness and desire to protect me made me feel calmer.

"Sloan Krause security detail. I'd do that job all day long, and here's the kicker—I'd do it for free. Or better yet, I'd pay to keep my eyes on you."

I smiled, grateful for him and a moment of normalcy.

Most people continued to sip and stroll, completely unaware that a crime had occurred nearby. It was better that way, but I couldn't recapture the magical feeling from earlier.

We bumped into Hans and Leah on our way to Greta's stall.

"Garrett!" Leah called, rushing up to hug her brother.

They danced and squeezed each other tight. I loved watching the two of them together. Growing up without siblings made me long for a relationship like theirs. I'd found it with Hans in my adulthood, so it was all the sweeter that he and Leah had found each other.

When Leah finally released her grasp on her big brother, she caught my eye. "Sloan, happy holidays. I can't believe I'm actually here. This is even more gorgeous than I imagined."

I gave her a big hug. "Now that you're here, the real fun can begin."

Hans motioned to the police lights. "Speaking of real fun, did things already get out of hand? I don't think of a holiday market drawing in the same drinking crowd as Oktoberfest. Guzzling the *Gluhwein* doesn't sound very appealing."

"Nor does guzzling anything," Leah added, sticking out her tongue and making a face. "I think college students should be forced to come clean up the patient rooms on Saturday nights when there are big frat parties. If I never have to pump another drunk student's stomach, that would be fine by me."

Garrett cleared his throat, turning solemn. "I'm afraid it's more than drunk college students. A man was stabbed."

"Oh no, that's terrible." Leah placed her hand over her heart. "The village is so small; I assume you all knew him?"

"Not well," Garrett admitted. "His name is Owen Kessler."

"Owen Kessler?" Hans repeated with shock, his mouth hanging slightly open as his eyes darted toward the emergency lights again. "Owen Kessler was stabbed? What happened?"

"I found him behind the food tents," I replied. "Someone stabbed him with a carving knife."

"How terrible." Leah shuddered. "Do they have a prognosis?"

I shook my head, wishing I could unsee Owen's pallid face. "Not yet."

She linked her arm through Hans's in a show of support. "Is Owen Kessler the woodworker you were telling me about?"

"Yeah. I can't believe it. I saw him shortly before I left to pick you up." Hans tugged off his Der Keller stocking hat and rubbed his head. "He and Pierce got into it. He broke a couple of Pierce's pottery pieces."

"Broke them? Leah asked.

"Smashed them is a better description." Hans's mouth remained open. A puzzled expression crossed his face. "You don't think Pierce could have done it?"

"Honestly, I'm not sure." I could hear doubt creeping into my tone. "I don't want to believe that, but the timing is more than a coincidence."

"And he was stabbed with a knife?" Leah shook her head side to side like she was shifting into work mode. "Puncture wounds to the brain cause TBI—traumatic brain injuries—they can be very serious, even fatal."

Carolers clad in Victorian-era costumes passed us, holding battery-operated tapered candles and humming melodically. It was a strange juxtaposition.

I exhaled slowly, watching my breath evaporate in cold puffs of steam. "The most likely scenario seems to be that Pierce—or whoever attacked Owen—did it in a moment of rage."

"Or there was a physical altercation before he was hurt," Hans added. "Were there any other signs of a struggle?"

"It was too dark, and I didn't get a good look at him, but there were no obvious bruises or other wounds, just the knife." Replaying the scene again made me shaky.

A group of Hans's friends spotted him and called him over to join them for drinks. He hesitated.

"No, go join them," I encouraged him with a genuine smile. "Garrett and I are going to wander a little. I'm in a bit of a daze, so walking around feels like it might help."

"That's a good idea," Leah said with approval, entirely switching into doctor mode. "Something sweet would also be good. Maybe a hot cup of apple cider and those donuts we passed on the way in."

"I like that plan." Garrett reached for my hand. "Doctor's order. You heard the expert. Let's get you some sugar."

We left Hans and Leah with a hug and promise to meet up tomorrow.

"How does a donut sound?" Garrett asked.

"Actually good. I think I can stomach a donut and hot cider now."

The crowds had swelled as the evening wore on. We waved to friends and familiar faces as we cut a path for the donut stand. The scent of the cake-like sweets wafted through the air, pulling me toward the booth. Hot from the fryer, the donuts were served with powdered sugar, cinnamon, or chocolate glaze. There were also filled options like apple spice, raspberry, and Bavarian cream. Holly, mistletoe, and poinsettias added a touch of seasonal color to the walk-up stand.

"We'll take one of each and two hot apple ciders, please," Garrett ordered before I had a chance to say that one donut would suffice.

I breathed in the scent of cinnamon sticks and simmering apples, a calming smell that reminded me of Ursula's kitchen. However, the calm was short-lived because a commotion broke out nearby at Pierce's stall.

"Not again," Garrett said with disbelief, handing me an apple cider topped with whipped cream and red and green sprinkles. "Should we go see what's up?"

"Yeah." I took the bag of donuts and followed him.

Chief Meyers was at the center of the commotion. She raised one hand. "Sir, I'm simply asking you to come with me to answer some further questions. You are not under arrest. This is standard procedure."

"I didn't do it. It wasn't me," Pierce shouted in return. His hands clung to the display ledge of his stall like he was going to force her to pry him away.

As we got closer, I noticed a large scratch on his cheek that hadn't been there earlier.

"Are you seeing what I'm seeing?" Garrett whispered.

I nodded. "It looks like he was clawed with someone's fingernails."

"I'm being set up. I didn't stab Owen. It wasn't me," Pierce yelled over the crowd noise and music.

Was he intentionally trying to cause a scene?

"Excellent. Then you should have no problem answering a few more questions at the police station." Chief Meyers took one step back and pointed to the far end of the park. "The question is, are you going to come willingly, or would you like me to handcuff you and escort you out of the market?"

"I want a lawyer. I know my rights." Pierce loosened his grip on the wooden stall. "We'll talk about all of that at the station." Chief Meyers remained composed and calm. "Let's head that way."

We watched her guide Pierce away. Could it be that easy? Had Chief Meyers already pegged him as Owen's assailant?

CHAPTER
SEVEN

GARRETT and I stayed near Pierce's stall, sipping our ciders and nibbling on donuts. The cinnamon sugar was my favorite. The cake-like donut was still warm and had a touch of nutmeg and the faintest hint of cloves. Leah's advice was right. The combination of the hot cider and the sweet donuts finally settled my stomach.

I exhaled a long, contented sigh.

"I like the sound of that," Garrett replied with a crooked smile. "Are the donuts the magic touch?"

"Yeah, I feel almost normal."

"Almost normal is a good day for me, so I'll take it," he said with a tender, concerned smile. "Do you think Chief Meyers suspects Pierce?"

"It appears that way. He's the most obvious suspect. Plus, where did the scratch come from? If he got into a physical fight with Owen like Leah suggested, that would explain his injury."

"And dozens of people witnessed Owen smashing his pottery. He has the most obvious motive."

"But almost too obvious, yeah?" I finished the cinnamon donut and tried the Bavarian cream next.

"Great minds think alike." He bit into a gooey raspberry-filled donut. "Although the scratch is hard to explain."

"I think we should wander over to Greta's booth and pick up our wreaths. I'd like to see if she'll say anything about what happened between her and Owen."

"Let's do it." He wiped a smudge of jelly from his bottom lip.

Greta was already packing up her stall, carefully packaging her sharp florist tools. "I'm so sorry. I have to go. Can I swing the wreaths by the pub tomorrow? I wasn't sure how long you were going to be. I know I said come by anytime, but something came up, and I really need to go, so I already boxed everything up."

It was true. Only the exterior decorations and her sign hanging from the top of the chalet booth remained. The arrangements, bouquets, centerpieces, and wreaths were tucked under the counter and put away for the night.

"No problem," I replied.

Greta closed the exterior shutters. Since Leavenworth was usually such a safe place, no one bothered to lock up their supplies or products. Two local security officers would patrol the perimeter overnight; otherwise, vendors wouldn't have to cart materials back and forth from their shops to the market.

"Thanks. I appreciate it. I'll drop in before I open tomorrow if that's okay?" As Greta tucked her tools into a canvas bag filled with gardening supplies on her shoulder, I noticed they included a set of knives similar to the one lodged in Owen's skull. "I really need to go now. See you then."

She raced off.

"Where's the fire?" Garrett asked once she was out of earshot.

"Yeah, that was quite a shift." I wondered if her speedy exit had anything to do with Owen. "Was she worried that the police were coming to question her?"

"She looked skittish, like the deer on Blackbird Island who freak out if you get too close," Garrett replied.

"I'm glad she's going to drop into Nitro tomorrow. That will give me an opportunity to think about what I want to ask her tonight, and she might be more likely to open up if it's just us."

"Yeah, I'll make myself scarce." Garrett brushed powdered sugar from his hands and put his gloves back on. "What next?"

"Should we see if Blake is still around?"

"You bet."

I appreciated that Garrett was always up for an adventure, whether that meant snowshoeing in the backcountry, testing unique beer combinations like a double blueberry pancake IPA, or supporting me in a bizarre situation like this. As much as I would have loved to go home, light a fire, and curl up on the couch with him, I knew I wouldn't be able to let Owen's attack go.

The thought that anyone was harmed during the most festive event of the year in our sweet village was unfathomable. Owen might not have been the most gracious or kind person, but he didn't deserve to be hurt.

We found Blake closing her booth, too. The market was open for another hour and a half, so I was surprised she decided to end the evening early unless her burn bothered her more than she originally thought.

She winced in pain as she tried to close the shutter doors.

"Let me get that," Garrett said, handing me his apple cider.

"Is it hurting?" I gestured to her bandages.

"Yeah." She gnawed on the inside of her cheek. Perhaps in an attempt to distract herself from the pain. "A lot more than I

252

thought it would. I tried to keep working, but you were right. I decided it's probably better to go home and rest, and I hope to put in a full day tomorrow. I really need the income. I was counting on sales from the market keeping me afloat through the end of the year, but now, I don't know—" she trailed off.

"My offer still stands. I got my start working at a farmers market. I'm not a professional barista, but I know how to operate an espresso machine and would be happy to help tomorrow."

Garrett finished securing the shutters. "Absolutely. We can rotate our staff if you want. I know Kat worked at a coffee shop in Oregon, so I'm sure she'd be willing to lend a hand."

Blake's wide eyes filled with tears. She blinked hard to hold them in but couldn't contain her gratitude. "I'm sorry to be such a blubbering mess. That's so nice of you both. I guess I had unrealistic expectations about how hard it was going to be to run a small business. I've spent the past two months preparing for this weekend only to end up like this." She raised her arm but quickly brought it down against her waist.

"Like we said earlier, owning and operating an independent business is a lot of work. It takes time to build up a client base and revenue," I said, feeling protective of her. Blake wasn't that much older than Alex. I remembered being in my early twenties, daydreaming of running my own small restaurant. Little did I know that a casual conversation with a charming German couple would lead me to a completely different life in Leavenworth.

"And we didn't go it alone," Garrett added. "You shouldn't have to either."

Blake placed her non-injured over her mouth and stifled a sob. "You're being too nice to me. I don't know what to say."

"Say that you'll accept our help. You'll be giving us a gift too. It's the spirit of the holiday season." I smiled kindly. I wanted to ask her more about Owen, but this wasn't the time.

"Okay. Thanks. As long as you're sure." She wiped away tears with the sleeve of her jacket. "I can be here for the duration of the day, and I have a friend who can help tomorrow night. It would be nice if someone could help steam milk and pull espresso shots, but I can oversee sales of whole beans and pour my holiday blends."

"Great. It's a plan," I said, wanting to confirm before she had a chance to change her mind. "The market opens at noon. Why don't we meet here a half hour before so you can run me through everything?"

"Are you sure? I feel bad taking you away from Nitro." She cradled her arm, holding it firmly against her in a protective stance.

It was clear that she was in more pain than she was willing to admit.

"This is what we do for each other in Leavenworth," I replied. "Otto and Ursula helped us open Nitro. We've collaborated with other local brewers, chocolatiers, honey producers, the list goes on and on."

"It's our way of paying it forward," Garrett added. "Selfishly, we want your holiday blend for our B and B guests, so it's a win-win."

Blake's shoulders slumped in relief. "I don't know how I'm going to repay you, but I'll find a way, I swear."

"No need." I tapped my wrist. "I'll be here for you to put me to work. Brushing up on my coffee skills will be fun, but now you should go home and rest your arm. Make yourself a nice cup of hot chamomile tea and try to get some sleep." I couldn't stop myself from mom-ing.

"I will. Thank you again for everything." Blake nurtured her arm as she walked away.

"Good move on not bringing up Owen," Garrett said once she was gone.

"She seems fragile right now. I think that might have put her over the edge. Hopefully, she'll open up tomorrow after a good night's rest." I pointed in the direction of our stall. "Should we go check in with Kat and then call it?"

"You took the words right out of my mouth." He pulled me close to his body. "Because you need to listen to your own advice. Let's say goodnight and get you tucked up cozy in bed."

I wasn't going to argue with him. We'd only been at the holiday market for a few hours, but it felt like a week had gone by. Hopefully, a night of sleep would give me a fresh perspective on Owen and put me one step closer to figuring out who stabbed him and why.

CHAPTER
EIGHT

THE FOLLOWING DAY, I was up with the pinkish blush of dawn to prepare a traditional German breakfast for our B and B guests. Garrett liked to sleep later, which was fine by me. I enjoyed the gentle calm of the kitchen and the smell of spiced holiday coffee and baked bread.

I cut myself a slice of Ursula's Christmas Stollen to enjoy while I decided what to serve for breakfast. The Stollen texture was rich, dense, and slightly crumbly. Ursula had generously filled the center with raisins, candied fruits, nuts, and marzipan. The dough was enhanced with cinnamon, nutmeg, and cardamom and frosted with a simple vanilla glaze.

My tastebuds thanked me as I savored a second piece. Every bite evoked a sense of nostalgia. The first year Mac and I were married, Ursula taught me how to make the traditional German treat. She explained that the sweet bread dates back to the 1400s. Its name originated from the German word *Stollen*, meaning "post," which represented its loaf-like shape. Stollen was prepared during Advent and a holiday staple in any German household, especially the Krause family.

Even though it was early, I texted Chief Meyers to see if there were any updates on Owen's status. She responded immediately that he remained in critical condition.

At least he was in good hands at the hospital.

I decided to start with *Griessbrei*, or semolina pudding, for our overnight guests. The fluffy and not overly sweet pudding was delicious and only required three ingredients—milk, sugar, and semolina. I placed a saucepan over medium heat and added semolina and sugar, whisking them together until the semolina was evenly coated with the sugar. Then I gradually poured in milk while stirring constantly. As the mixture heated up, it began to thicken. I reduced the heat and stirred until a thick pudding had formed.

Next, I added a splash of vanilla and rum extracts and scooped the creamy pudding into individual glass bowls. Right before I served the puddings, I would top them with a drizzle of honey and my orange, cranberry, and IPA compote.

I let them cool on the counter and made the compote by zesting oranges. I combined the zest and juice of each orange, along with whole cranberries, sugar, salt, a pinch of ground cloves, and a splash of our citrus IPA in a new saucepan and let the mixture come to a boil. Then, I turned the heat to low and let it simmer until the cranberries began to burst with a pop.

Soon, the kitchen smelled like Christmas morning, but my thoughts kept returning to Owen's attack. A good night's sleep hadn't provided me with any new insight into who might have stabbed him. Chief Meyer's taking Pierce to the station for further questioning could mean she suspected him and was buying her team time to gather evidence. It could also be that she simply had more questions she needed answered. I considered texting her again but knew she was likely deeply immersed in the investigation.

I intended to ask Blake about the exchange I witnessed

right before she burned her arm. And, hopefully, Greta would come by with our wreaths before I had to leave. I was curious about her relationship with Owen. She certainly seemed the most emotionally invested, and if his assault had been a crime of passion, she had displayed magnitudes of passion right before I found him.

I sighed and topped off my coffee.

It had to be Pierce. Owen intentionally shattered Pierce's art, giving him a clear motive, and how else could he have gotten the scratches on his cheek?

Maybe once the village was up and moving, we'd get word from Chief Meyers that she'd made an official arrest.

That would be a relief.

I checked my compote, which had bubbled into a thick, rich sauce. In addition to the semolina pudding, I sliced our sweet bread into slabs and brushed them with melted butter, cinnamon, and sugar. I set them in the oven to toast and arranged a platter of fruits, berries, *Weisswurst* (or white sausages), cheese, and apple custard cake.

Once I heard footsteps and movement above, I took my spread upstairs to the dining area. We had transformed the alcove with bookcases filled with books and games for guests to use during their stay. An antique buffet salvaged in the demolition served as our coffee and tea bar. We kept it stocked with an assortment of teas, hot chocolates, coffee, apple ciders, and cookies for guests to help themselves.

I placed the platter on the long shared table and made sure we had enough plates and silverware for each guest. We draped the bookcases in fairy lights and fragrant evergreen boughs to make the space extra special for the holiday season. Garrett hallowed out the bottom of beer bottles for a center-piece and filled them with golden tea lights.

"Good morning, Sloan," Kat called from the end of the hallway. Part of her salary included room and board. "Can I help with anything? I didn't realize it was already breakfast time. I guess I slept in, sorry." She rubbed the corner of her eye and fluffed her curls.

"No need to apologize. I was up early and knew you closed the market last night." She followed me downstairs. "How did the rest of the night go?"

"Nothing like the start of the evening, fortunately. I still can't believe a guy was stabbed. The police were still there when we closed. Did you know him?"

"I knew of him from Hans but didn't know him well." I began setting the glasses of puddings on a tray. "Can you scoop the compote onto these, and I'll finish them with honey?"

"Sure." Kat's dimples became more pronounced when she smiled. "Although, can I just eat this with a spoon? It smells like Christmas morning."

"Good, that's the goal."

She finished each pudding with a hearty scoop of the cranberry orange compote. "Does Chief Meyers have a potential suspect? I heard that they arrested Pierce, but you know Leavenworth, that could be a rumor."

"Could be, but she did take him in for questioning. I didn't hear after that," I said, drizzling locally sourced honey on the colorful puddings.

"I heard he went through a nasty breakup recently." Kat scooped the last of the compote onto the final pudding. Then she dipped her pinkie into the sauce. "Oh my God, I don't know how you do it, but this tastes even better than it smells. Yum."

"I'm glad you like it." I nodded to the far counter. "I set aside portions for you and Garrett."

"You're the best boss ever, you know that, right?" Kat beamed.

"Right back at you." I grinned. "Are you looking forward to visiting your family for the holidays?"

"My mom is so excited. She's texted me at least twenty times to remind me to bring samples of all our beer for everyone to taste."

"That's so sweet, and don't worry, we'll hook you up before you leave."

"I'm going to be the most popular cousin at Christmas when I show up with beer." Kat chuckled.

"That reminds me, after all of the chaos last night with Owen's attack, I forgot to ask about the beer. It seemed like the holiday ale was the most popular. Should we bring a couple of extra kegs today?"

"Probably." Kat nodded. "There might be a quarter of it left, but we were pouring a lot of pints, at least until the police showed up. Then there was a lull because everyone went to see what was happening, and it picked up again before the last call."

"Okay, I'll have Garrett bring at least two. We want to keep enough on hand for the tasting room, but we should be good." I lifted the tray. "Did you hear anything specific about Owen's breakup?"

"No. A woman came by right when all of the commotion broke out. She was the only one not over by the entertainment and food tent. Everyone rushed over in that direction, and she was fleeing the area."

"Fleeing?" I raised one eyebrow.

"Well, not technically. At least, I don't think so. She was just coming from that area and stopped for a pint. She mentioned something about breaking up with Owen."

"Wait, *she* broke up with Owen? Do you know who it was?"

"She owns the flower shop. What's her name? Gretchen? Gretel?"

"Greta," I offered.

Kat snapped her fingers together. "Yeah, Greta. She was acting weird. She kept saying how karmic it was that Owen was on his way to the hospital after breaking her heart."

"She said she broke it off with him?"

"Exactly. She wasn't making sense. I figured it was the shock of learning that he had been stabbed. I think everyone was stunned."

"Right." I nodded. This changed everything. Greta and Owen had dated? She claimed to have broken up with him, but from what I'd witnessed, the opposite seemed much more likely. Plus, other questions loomed, like why was she running away from the crime scene? And how did she know that Owen had been stabbed?

CHAPTER
NINE

AFTER BREAKFAST, we prepped the bar and tasting room and reviewed the day's schedule. Garrett and Kat would rotate between the market and Nitro, overseeing the volunteers pouring at the booth. It was unlikely that Nitro would be very busy. Everyone would be at the Christmas market, but it was good to keep the taproom open for anyone who wanted to sample a broader line of our craft beers or for any locals who might want to seek refuge from the crowds for a moment.

Nitro glimmered as sunlight streamed in through the front windows. Dawn broke over the horizon of the surrounding peaks, casting a soft golden hue over the village. A fresh coat of pristine snow blanketed the rooftops, glistening like a field of sparkling gems under the gentle morning light. Chimneys puffed out smoke. A sense of stillness permeated everything. Families were still snug in their homes, savoring the tranquility of a lazy Saturday with cups of cocoa and cinnamon buns.

There was nothing that compared with the bucolic view from our front windows. I took a minute to soak it in while circling through the dining room, ensuring the high-top tables and barstools were arranged for customers. I turned on the fairy lights on the beer bottle tree and plugged in the overhead Christmas lights.

My thoughts drifted to Blake. I could clearly remember the first day I stepped inside Nitro and almost considered turning around and walking back out the door. I'm so glad I chose to stay. Starting over with something entirely new forced me out of my comfort zone. It was hard to believe the transformation the brewery and I experienced together.

Nitro had been a sterile and not very welcoming space with its stark white walls, cavernous exposed ceilings, and subtle nods to chemistry. Garrett had poured his energy into creating a functional brewery and taproom and brewing a debut line of quality craft ales. It was funny to reflect on how I had approached him gingerly with the idea of making the taproom more inviting by adding lighting and greenery and hanging old family photos on the walls.

He had been extremely receptive to my suggestions, including putting together a pub menu with small bites, daily soups, and beer-forward desserts.

None of the changes had taken place overnight. Nitro was a labor of love and mirrored my internal metamorphosis. Mac cheating on me had been my catalyst for seeking change, but really, it was so much deeper than that. I'd spent the last couple of years getting to know myself for the first time. Opening up to my past—the good parts and the painful parts. If I hadn't taken a leap of faith with Nitro and Garrett, I might still be stuck in an unhappy marriage and doubting my worth and value.

I felt for Blake. She was launching a business on her own with the added pressure of needing immediate revenue to survive. I hoped that she would take us up on our offer to help guide her beyond just this weekend, but I also had to wonder if the stress of keeping Kunst and Kaffee afloat could have led her to do something drastic—like stab Owen, although I hadn't figured out a motive or connection.

I would have to get her to open up while we worked together later. With that thought in mind, I returned to the kitchen to start on the soup of the day—a traditional German goulash. I began by sautéing onions, carrots, celery, peppers, and garlic until they were soft and translucent. Then I added stew meat, sweet paprika, dried herbs, and salt and pepper. I covered the mixture with beef stock, crushed tomatoes, and our dark ale. It would simmer on low for an hour until the meat was so tender you could cut it with a fork. We would serve it with a dollop of sour cream and a slice of rustic bread.

Since my cookies had been such a hit last night, I decided to bake another round for the market and our dessert special.

Kat came into the kitchen carrying a tray of dishes from breakfast. "What smells so good, Sloan?"

"I made a batch of goulash soup," I replied, motioning to the stock pot on the stove. "And these are more Christmas stars." I used a condiment bottle to flood the cinnamon cookies with meringue icing.

"That's awesome, except I'm going to have a problem not inhaling all of them. I don't know why, but those are my weakness."

"I'll be sure to save a few extra just for you." I winked.

Once everything was ready, I washed my hands and returned to the tasting room. I set out bowls of Doritos and nuts and gave the bar one last polish before flipping the sign on the door to OPEN.

A handful of customers trickled in, mainly tourists who had come for opening night of the markets and wanted six packs of beer to take home. Shortly after opening, Greta showed up as promised with a box of miniature wreaths.

"I'm so sorry about last night. I had to get out of there. I couldn't take it. Not after I learned that Owen was seriously injured. I tried to call the hospital, but they won't tell me anything," Greta said, resting the box on the bar. Her left eye twitched as she continued. "It doesn't feel real."

"Did you know him well?" I asked, glad that she brought up the topic first.

"Uh, is that what you heard?" Greta unzipped her coat and reached into her gardening apron for a pair of shears she used to slice the box. "Does everyone know?"

"Know what?"

"About me and Owen." She lifted the first wreath from the box. It was six inches in diameter with interlacing evergreen and eucalyptus branches tied with dried orange and lemon slices, bunches of cinnamon sticks, and red berries. "I didn't think the village knew about us."

I made space on the bar for her. "I'm not sure what the village knows. I heard a rumor that you two might have dated, but rumors aren't something I repeat."

She tucked an errant lemon slice between two branches and reached for the next wreath. "I appreciate that, although I'm sure if you've heard it, everyone has. That's how gossip works in this town."

She was right about that. Living in a small town where everyone knew your name came with many rewards, but on the flip side, it was hard to retain much (if any) autonomy in a village our size.

"I never should have gotten involved with Owen. Nothing good came from our relationship. If you could even call it a relationship." She shook her head in disgust and reached for a Dorito. "May I?"

"Help yourself."

"So everyone knows?" She crunched a chip and closed her eyes as if trying to force herself to remain in control.

"Were you dating for long?" I asked, trying to steer the conversation.

"No, not long. Or, actually, I should say too long. Our first date should have been my warning. There were so many red flags, but I ignored all the signs because he was a masterful gaslighter. He made me think I was the one with a problem." She licked Dorito dust from her finger and let out a sarcastic laugh. "He manipulated me, belittled me and my work, and crushed my self-esteem, and the worst thing about it is that until last night, I still thought I loved him. Talk about an unhealthy relationship."

"Did something change last night?"

She took the next wreath out of the box. It was similar to the first, except instead of fruit and berries, it was decorated with pinecones, bark, and moss. "I finally came to my senses and put my own needs first. Owen didn't like that at all. He wanted me to stay unhappy. He thrived on being in control. He loved making me feel small. I don't know why, but I had what I can only describe as an out-of-body experience last night. I watched cheerful families and couples dancing to the music and enjoying the festive atmosphere, and it clicked together. I knew I was done. I knew I had to end it with Owen for good."

I was glad to hear that she stood up for herself, but her story didn't align with what I'd observed. I opened one of the drawers behind the bar, searching for scissors and hanging wire to buy myself time to think of how to ask her about their exchange. I didn't want to interrupt the conversation or put her on the defensive.

"I understand the feeling of putting yourself second in a relationship. I did that for a long time, and it isn't easy to shed those patterns," I said, snipping off a piece of hanging wire. "It seemed like things were intense with you and Owen last night."

"That's an understatement. I was ready to break up with him for good last night. He came by the flower booth and told me I needed to shut it down and get a drink with him. I told him to go to hell, and he could drink himself to death for all I cared. Do you know what he said?" Her voice turned shrill.

I shook my head.

"He told me he was breaking up with *me*. The nerve. What an asshole. He wasn't going to break up with me. I was going to end it with him, and he knew it, so he did it first just to have the upper hand. I ran after him because I was so upset. I wasn't going to let him get away with his stupid, childish games. I needed to end it. I needed that for myself, and I wasn't going to let him take that away from me." She massaged the side of her eye with her index finger to try and stop the twitching.

I wanted to believe her. It sounded like their relationship had been tumultuous. Her description of how Owen treated her matched his behavior at the market last night, but I wasn't convinced she was telling me the truth.

She had run after Owen, begging him not to go, and when he ignored her pleas, she had broken down in front of me. Was it because she wanted to break up with him first? Or was it because he had ended things with her, and she was still desperately in love with him?

As much as I was a champion of women standing up for themselves, I couldn't take Greta off my suspect list. Her rocky relationship with Owen gave her a clear and powerful motive for wanting to hurt him.

She easily could have followed him around the other side of the tent, stabbed him, and returned to her booth without anyone noticing. The fact that he had been hurt in such a dramatic fashion also made her the more likely suspect. If she had tried to reason with him and they got into a scuffle, it was a reasonable leap to imagine her stabbing him. The only question was how she got ahold of the knife. Or could she have planned to try to stab him all along? She could have used the gardening knives I'd seen in her bag last night or stolen the knife from Pierce's stall after seeing their argument. She might have seized the opportunity to implicate Pierce by using his knife.

Any of my theories at the moment were plausible, which unfortunately put me no closer to figuring out who had attacked Owen.

TEN

GRETA'S NOSTRILS FLARED. "Owen enjoyed playing mind games, but I wasn't going to let him manipulate me any longer. He had the nerve to say there was someone else. Like I would ever believe that, it was another one of his ploys to get me to stay." Her phone rang. She fumbled through the box until she found it at the bottom. "Sorry, I need to take this. Enjoy the wreaths."

"What about payment?" I asked.

"Swing by the shop tomorrow. Or find me at the market. I'm not worried about it." She lifted the phone to her ear and walked outside.

Had I gotten the full story? How much self-editing had Greta done? From what I'd observed, their relationship seemed one-sided, but it wasn't fair to make that judgment based on seeing them interact one night. There was a chance that Owen reciprocated Greta's feelings, or at least once had. Their argument at the market might have been the final straw. Maybe they both realized they were poorly matched or maybe Greta was re-writing the story and penning herself as the victim.

"Hey, Sloan, it smells like a winter pine forest," Garrett

said. He was wearing a pair of jeans with a thick navy screen-printed hoodie. The design was perfect for the Christmas market. It had a frothy pint of beer, snowflakes, and the words: WISHING YOU A HOPPY HOLIDAY.

"Classic pun," I said with a half laugh. "Even for the holidays."

"Especially for the holidays. I pre-ordered at least six different T-shirts and hoodies for the season. I have to give the people what they want." His eye glinted with mischief.

"I thought they wanted beer."

"Beer and puns." He lifted the first wreath and held it to the light. "This is the source of the winter wonderland smell in here."

"Greta just dropped them off." I glanced at my watch. "Do you mind hanging them? I promised Blake I'd be there early for her to show me the ropes."

"No problem." His tone turned serious. "Be careful, though. I know you're a strong, capable, confident woman, but Owen's attack has me feeling unsettled. It's still shocking to think that someone drew a knife out in the open at the market last night with so many people around."

"It wasn't exactly in the open. He was stabbed behind the tent."

Garrett tilted his head to one side. "You know what I mean, Sloan Krause. Don't go chasing off behind any tents, okay?"

"Okay." I gave him my most sincere face. "Same for you."

"Have you heard anything about how Owen's doing?" Garrett flicked a pine needle from the bar.

I pressed my lips together and shook my head. "Nothing yet."

"Hopefully, no news is good news." He kissed the top of my head. "I'll stop by Blake's booth for a coffee before my shift. Good luck."

"Thanks. See you soon." I grabbed my hat, parka, and gloves from the coat rack near the front door and stepped outside into the frosty air. The cobblestone streets, usually well-trodden, were untouched except for the footprints of a few early risers. The street lamps were still dusted with snow, giving them a whimsical appearance. The distant peaks touched the brilliant blue sky, creating a breathtaking backdrop.

I turned onto Front Street, where woodsy smoke mingled with the aroma of fresh from the oven bread and pastries. Vendors were setting up for the day, opening their shutters, turning on their twinkle lights, and refreshing their decorations.

Blake was already waiting for me at the coffee stall. She wore a crisp red and white checkered apron and a knitted wool sweater, but I could tell from the bulk of her left arm that her bandages were still in place.

"Good morning," I called with a wave. "I'm impressed. You look like you're ready for business."

She unwrapped a mint green ceramic mug with hand-painted holly berries and set it next to the other art pieces for sale. "It wasn't hard. Everything was pretty much ready to go from last night."

"How's your arm feeling?"

"Not great. I'm happy you talked me into helping because I can't run the espresso machine. It's fine as long as I'm not moving it, but it hurts, and my entire arm is throbbing."

"Did you take any pain medication before you came?"

"Yeah. Hopefully that will help." She took off her gloves and handed me an apron.

I noticed her right hand was bandaged, too. "Did you burn both arms?"

"Huh?" She looked at her hand, shook her head, and

motioned to a knife near a large bag of whole beans. "No, I cut myself trying to open a bag of beans this morning. I should get the klutz of the year award."

"I hear you. When I give brewery tours, people always laugh about having to wear safety vests and goggles, but commercial kitchens, breweries, and roasteries can be dangerous."

"Especially if you're accident-prone like me," Blake laughed at herself. She showed me how to use her espresso machine, a significant upgrade from our small machine at Nitro.

"Do I need to know anything special about the grinder?" I asked, motioning to the grinder next to the machine.

"It's all preset, so you just have to pour the beans and let it do its thing. When I opened the shop, I used my old grinder, but Owen insisted that we get something that would ensure consistency across every cup of coffee we serve."

I wondered how to bring Owen up in the conversation, and she gave me the perfect opportunity.

"I didn't realize Owen is involved in the business."

"Unfortunately, yeah." She kept unpacking coffee cups. "He *was* involved. He's not anymore."

"What was his role?" I filled a stainless-steel pitcher with whole milk and practiced using the steaming wand.

"He gave me a small loan. I already paid it back in full, though. That's one of the reasons I need the market and the rest of the holiday season to be successful. He was horrible to work with. I realized that too late. When he approached me about the loan, it seemed like a shiny present wrapped with a bow, but I quickly learned that Owen only cared about Owen and padding his bank account."

The milk began to bubble. I turned off the steam wand and consulted Blake's recipe for her Bavarian Cream Latte. I poured two espresso shots and a tablespoon of *Eierlikor*, or Bavarian cream liqueur, into a mug. Then, I added the steamed milk and topped the drink with whipped cream, chocolate shavings, and a dusting of nutmeg.

"Did he ask for a percentage of the business in return for the loan?"

"No. He wrote me a check with 'no strings attached.' Only every string was attached. He would come into the shop every day and make snide comments about my menu, my inventory, my customer service—everything."

I tasted my sample drink to make sure the proportions were correct. It was creamy and rich with a distinctly German flavor. Ursula would love this coffee. "Did he have any advice that was helpful at all?"

"Not really. Unless you define advice as ordering me around. Maybe it was his name, but it was like he felt like he owned me. Like the business was his because he gave me a few thousand dollars. I gave him free coffee and pastries whenever he stopped in. I tried listening to his advice and input, at least at the beginning. He was supposed to be this successful businessperson and investor, but his ideas were super outdated and not at all relevant to my vision for the shop."

There seemed to be an ongoing theme concerning Owen and his need to control people. Blake's experience aligned with what I'd heard from Greta and what I suspected was the case with Pierce.

"And paying back the loan didn't change things?"

"It only made it worse." She let out an involuntary moan as she twisted open a container of chocolate syrup. "I don't think he wanted me to be able to pay him back. I think he was counting on the fact that I was going to keep struggling, and he would keep bailing me out just to be able to lord it over me, you know what I mean?"

I knew the type.

"Last night, I noticed him trying to intimidate you. What was that all about?" I wiped whipped cream from the side of my mouth.

"You did? When?" She sounded casual, but I caught a look of concern flash across her face.

Was it my imagination, or did she sound nervous?

"Right before you burned yourself. He was standing over there." I nodded across the market to where I'd seen Owen.

"Weird. I never saw him."

"You didn't?"

"Nope. I was probably too busy with customers or trying to spill hot coffee all over myself, but the last time I saw Owen was at the shop."

Was she telling me the truth? I would have sworn an oath that Owen's menacing gesture was the reason she had spilled the coffee. She had been distracted. She wasn't paying attention to what she was doing because she had been laser-focused on Owen.

But why would she lie about that?

"I should probably show you how to mix the dark chocolate for our mochas," she said, changing the subject.

I didn't press the issue. The market would open shortly, and I wanted to be prepared.

By the time we finished going over everything, a small line had formed.

Blake poured samples of her holiday blends while I steamed eggnog, oat milk, and chocolate milk for lattes and mochas. She was upbeat and cheerful with everyone. She certainly didn't present like someone who had brutally stabbed Owen last night, but her confession made me realize that she had a motive for wanting to hurt him, too. Money. And money was a powerful motivator.

CHAPTER
ELEVEN

THE REST of the morning and afternoon flew by. Working at the coffee cart was a different energy than pulling pints at Nitro. Or maybe I was picking up on Blake's energy. She had changed since she brought up Owen and his involvement in her burgeoning business. She seemed more closed off and nervous.

Sales seemed to be successful, though. My fingers flew between steaming milk and pulling shots of espresso. Blake sold out of her holiday blend and packaged dozens of her ceramic mugs and bowls in gift boxes.

I was glad to be able to lend my support, but by the time her afternoon help came to relieve me, I was exhausted.

"Thanks again, Sloan. You're the best," she said as I untied my apron and handed over the reins. "You have free coffee on me for life."

"No, there's no need for that. It was a pleasure, and it reminded me how hard baristas work. Baristas and beer-tenders have to stick together. Those of us in the service industry understand the toll a long shift takes on your body."

"Yeah, well, I couldn't have done it without you." She

reached under the counter and handed me a bag of her holiday blend. "Take this. I saved it for you, and I'll come by the taproom to talk about getting you all set up with your own Nitro blend. Maybe on Monday, if that's okay?"

"Perfect." I held the bag to my nose and inhaled the scent. "Thank you for this, and good luck with the rest of the market. Don't overdo it."

"I won't."

I was famished. I could eat an entire platter of sauerbraten and potatoes and finish it off with a hot apple strudel, so I wound my way to the Nitro stall to find Garrett.

The atmosphere during the daytime was different than last night. The high school choir sang carols in the gazebo, and kids ran free on the sledding hill while their parents enjoyed an afternoon pint in the beer tent. The entire village was alive with energy and excitement.

Nitro was equally buzzing. Two queues wrapped almost to the food and entertainment tent, but Garrett and our volunteer crew kept the line moving.

"Do you need me to jump in?" I asked.

Garrett expertly held a pint glass at an angle and filled it with dark chocolate stout while answering. "Not a chance, Sloan. It's nearly five. You've been slinging coffee all day. Take a break. Get something to eat. Kat should be here in about thirty minutes. I'll come find you."

I didn't bother to protest.

The Krause family, including Alex, were all working the Der Keller tent, which was three times the size of our stall. Der Keller had a full beer tent with long tables and benches humming with happy customers swaying with raised pint glasses to the German polka band. A canopy of twinkle lights and German flags fluttered on the ceiling. Twenty-foot spruce trees adorned with more lights and vintage Bavarian ornaments flanked each side of the stage.

Staff were dressed in classic blue and white checkered trachten shirts, suspenders, and barmaid dresses with embroidered Der Keller logos.

Alex weaved through the tables, clearing plates and empty glasses. Mac, Hans, and Leah poured beer while Otto and Ursula stood at the end of the massive bar, posing for pictures with tourists in their traditional red and cream German wool outfits.

"Sloan, where have you been all day?" Mac asked. His cheeks and the tip of his nose were ruddy from the cold.

"I've been helping Blake with her coffee cart." I told them about Blake's injury yesterday.

Leah handed a customer a tasting tray. "You better get out of here fast. I had no idea the Krause brothers would put me to work. I thought I was coming up for a holiday getaway. Little did I know I have to earn my keep." She winked at Hans.

He beamed at her with such adoration it took my breath away. "It's a Krause custom, right, Sloan? We welcome people into the family by testing their beer-pouring skills."

I laughed and gave Leah a conspiratorial smile. "I'm afraid it's true. But free beer and Ursula's potato dumplings are pretty great perks."

"Uh, I think you forgot a key perk," Hans interrupted.

"What's that?"

"Me." He tapped his chest and pulled Leah in for a kiss.

"He's not wrong about that either," I said quietly, checking to make sure no one could hear us. "Don't let this go to his head, but April Ablin once declared him Leavenworth's most eligible bachelor."

"If April says it, it has to be true." Mac caught my eye. We shared a familiar look. I appreciated that we had come to a place in our relationship where we could enjoy each other's company and our shared past.

"Watch out, brother, you might be next." Hans clapped Mac on the back.

Mac's cheeks turned a deeper shade of red. "What can I pour you, Sloan?" he asked, intentionally changing the subject.

I hoped that Mac would find someone new. Not April, but someone who would bring out his best qualities, like his ability to charm strangers, his love for food, and his commitment to his family. He deserved happiness.

"I'm actually on the hunt for food," I replied, studying the Der Keller menu. It was a very pared-down version of the restaurant's full-service menu. "I was going to head to the food tent but didn't realize the kitchen was doing *Königsberger*. Sold. I'll take a plate."

The German meatball dish was served in a rich, creamy gravy made with lemon, capers, and spices over potatoes. My mouth began to water at the thought of the savory dish.

"Go have a seat. I'll bring it out to you," Mac said. "You look tired."

"That's sweet. Thanks." I started to leave, but Hans stopped me.

"Hey, before you go. Are you and Garrett free for dinner tomorrow evening at my parents' house? We're going to do a full Christmas feast before Leah has to return for her last week of work in Portland."

"Yes, I can't think of anything pressing. Count us in, and let me know what we can bring."

"Great. Just bring yourselves." Hans smiled at Leah. "We'll take care of the rest."

"Okay, see you then." I went to find a seat. I knew Garrett would want to have dinner with Leah and the Krause family, but I had to think of something to bring.

A spot opened up near the stage. I hurried over to grab it and let out a little gasp when I sat down and realized that Pierce was seated next to me.

"Oh, hi, how are you?" I asked, trying to recover. When I'd last seen him, he was being taken to the police station for further questioning. Part of me had convinced myself that he had to be guilty, given his argument with Owen and the scratch on his face.

"I'm not sitting in a jail cell, so I guess I'll drink to that." He lifted his heavy beer stein.

If Chief Meyers had released him, she must not have thought he was a flight risk or dangerous. Maybe she wanted to detain him and didn't have enough evidence to keep him in custody.

"How are you doing?" I asked again, hoping he might open up if I created a safe space for him to talk.

"Better now that I'm not stuck at the police station." He chugged his beer. "Did you hear that Owen's in stable condition?"

"No, that's good news." In the rush of the day, I hadn't heard any updates.

"Everyone thinks I did it. God, I would think I did it. I get why people are suspicious of me, but this village can be brutal when it comes to rumors. Isn't the saying that we're supposed to be assumed innocent until proven guilty? It's the opposite for me. I'm like a piranha. No one will even sit next to me. I see their stares. I know what they're thinking.

"Pierce did it. Pierce snapped. Pierce is a starving artist who couldn't hack it. I've heard it all. The evidence points to me, too. Owen was stabbed with my ornament carving knife. I'm sure you've heard that."

I shook my head, trying to keep my composure. This was a

major revelation, and yet Pierce sounded casual about it. "No, really?"

"Yeah, which somehow means I'm to blame. Owen tried to start a fight. He smashed my pottery shortly before he was stabbed. I could have gone after him, but I didn't because I'm not violent. I see how the evidence looks—my knife, this huge scratch on my cheek, but I didn't do it. I didn't hurt him. Now that he's awake, hopefully, he'll confirm it wasn't me. I'm fairly sure that Chief Meyers believes me, but hearing it from him should put an end to any questions."

"She must have if she let you go." I considered my words carefully. "If you don't mind me asking, why did Owen break your pieces? It's fine if you don't feel comfortable talking about it; I completely understand."

"No, hey, at least you're speaking to me. Everyone else is giving me a wide berth, like at any moment I'm going to pull a hatchet from behind my back and go on a stabbing spree." He sighed and ran his finger around the rim of his stein. "Owen was furious because he learned I'm going into business with a friend in Wenatchee."

"Why did that upset him?" My feet tapped to the beat of the holiday polka.

"He's been trying to buy me out for months. I refused. I could tell he was not going to be someone I wanted to deal with when it comes to business—or really, anything." Pierce took another drink of his ale, leaving a thin foam mustache above his lip. He wiped it off with the edge of his napkin. "I don't think he was used to people saying no to him much. He wouldn't accept that I didn't want to sell the business to him. He kept coming back and bumping up his offer little by little. Then, he claimed that I was playing games to get him to bid higher. I wasn't. I just didn't like the guy, and I had other offers on the table."

"That's why he broke your pottery?"

"Yeah. He claimed that I was doing clandestine deals behind his back. He tossed around some veiled threats like he was going to make me 'pay for what I'd done' and that I would regret crossing him. But the thing is, I was upfront and honest with him from the first day he sauntered into my pottery studio. It probably sounds too out there, but I'm an artist. I feel people's energy. It affects me. Owen's energy was dark. No amount of money would have swayed me to work with him."

"I know exactly what you're talking about. I've had similar experiences where people's energy can either be magnetic or polarizing."

"Yeah, Owen's was polarizing." He swirled his beer. I wanted to tell him it was unnecessary, but I didn't think this was the appropriate time to share my beer knowledge. I wanted to keep him talking about Owen.

"In some ways, I don't blame whoever stabbed him. Not that I would wish him harm, but given my interactions with the guy, I can imagine that someone might have finally had enough. I just wish they hadn't framed me."

"How do you think they got your knife?" I spotted Mac heading our way with my meatballs and a pint of beer.

"They probably swiped it from my booth. It wouldn't have been difficult. I was throwing pottery for part of the night. People were streaming in and out. Anyone could have grabbed it and tucked it in a pocket or a purse."

"Dinner delivery," Mac announced, placing a steaming plate of meatballs and a pint of amber ale in front of me. "Prost." He noticed Pierce's stein. "That's looking a bit low. Can I top you off?"

Pierce covered the top of his glass with his hands. "Thanks, but I'm good."

281

"You good otherwise, Sloan?" Mac sounded casual, but I caught his drift and his sharp glance at Pierce.

"I'm great. Thanks for this; I can't wait to dive in." It was nearly impossible to resist the urge to devour one of the meatballs whole, but the plate steamed like an erupting volcano. They needed a minute to cool, and I needed to hear the rest of Pierce's story.

"Anyway, like I told Chief Meyers, it wasn't as if I had my carving tools locked up. They were sitting out next to my wheel. I'm guessing that whoever stabbed him saw him wreck my pottery and recognized they had a chance to pin this on me." He tipped his stein to finish the last few sips of his beer.

"Do you remember seeing anyone hanging out by your tools?"

"Chief Meyers asked me the same thing. Unfortunately, no. It was so busy. I must have had close to a thousand people through my booth. I was making sales, talking to customers about special holiday orders, and doing demos on the wheel. I wasn't paying any attention to my tools because I never considered they'd be used to stab someone."

He sounded distraught. I was inclined to believe him, especially since Chief Meyers had let him go, but there was still the issue of the scratch on his face.

"I implicated myself with this." He touched the scratch on his cheek and answered the question I hadn't asked. "I had to go out to my truck to get another box of vases because I went through inventory faster than planned. I ran into a branch on Greta's booth. It wasn't her fault. I moved out of the way for a family passing by, and my cheek skimmed her garlands. It caught on a sharp piece of the wire she used to string them together. It bled for about ten minutes, but it's already scabbed over now. I had to call my doctor's office to make sure I was up to date on my tetanus shot."

It seemed like a reasonable explanation.

I didn't envy Chief Meyers. Pierce was the easiest suspect. Everything appeared to point to him, but he had logically broken down each of the things that had led me to believe he could have done it. That was good for him, but it meant that I was no closer to figuring out who stabbed Owen.

CHAPTER

TWELVE

"THANKS for not treating me like an outcast," Pierce said, standing and picking up his empty stein. "You're one of the good ones, Sloan. Have a happy holiday."

I watched him return his glass. He scored points from me for that small act of kindness alone. Bussing tables came with the territory when running a brewery—or a holiday festival—but I was always touched by customers who made a point of helping out.

Everything Pierce shared made me ready to take him off my list of potential suspects, but until Chief Meyers made an official arrest, I wasn't crossing off any names.

My dinner had cooled enough to eat. I devoured the savory meat bathed in the tangy cream sauce. They melted in my mouth. I used the potatoes to scrape up more of the sauce and washed it down with the amber ale. I knew I wasn't the best judge since my stomach had been rumbling for hours, but this might be my favorite holiday meal—ever.

"Now you look more like the Sloan I know and love,"

Garrett interrupted my love affair with my dinner and slid on the bench across from me.

"I would offer you a bite, but I've basically licked my plate clean." I pointed to the evidence with my fork.

"That means you'll be ready for dessert soon." Garrett helped himself to a sip of my beer. "Der Keller's amber is always solid."

"I told Mac the other day that I think it's even better. You know what he told me?"

"I'm all ears."

"They changed the malt. You can taste the difference, can't you? It's subtle, but there's a touch more caramel and almost a burnt butter note." I pushed the pint toward him again to try.

He closed his eyes and savored another taste, swishing the liquid on his tongue. "I'm also getting toffee."

"Maybe we'll have to brew a hoppy red for our winter rotation," I suggested. "Something like this, but punch up the hops for the hop heads. Maybe a trio of Northwest hops—Cascade, Simcoe, and Centennial." The nearby Yakima Valley was the world's largest hop-growing region. It had surpassed Germany in production a few years back, a stat that Otto and Ursula enjoyed teasing their friends back in their motherland about.

"You had me at hops," Garrett retorted with a goofy grin. "In all seriousness, you look like you have a lot more color in your cheeks. Are you up for hunting down some dessert and doing a little shopping, or are you ready to call it a night?"

"The meatballs were magic. I'm up for anything, although you just missed Pierce."

"Pierce?" Garrett glanced around us like he expected Pierce to be hiding behind the Christmas trees. "So he's not being detained any longer? Does that mean that Chief Meyers doesn't think he did it?"

"I'm not sure."

We split the rest of my beer while I filled him on everything that Pierce had told me, as well as my earlier conversations with both Blake and Greta.

"That leaves us with Blake or Greta," Garrett said when I was done. "Assuming that Pierce is telling the truth, that is."

"Exactly. Blake's desperation to make Kunst and Kaffee successful gives her a viable reason for stabbing him."

"Same for Greta," Garrett added. "If she was in love with him and realized that he didn't reciprocate her feelings or was having an affair with someone else, I can imagine that she might have done something drastic, like stab him."

"And both of them could have stolen the pottery knife from Pierce's booth," I said, wiping my hands on a napkin and stretching.

"You know what might help us? German chocolate almond cookies. The bakery has them fresh from the oven." Garrett held out his hand to help me up. "What do you say? Chocolate?"

"Always chocolate." I laced my hand through his.

Kuchen, an authentic German bakery in the village, smelled like it belonged in the pages of *Charlie and the Chocolate Factory*. In addition to the chocolate almond cookies, there were cake stands displaying apple cinnamon crumble cakes, jam-filled Linzer cookies, Sacher torte, and plum tarts.

"Should we do a repeat of donuts and get one of everything?" Garrett leaned closer to get a better look at the tarts.

"You mentioned chocolate, so I'm going for the cookie," I said, practically salivating at the chewy chocolate cookies decorated with toasted almonds and powdered sugar.

"Me too, although the plum tart is tempting, we had pizza for lunch, so I don't think I can handle a whole tart." He rubbed his stomach with his free hand.

"Hans and Leah invited us to dinner at the Krause's

tomorrow night. Why don't I make a tart to bring to share?" I had a recipe that would serve a crowd and didn't take hours to bake.

"A plum tart will go perfectly with a growler or two of our baked tart sour ale."

Garrett and I had brewed a small batch of an experimental sour with tangerines, candied orange peel, cinnamon, vanilla, and milk sugar. It turned out so well we wanted to recreate it on our main brewing equipment to add to the December tap list.

We got our cookies and strolled through the stalls, taking our time to stop and enjoy each booth. It felt nice to carve out a little normalcy after everything that had happened. Harmonic melodies of a youth choir rang through the air as the sun sunk behind the mountain, giving way to a dazzling display of stars and a golden winter moon.

Our feet crunched through the snow, and our breath puffed out in bursts of steam.

But the peaceful moment was cut short by the sound of screams.

We didn't hesitate. We ran toward the screaming. It was coming from Greta's booth.

A small crowd had formed in front of the colorful flower stall.

"Back away. Everyone, back away," Greta commanded. She held a sharp pruning knife and lifted it to her neck. "Get away from me. I mean it."

I dropped Garrett's hand and pushed through the bystanders. "Let's give her some space, okay?" I hoped that my voice sounded calm. I felt anything but inside. My heart thudded against my chest. My neck was damp. Heat rose to my cheeks like a spreading wildfire.

Why was Greta threatening to hurt herself?

I looked for any sign of Chief Meyers or her team, but no officers were in sight.

"Greta, can you put the knife down?" I asked, taking a small step forward.

She dug it into her skin. A tiny drop of blood pooled at the knife's edge and trickled down her neck. "No. Back up. I'm not kidding. I'd rather die than be arrested. Just leave me alone." I'd lost Garrett in my hurry to help. Surely, he would have the wherewithal to call Chief Meyers. I'd seen officers in the beer tent earlier. They would respond to the commotion.

But for the short term, it was just me.

I wasn't trained in negotiating a situation like this. Would continuing to try to calm Greta down make it worse? I wished I knew the protocol, but I went with my gut since I didn't.

"Greta, I'm here to help. I don't want to see you get hurt."

"My life is already ruined. I have nothing to live for anymore." Her grasp remained firmly on the knife.

"It might not feel that way now. I understand. I've been through some dark and very lonely times in my life. There were days when I was in foster care that I thought I would be alone forever. If you had told me then that I would have a family and this community that I love, I never would have believed you. The same is true for you. Things might feel bleak, but that's not a permanent feeling."

"No, you don't understand," she wailed; her eyes were wild, darting from side to side like a stunned animal. "They're going to arrest me. I stabbed him. I didn't mean to. I just wanted to hurt him, to wound him the way he wounded me. I didn't know it would turn so serious. There was so much blood. We got in a fight. He tried to hit me. I swear. I used the knife for self-defense, but the police will never believe that."

"I've known Chief Meyers for many years and can assure you that she will listen, but you have to give her a chance to do that, okay?" I raised my hands to show her that I wasn't a threat. "If you want, we can go find her together."

Greta's hand trembled. The knife shook against her neck like she was lifting a heavy weight she could no longer hold.

I took a tiny step forward. "You're not alone, Greta. I can't promise there won't be consequences, but I can promise you that you don't have to go through this alone."

She released her grip on the knife. It dropped on the snow just as Chief Meyers and two officers raced forward and contained her.

THIRTEEN

I KEPT my promise to Greta and accompanied her to the police station with Chief Meyers's permission. She confessed to stabbing Owen but continued to insist that it had been an act of self-defense. Not coming forward immediately probably didn't do her many favors, but after she had calmed down and a lawyer had been called to represent her, Chief Meyers walked me outside.

"I appreciate your willingness to jump in, Sloan. You were composed and collected and met her where she was at. It's like I always say to my cadets: empathy is your greatest asset." She scanned Front Street as we spoke.

I couldn't imagine what it must be like to be in her shoes. She was constantly on watch, protecting our community.

"What's going to happen to her now?" It was strange to watch a picture-perfect snapshot of the village glowing beneath millions of twinkling lights. The snow on the sledding hill sparkled like it had been sprinkled with stardust. Families gathered around a bonfire at the base of the hill, roasting marshmallows in the flickering flames.

The laughter of sledders echoed as they ascended the hill, getting ready for a thrilling descent down the icy slope. A new group of carolers took center stage in the gazebo as a horse-drawn carriage decked out in holiday greenery paraded down the street, leaving a trail of jingling bells.

"I don't need to tell you that the charges against Greta are serious. We have been able to obtain two eyewitness statements that corroborate her story. Both witnesses observed a man and woman who matched Greta's and Owen's descriptions arguing. According to the witnesses, he threatened her first, and then she stabbed him with the knife. She claims he took out the knife first but dropped it. According to her, she grabbed it and stabbed him before he had a chance to react. We're considering a lesser charge in light of the witness testimony. Owen is in stable condition. It sounds like the prognosis is good, but we'll have to wait until he's discharged before we pursue charges against him as well."

"What does that mean?"

"Assault and battery versus assault with a deadly weapon," Chief Meyers responded matter-of-factly. "There's a range of potential sentences and penalties if self-defense is involved."

That was a glimmer of positive news in an otherwise tragic situation.

A vision of Owen grabbing something from Pierce's booth flashed in my head. "You know, Owen might have taken Pierce's knife," I said, explaining what I'd witnessed.

"That could be the confirmation we need. I'll make a note of it. You may be called for further statements." Chief Meyers silenced her walkie-talkie. "I'm sorry if that might impact your holiday."

"It's no problem. I'll do whatever I can to help."

"As will we." She tipped her head. "Goodnight, then."

"*Gute Natch.*" I felt German slip out of my lips.

Chief Meyers couldn't conceal a half grin. "Oh dear, Sloan. April Ablin's gotten to you."

I clasped my hand over my mouth. "Never. Say it isn't so."

She laughed as she returned inside.

I went to find Garrett but didn't have to look long. He was waiting for me at the base of the sledding hill.

"How did it go?" he asked with genuine concern.

"She confessed," I sighed. My teeth stung from the plummeting alpine temps. "I feel sorry for her. It sounds like it was self-defense. Chief Meyers is considering reducing the charge because a couple of people saw them fighting."

"I guess that's something." Garrett pulled me toward him and rubbed my shoulder.

I leaned against his chest. "It's so sad that it had to come this. Greta wasn't the only person he harmed. Don't get me wrong, I'm not trying to justify her decision to resort to violence, but if he came after her first, it doesn't seem like she had the intent to hurt him seriously."

"Yeah, but what about Pierce's pottery knife?"

I relayed what Chief Meyers told me.

"Well, I'm just glad it's over, and it sounds like Owen will recover, and hopefully, Greta will get the help she needs." Garrett scowled. "I can't imagine what might have happened if you didn't jump in. Actually, let's not think about that."

"No, let's not." I leaned into his chest. "The only thing I want to imagine now is a hot bath, a cup of tea, and my bed."

"Then, let's make that a reality."

CHAPTER
FOURTEEN

THE NEXT DAY, news of Greta's arrest blew through the village faster than the howling winter storm rolling into the village from the high Cascades. I spent the bulk of the day baking a plum tart with fresh plums, ground almonds, and a splash of our sour ale and running back and forth between the tasting room and the brewery. Most tourists were already on their way home, but we had a steady stream of regulars come in for a pint with a side of gossip.

At the dinner hour, we left Nitro in Kat's capable hands, packed my plum tart, and took an evening stroll to Otto and Ursula's house. Mac and Hans had put up retro Christmas lights and a golden star along the roofline.

Otto greeted us with big hugs and hung our coats near the rack by the front door. "Come in, come in. It is bitter cold. Ze snow has been coming down sideways all day. Warm up by ze fire."

Their cozy living room was bathed in warmth from the crackling fire. There were assorted crocheted throw blankets and pillows on the couches and chairs, all stitched by Ursula. A holly wreath adorned the mantel with photos of Mac, Hans, Alex, and me. Every corner of the room was filled with hand-crafted decorations. Paper stars hung from the ceiling. Wooden nutcrackers lined the windowsill and side tables.

The Tannenbaum stood in the far corner of the room. Twinkling candles and paper garlands stretched around its fragrant branches. Popsicle stick ornaments made by Alex in preschool and more family photos hung from the tree.

The attached dining room was set with a festive tablecloth and holiday-themed porcelain. Their collection of fine china, passed down for generations, graced the table. Soft strains of German carols played on their vintage record player.

"Ziz smells wonderful, Sloan," Ursula said, praising my plum tart. "You didn't need to bake, but we will certainly enjoy ziz."

Intoxicating aromas of cinnamon, spices, and her sauerbraten stewing on the stove wafted from the kitchen.

"Where should I put it?" I asked.

"On ze buffet would be good." She motioned to the buffet set with dainty Christmas dessert and tea plates. "We will start in ze living room with some snacks and beer if zat sounds good."

"We brought one of our experimental brews to share." Garrett lifted the growler.

"Did someone say experimental beer?" Mac called from the kitchen. "I'm pouring the first round. Bring that back here."

Alex came out from the kitchen, balancing a tray of meats, cheeses, pickles, liverwurst, pates, and assorted bread. "Hey, Mom, I thought I heard you come in. Oma put me to work in exchange for an extra root beer. Is Uncle Hans here yet?"

"Not unless he's in the kitchen with you."

I loved seeing how comfortable Alex was in his grandparents' house. This was his second home growing up. It was a happy reminder of how I had changed the narrative and created a family for him and me.

He set the platter on the coffee table and stood with his back against the fireplace. We caught up on his day while we waited for Leah and Hans to arrive.

They showed up just as Mac and Garrett brought out a round of drinks.

"Happy Christmas, everyone." Hans shook snow from his coat and ushered Leah into the living room. "Sorry, we're late."

Their cheeks were bright with color.

"How was ze skiing?" Ursula asked, lowering herself into a chair next to the fireplace.

"Really great." Leah couldn't take her eyes off Hans. "So great. I can't even form a complete sentence."

Mac passed around pints while Garrett came to stand next to me. "I'm surprised to hear that. With it gusting outside, I would have thought the skiing would have been brutal."

Leah giggled.

Hans put his arm around his waist and cleared his throat. "We were going to wait until after dinner to do this, but we're both so excited that I can't wait."

Leah bobbed her head in agreement.

"We didn't get much skiing done today because I proposed at the ski lodge, and Leah said yes," Hans gushed.

Leah held out her hand to show off a sparkling engagement ring.

The room erupted with hugs and congratulatory cheers.

Once we had settled down a little, Otto stood next to Ursula. "I zink zis calls for a toast, *ja?*" His pale blue eyes misted with happiness. "We are lucky to have ze family together here around ze fire. Ze holidays are special for Ursula and me because of all of you." His hand quivered slightly as he raised his Christmas stein. "To Leah and Hans and our beautiful growing Krause family."

Everyone followed suit and cheered "Prost" as we clinked our glasses in celebration.

"And ze wedding it will be here, *ja*?" Ursula's apple-like cheeks dimpled when she smiled.

"We're going to need to brew a special wedding beer," Garrett said.

"Yep." Mac nodded in agreement. "Another collaboration starts tomorrow."

"I don't know if it needs to start tomorrow," Leah protested. "We haven't even set a date."

We all laughed and peppered them with dozens of questions while we enjoyed our drinks and Ursula's pre-dinner feast.

When everyone moved to the dining room, Garrett gently tugged my arm to stop me. "Hang one on second. There's a question I've been needing to ask you."

For a minute, my heart lurched. He wasn't thinking of proposing, too?

Not that I couldn't imagine that one day, but tonight was about Leah and Hans, and I was content with our relationship at the moment. My divorce with Mac was final. We had found a new common ground and routine with Alex. I wasn't ready for anything more. Not yet.

"I'm excited about spending the holidays with you, Sloan," Garrett's voice was husky and filled with emotion. "But you haven't told me what's on your wish list."

I let out a small sigh of relief and smiled. "I don't need a list because everything I want and could ever need is right here in this room."

He kissed my head and whispered, "Me too."

ACKNOWLEDGMENTS

Writing a holiday mystery short in six weeks definitely challenged me. It was a good challenge and one that I didn't embark on alone. First and foremost, I must thank Gordy Seeley, my beloved Tech Guy, who is always up for any adventure, especially if it involves beer, and is my constant hype man. Not only did he convince me that I could write this short in a tight timeline, but he was also responsible for the backend of publishing this book—the cover art design, formatting, page proofing, and distribution.

A huge thank you to my patrons on Patreon, who were instrumental in providing feedback and input, weighed in on story ideas and recipes and encouraged me to keep writing when my eye started twitching and my hair looked like something out of a horror film. A special shoutout to Flo Cho, Courtny Drydale, Lily Gill, and Kat Webb for your constant encouragement and support. It means the world to me.

Every book, even a short book, needs a stellar editor. I had that in Melinda Hamilton, who enthusiastically agreed to lend her editorial eye to the manuscript and get it back to me at lightning speed. It just so happens that Mel is very well-versed in Bavarian culture, which was such an awesome bonus for making sure that the recipes and traditions were spot on. Thank you for caring about Sloan and making this short story the best it can possibly be.

And, finally, to you. I'm hugely grateful for our connection and this fantastic book community. In a world of disconnection, finding your people is so important, and I'm so happy you are my people.

XOXO,
    Ellie

RECIPES INSPIRED BY SLOAN KRAUSE

The following are a collection of recipes featured in the Sloan Krause Mystery Shorts: *Hold on for Beer Life*, *A Brew to a Kill*, and *Ale I Want for Christmas is a Clue*.

Happy baking!

RECIPES

HOLD ON FOR BEER LIFE

Delight in these tasty recipes featuring the crisp, warm, and citrusy flavors of summer.

BRUSCHETTA TRIO PAIRED WITH A HONEY ALE

Ingredients:

For the base:

    1 loaf of French bread—cut into ¼ inch slices

    ¼ cup olive oil

For the toppings:

    1 8-ounce jar of apple chutney

    1 6-ounce container walnut pesto

    4 ounces of goat cheese

    1 large tomato, diced

    2 cloves garlic, minced

    ¼ cup chopped fresh basil

    1 tablespoon olive oil

    1 tablespoon balsamic vinegar

    ½ teaspoon salt

    ½ teaspoon pepper

Directions:

Preheat the oven to 400° F. Brush both sides of the bread slices with olive oil and place them on a baking sheet. Bake for five minutes, then turn slices over and bake for another five minutes until the bread is toasted on both sides. While the bread is toasting, toss diced tomato, garlic, basil, olive oil, vinegar, and salt and pepper together in a mixing bowl.

Remove the bread from the oven. Divide into three equal portions. Spread a generous layer of apple chutney on a third of the slices. Spread walnut pesto over the next third and crumble goat cheese over the top. Scoop the tomato mixture onto the remaining slices and serve immediately.

SUMMER SALAD PAIRED WITH A ROSEHIP PALE ALE

Ingredients:

For the salad:

    16 ounces contain spring lettuce mix

    1 cup candied pecans

    2 beets, sliced and grilled

    8 ounces goat cheese

    Fresh dill, chives, and thyme chopped

For the dressing:

    3 ounces rosehip pale ale

    4 tablespoons olive oil

    1 tablespoon apple cider vinegar

    1 tablespoon honey

    Salt and pepper

Directions:

Toss salad greens with pecans, grilled beets, goat cheese crumbles, and fresh herbs in a large bowl. For the dressing, add rosehip pale ale, olive oil, apple cider vinegar, honey, and salt and pepper (to taste) to a small mixing bowl and whisk together. Drizzle over the salad and serve immediately.

YELLOW SQUASH SOUP PAIRED WITH A NORTHWEST RED ALE

Ingredients:

2 tablespoons olive oil
2 white onions, chopped
5 cloves garlic, minced
5-6 cups yellow squash, seeded and cubed
4 sprigs fresh thyme, finely chopped
5 cloves garlic, minced
4 cups chicken broth
½ cup NW red ale
1 teaspoon salt
1 teaspoon white pepper
¼ cup heavy cream

Directions:

Heat olive oil in a large saucepan over medium heat. Add onions, squash, and fresh thyme and cook for 5 minutes stirring frequently. Add the garlic and stir for one more minute.

Then add chicken broth, NW red ale, and salt and pepper. Bring to a boil. Cover, reduce heat to low, and let the soup simmer for 20 minutes or until squash is tender.

Remove from heat. Add one cup of soup at a time to a blender and blend in batches until soup is smooth. Return to the saucepan, add heavy cream, and heat through. Serve hot.

GRILLED CITRUS
CHICKEN PAIRED WITH
AN IPA

Ingredients:

1 cup IPA (or any kind of citrus beer)
    4 large chicken breasts
    1 red onion, sliced into rings
    1 orange
    1 large bunch of cilantro, chopped
    1 teaspoon pepper
    1 teaspoon salt

Directions:

Pour beer into an 8-inch by 8-inch baking dish. Grate orange rind and sprinkle into baking dish. Place chicken breasts in the beer bath. Poke holes in the chicken with a fork to allow the marinade to be absorbed. Peel and slice red onion in rings and place over chicken. Squeeze in the juice of the orange. Wash and chop the stems from the cilantro and add them to the mixture. Sprinkle with salt and pepper. Marinate for 8 hours or preferably overnight. Heat gas or charcoal grill to medium heat (approximately 350-400° F). Grill chicken breasts for 20 to 30 minutes or until internal temperature reaches 165° F. Serve hot.

VANILLA CUSTARD PAIRED WITH A CHOCOLATE RASPBERRY STOUT

Ingredients:

2 cups milk
2 tablespoons cornstarch
½ cup sugar
2 eggs, lightly beaten
1 teaspoon vanilla extract
1 teaspoon vanilla bean paste

Directions:

Combine milk, cornstarch, and sugar in a saucepan and whisk together over medium heat. Allow the milk to start to bubble; careful not to let it scorch on the bottom of the pan. Once the milk has reached a low boil, remove the pan from the heat. Beat eggs in a separate pan. Add two tablespoons of milk mixture to the eggs, whisking constantly. Repeat until all of the milk has been added, then return the pan to the heat and whisk over medium heat until custard begins to thicken. Do not boil. Once the custard has thickened, remove from the heat and whisk in vanilla extract and paste. Chill for one hour and serve cold.

RECIPES

A BREW TO A KILL

Enjoy this taste of Nitro's menu from the cozy comfort of your own kitchen. Read on for the recipes.

WHITE VELVET COOKIES

Ingredients:

1/2 cup unsalted butter, at room temperature
1/2 cup granulated sugar
1 large egg
1 teaspoon pure vanilla extract
1 and 1/2 cups all-purpose flour
1/2 teaspoon baking powder
1/4 teaspoon baking soda
1/4 teaspoon salt
1/4 cup sour cream

Directions:

Preheat oven to 350°F and line a baking sheet with parchment paper. In a large mixing bowl, cream the butter and sugar together until light and fluffy. Add the egg and vanilla extract and mix well. In a separate bowl, whisk together the flour, baking powder, baking soda, and salt. Gradually add the dry ingredients to the wet mixture, mixing until just combined. Stir in the sour cream until the dough is smooth. Scoop out the dough by the tablespoonful and roll into balls. Place the balls on the prepared baking sheet, leaving about 2 inches of space between each cookie. Bake for 12-15 minutes, or until the cookies are lightly golden around the edges. Remove from the oven and allow the cookies to cool on the baking sheet for a few minutes before transferring them to a wire rack to cool completely.

RHUBARB-FILLED CRUMBLE COOKIES

Ingredients for the filling:

4 cups chopped fresh rhubarb
1/2 cup granulated sugar
1 tablespoon cornstarch
1 teaspoon vanilla extract

Ingredients for the crumble topping:

1 cup all-purpose flour
1/2 cup rolled oats
1/2 cup brown sugar
1/2 teaspoon ground cinnamon
1/2 cup unsalted butter, cold and cubed

Directions:

Preheat oven to 375°F and grease a baking dish with butter. In a medium bowl, mix together the rhubarb, sugar, cornstarch, and vanilla extract until well combined. Pour the mixture into the prepared baking dish and set aside. In a separate bowl, mix together the flour, oats, brown sugar, and cinnamon. Add the cubed butter and use your fingers to rub the butter into the dry ingredients until the mixture resembles coarse breadcrumbs. Sprinkle the crumble mixture evenly over the top of the rhubarb mixture. Bake for 30-40 minutes, or until the crumble is golden brown and the rhubarb filling is bubbling. Remove from the oven and allow the crumble to cool for a few minutes before serving.

CHOCOLATE
SHORTBREAD COOKIES

Ingredients:

1 cup (2 sticks) unsalted butter, at room temperature
1/2 cup granulated sugar
1/4 cup unsweetened cocoa powder
2 and 1/4 cups all-purpose flour
1/2 teaspoon salt
1 teaspoon vanilla extract

Directions:

Preheat oven to 350°F and line a 9-inch square baking pan with parchment paper. In a large mixing bowl, cream the butter and sugar together until light and fluffy.

Add the cocoa powder and mix until well combined. In a separate bowl, whisk together the flour and salt. Gradually add the dry ingredients to the butter mixture, mixing until the dough comes together and is well combined. Stir in the vanilla extract. Press the dough evenly into the bottom of the prepared baking pan. Bake for 25-30 minutes, or until the shortbread is firm to the touch and slightly browned around the edges. Remove from the oven and allow the shortbread to cool in the pan for 10 minutes before slicing it into bars or squares.

STRAWBERRY FRENCH TOAST

Ingredients:

1 loaf of bread
4 eggs
1/2 cup heavy cream
1/4 cup IPA (or substitute with milk)
1 teaspoon vanilla extract
1 teaspoon lemon zest
1 tablespoon brown sugar
4 tablespoons unsalted butter
2 cups fresh strawberries, sliced
1 tablespoon fresh lemon juice
1/2 teaspoon vanilla extract

Directions:

Preheat oven to 350°F. In a mixing bowl, whisk together the eggs, heavy cream, IPA, vanilla extract, lemon zest, and brown sugar until well combined. Cut thick slices of the bread and soak them in the egg mixture for a few minutes. Heat a large sauté pan over medium-high heat and add a tablespoon of butter. Once the butter has melted and the pan is hot, add a few slices of the soaked bread to the pan and cook until the bottom is golden brown, then flip and cook until the other side is golden brown and crispy. Repeat with the remaining slices of bread, adding more butter to the pan as needed. Place the cooked French toast slices on to a parchment-lined baking sheet and put them in the preheated oven to warm while you make the strawberry compote.

In the same sauté pan, add another tablespoon of butter and the sliced strawberries. Cook over medium heat until the strawberries start to break down and release their juices. Add the lemon juice, vanilla extract, and brown sugar to the pan and stir to combine. Reduce the heat to low and let the strawberries simmer until they have softened and a thick sauce has formed. Remove the French toast from the oven and serve with the warm strawberry compote on top, and finish with a dollop of lemon-infused whipped cream.

CHICKEN ARTICHOKE SOUP

Ingredients:

2 tablespoons olive oil
1 large onion, diced
2 large carrots, peeled and diced
2 stalks celery, diced
4 cloves garlic, chopped
1/4 teaspoon red pepper flakes
1 teaspoon salt
1/2 teaspoon black pepper
8 cups chicken broth
1 can (14 ounces) artichoke hearts, drained and chopped
2 boneless, skinless chicken breasts
1/2 cup heavy cream
2 cups baby spinach leaves
1/4 cup grated Parmesan cheese
1/4 cup grated Romano cheese
1/4 cup grated Asiago cheese

Directions:

In a large pot or Dutch oven, heat the olive oil over medium heat. Add the diced onion, carrot, and celery and cook until the vegetables start to soften, about 5 minutes. Add the chopped garlic, red pepper flakes, salt, and black pepper and cook for an additional 2 minutes. Pour in the chicken broth and bring the soup to a boil. Add the chopped artichoke hearts and chicken breasts to the pot. Reduce the heat to low and let the soup simmer for 20-25 minutes, or until the chicken is cooked through and tender. Remove the chicken breasts from the soup and shred them with two forks. Return the shredded chicken to the pot. Stir in the heavy cream and baby spinach leaves and let the soup simmer for an additional 5 minutes. Finish with grated Parmesan, Romano, and Asiago cheeses and serve hot.

RECIPES

ALE I WANT FOR CHRISTMAS IS A CLUE

Enjoy this collection of holiday Krause Family favorites.
Wishing you a season filled with love, light, joy, and lots of
Bavarian baking.

ZIMTSTERNE (CINNAMON STARS)

Ingredients:

For the Dough:
    2 cups ground almonds
    1 1/2 cups powdered sugar
    2 teaspoons cinnamon
    1/4 teaspoon cloves
    2 large egg whites
    1 teaspoon almond extract
    A pinch of salt

For the Icing:
    1 cup powdered sugar
    1/2 teaspoon almond extract
    2 tablespoons dark chocolate stout

Directions:

In a large mixing bowl, combine the ground almonds, powdered sugar, cinnamon, and cloves. In a separate bowl, whisk the egg whites with a hand mixer or whisk until they become frothy and form soft peaks. Gently fold the egg whites into the almond mixture. Add the almond extract and a pinch of salt. Continue to fold and mix until a soft, sticky dough forms. Form the dough into a ball and wrap it in plastic wrap. Place it in the refrigerator to chill for at least 1 hour.

Preheat the oven to 325°F and line a baking sheet with parchment paper. Roll out the chilled dough to a thickness of about 1/4 inch on a surface lightly dusted with powdered sugar. Use star-shaped cookie cutters to cut out the cookies. Place the stars on the baking sheet. In a small bowl, mix the powdered sugar, almond extract, and stout to create a thick but spreadable icing. Adjust the stout to achieve the desired consistency. Use a small brush or a spoon to ice the tops of the stars with a thin layer of icing. The icing should cover the entire surface but not be too thick. Place the baking sheet in the oven and bake for about 12-15 minutes or until the Zimt-sterne bakes to a pale golden color. Remove from baking sheet and allow to cool before serving.

SEMOLINA PUDDING

Ingredients:

1/2 cup semolina
2 cups milk
1/4 cup sugar
1/2 teaspoon vanilla extract
Pinch of salt

Directions:

In a medium-sized saucepan, add the semolina and sugar. Mix them, ensuring the semolina is evenly coated with sugar. Gradually pour in the milk while stirring continuously to avoid lumps. Combine the semolina and milk thoroughly with a whisk or a wooden spoon. Place the saucepan over low to medium heat and continue stirring until it thickens. Reduce the heat to low, continue to simmer, and stir gently. It should take about 10-15 minutes. When the pudding is almost ready, stir in the vanilla extract and a pinch of salt. Remove the saucepan from the heat and allow the pudding to cool slightly. Serve with cranberry orange IPA compote (recipe below).

CRANBERRY ORANGE IPA COMPOTE

Ingredients:

2 large oranges, zested and juiced
2 cups fresh or frozen cranberries
1 cup sugar
Pinch of salt
Pinch of ground cloves
1/2 cup citrus IPA (or any citrus-flavored beer)

Directions:

Zest both oranges using a zester or fine grater, and set the zest aside. Squeeze the juice from both oranges, straining out any seeds. In a small saucepan, combine the orange zest, orange juice, fresh or frozen cranberries, sugar, salt, and ground cloves. Pour in the citrus IPA, place the pan over medium-high heat, and bring the mixture to a boil while stirring gently. Once the mixture comes to a boil, reduce the heat to low to maintain a gentle simmer. Allow the compote to simmer, uncovered, for about 10-15 minutes or until the cranberries begin to burst. Remove the saucepan from heat and let the compote cool to room temperature. Serve warm over pudding.

URSULA'S CHRISTMAS STOLLEN

Ingredients:

For the Stollen:
1 1/2 teaspoons active dry yeast
1/2 cup warm milk
1 teaspoon sugar
3 cups all-purpose flour
1/2 cup sugar
1/2 cup unsalted butter, softened
2 large eggs
1 teaspoon cinnamon
1/2 teaspoon nutmeg
1/4 teaspoon cardamom
1/2 cup golden raisins
1/2 cup dried cranberries
1/2 cup chopped nuts (e.g., almonds, walnuts)
4 ounces marzipan, diced into small pieces

For the Vanilla Glaze:
- 1 cup powdered sugar
- 1/2 teaspoon vanilla extract
- 2-3 tablespoons milk

Directions:

In a small bowl, dissolve the yeast in warm milk with 1 teaspoon of sugar and let it sit for about 5-10 minutes until it becomes frothy. While the yeast activates, combine the flour, granulated sugar, cinnamon, nutmeg, and cardamom in a separate bowl. Add the softened butter and eggs to the dry ingredients. Pour in the activated yeast mixture as well. Mix everything until it forms a rough dough.

Turn the dough onto a floured surface and knead it for about 5-7 minutes until it becomes smooth and elastic. You may need to add a little more flour if the dough is too sticky. Incorporate the raisins, cranberries, chopped nuts, and diced marzipan into the dough. Knead until the ingredients are evenly distributed throughout the dough.

Place the dough in a greased bowl, cover it with a clean kitchen towel, and let it rise in a warm, draft-free place for about 1-2 hours or until it has doubled. After the dough has risen, punch it down to remove excess air. Shape it into an oval or oblong loaf, resembling the traditional Stollen shape, on a baking sheet lined with parchment paper. Cover the shaped Stollen with a kitchen towel and allow it to rise for an additional 30-45 minutes.

Preheat your oven to 350°F. Bake the Stollen for 30-35 minutes or until it's golden brown and sounds hollow when tapped on the bottom. While the Stollen is baking, prepare the vanilla glaze by mixing powdered sugar, vanilla extract, and enough milk to create a smooth and pourable glaze. Set it aside. Once the Stollen is done baking and still warm, brush it generously with the vanilla glaze. Allow the glaze to set before slicing and serving.

Holiday Goulash Soup

Ingredients:

2 tablespoons vegetable oil
1 large onion, finely chopped
2 carrots, diced
2 celery stalks, diced
1 bell pepper (any color), diced
4 cloves garlic, minced
2 pounds stew meat (beef or pork), cut into bite-sized cubes
2 tablespoons sweet paprika
1 teaspoon thyme
1 teaspoon oregano
Salt and black pepper to taste
4 cups beef stock
1 can (14 ounces) crushed tomatoes
1 cup dark ale (such as a stout or a dark lager)
2 bay leaves

Directions:

In a large soup pan, heat the vegetable oil over medium-high heat. Add the chopped onions, carrots, celery, and bell pepper. Sauté them for about 5-7 minutes or until they become soft and translucent. Stir in the minced garlic and sauté for an additional minute until fragrant. Add the bite-sized stew meat to the pot. Brown the meat on all sides, stirring occasionally, for about 5-7 minutes. Sprinkle the sweet paprika, thyme, oregano, salt, and black pepper over the meat and vegetables. Stir well to evenly coat everything with the spices. Pour in the beef stock, crushed tomatoes, and dark ale. Stir to combine all the ingredients. Toss in the bay leaves for extra flavor. Reduce the heat to low, cover the pot, and let the goulash simmer gently for about 1.5 to 2 hours, or until the meat becomes tender and the flavors meld together. Stir occasionally during cooking. Serve with a dollop of sour cream and a slice of rustic bread.

BAVARIAN CREAM LATTE

Ingredients:

2 shots of espresso
1 tablespoon Bavarian Cream liqueur (*Eierlikör*)
1 cup steamed milk
Whipped cream, for topping
Chocolate shavings, for garnish
Ground nutmeg, for dusting

Directions:

Brew two shots of espresso using an espresso machine. You can use strong brewed coffee as a substitute if you don't have an espresso machine. Pour the Bavarian Cream liqueur (*Eierlikör*) into a large mug or latte glass. Add the freshly brewed espresso shots to the mug with the liqueur. Give it a gentle stir to combine. Steam and froth the milk using a milk frother or by heating it gently in a saucepan while whisking. The milk should be velvety and creamy. Slowly pour the steamed milk into the mug over the espresso and liqueur mixture, holding back the foam with a spoon to add it as the final touch. Generously top with a dollop of whipped cream. Sprinkle chocolate shavings over the whipped cream. You can use a fine grater or a chocolate bar with a peeler to create the shavings. Finish with a light dusting of ground nutmeg.

Sloan's Holiday
Plum Tart

Ingredients:

For the Tart Crust:
- 1 1/4 cups all-purpose flour
- 1/4 cup sugar
- 1/2 cup unsalted butter, cold and diced
- 1 large egg yolk
- 2 tablespoons cold water
- A pinch of salt

For the Plum Filling:
- 1 1/2 pounds (about 4 cups) ripe plums, pitted and sliced
- 1/4 cup sugar
- 1 tablespoon cornstarch
- 1/4 teaspoon cinnamon
- A splash of your favorite beer (approximately 2-3 tablespoons)

For the Base:

2 tablespoons breadcrumbs

2 tablespoons ground almonds (optional, for extra texture)

Directions:

Preheat your oven to 375°F. Combine the flour, sugar, and a pinch of salt in a food processor. Pulse briefly to mix. Add the cold, diced butter to the flour mixture in the food processor. Pulse until the mixture resembles coarse crumbs. In a small bowl, mix the egg yolk and cold water. Gradually add this mixture to the food processor and pulse until the dough starts to come together. Be careful not to overmix; stop as soon as the dough forms. Turn the dough onto a lightly floured surface and gently knead it until it comes together. Shape it into a disk, wrap it in plastic wrap, and refrigerate for at least 30 minutes.

While the dough is chilling, slice the plums and remove the pits. Place them in a large bowl. Mix the granulated sugar, cornstarch, and cinnamon in a small bowl. Sprinkle this mixture over the sliced plums and gently toss to coat. Roll out the chilled tart dough on a lightly floured surface into a circle about 12 inches in diameter. Transfer it to a tart pan or pie dish and press it gently into the bottom and sides. Trim any excess dough. Sprinkle a thin layer of breadcrumbs (this helps absorb excess moisture from the plums) and ground almonds (for extra texture) over the bottom of the tart crust. Arrange the sliced and coated plums in the tart crust, slightly overlapping them in a circular pattern. Drizzle a splash of beer evenly over the plum filling. Place the tart in the preheated oven and bake for 30-35 minutes, or until the crust is golden brown and the plum filling is bubbly and slightly caramelized. Allow the plum tart to cool for a bit before serving.

ABOUT THE AUTHOR

Ellie Alexander is a voracious storyteller and a lover of words and all things bookish. She believes that stories have the ability to transport and transform us. With over thirty published novels and counting, her goal is to tell stories that provide points of connection, escape, and understanding.

STAY IN TOUCH!

Connect with Ellie on her social media channels and scan the QR code below with your phone's camera to subscribe to her email newsletter:

patreon.com/EllieAlexander

instagram.com/ellie_alexander

tiktok.com/@elliealexanderauthor

youtube.com/elliealexanderauthor

amazon.com/author/elliealexander

facebook.com/elliealexanderauthor

pinterest.com/elliealexanderauthor

goodreads.com/elliealexanderauthor

bookbub.com/authors/ellie-alexander

ELLIE ALEXANDER'S AUTHOR ACADEMY

COURSES AND COACHING TO HELP ASPIRING AUTHORS WRITE, PITCH, AND MARKET THEIR BOOKS ON THE WAY TOWARD REALIZING THEIR DREAMS OF BECOMING PUBLISHED

Are you struggling with where to start when it comes to writing? Or maybe you've gotten partway through a draft and don't know what comes next? Perhaps you've finished a book and need help navigating the path to publication.

I love teaching and sharing the vast amount of knowledge that I've acquired publishing 29 books and counting. I've been in your shoes, and I have stacks and stacks of unfinished, terrible, horrible, no good first drafts that will never see the light of day. I've taken everything I've learned (the good and the bad) and transformed it into a mystery series masterclass. My comprehensive course takes the mystery out of how to craft, edit, and publish a novel with step-by-step videos, tangible assignments and activities, and an engaged and activity private community of writers just like you who will help cheer you on as you pound out that word count.

You can write that novel! It's time to stop dreaming about finishing the book that's been taking up space in your head and to start realizing your dream! I'm so excited to help guide and champion you, and can't wait to see your book on the shelves!

Sign Up Today!

Made in United States
Troutdale, OR
04/12/2024

19132532R00217